Aunt Pleasantine

Also by Ruth Doan MacDougall:

The Lilting House
The Cost of Living
One Minus One
The Cheerleader
Wife and Mother

"Me and my sweet wife Martha was standing upstairs.
I heard a white man say I don't want no niggers up there.
  Lord, he was a bourgeois man!
  Hoo! In a bourgeois town.
I got the bourgeois blues, I'm gonna
Spread the news all around."

To Harvey Ginsberg

Aunt Pleasantine

The sun was hot in the blueberry field.

Mary tilted her straw hat down over her eyes and duckwalked to a new bush and picked the low-bush berries.

She said, "You spend the first part of your life trying to get a tan, and then they tell you it's bad for your skin, so you spend the rest of your life avoiding a tan."

Nearby, Aunt Pleasantine said gently, "I thought I once warned you that the sun ruins complexions."

"But kids never listen."

Aunt Pleasantine was sitting in a blue canvas deck chair, in the shade of a gray birch. Her hands were folded on her lap. She wore Mary's other straw hat, the conical Oriental one which emphasized Aunt Pleasantine's air of privacy and made Mary even more hesitant to ask why she was here.

Mary plunked blueberries into the bucket.

Aunt Pleasantine said, "I divorced James fifty-four years ago this month. I divorced him because he was a woman chaser—and catcher, and not always particular about what he caught."

Mary was so startled by this remark that she momentarily hid from it in thoughts of hats. She remembered once writing Aunt Pleasantine to ask about an old photograph she'd found among others in a blanket chest after Mother died. Aunt Pleasantine wasn't Mary's aunt, she was a close friend of Mary's dead grandmother, and Mary recognized her in the photograph and thought she might be able to identify the other people in it who weren't family members. Aunt Pleasantine could and, knowing Mary was a photographer and painter, wrote a detailed reply, describing it from memory.

The picture you mention is one I gave your grandmother when I left Brandon to go to work for the Websters.

It must have been taken about 1909, because it was before I was married and that momentous event occurred in 1910.

The picture was taken during a drive. We stopped and got out of the automobile to have our picture taken by your grandmother's brother.

From left to right:

Your grandmother is wearing a blue and white checkered taffeta dress. Her bonnet is blue, with white ties.

Next, my father, whom I adored, in his auto cap and duster, the latter oil-spotted because he always rode in the front seat.

Next, my poor grandmother, whose life I made miserable. As you probably know, my grandmother brought me up after my mother died, when I was five years old, of the then called "galloping consumption." Grandma is wearing a blue and green silk foulard dress with a light straw bonnet.

The coy one is, of course, me. My bonnet was black with bunches of violets, supposed to add greatly to my appearance, when the ribbon ties held them securely over my ears.

I believe that in the background there is a Rah-Rah boy? And a "smoothie" who is smoking a "seegar"? They were your grandmother's and my beaux, but I can't remember their names.

We ladies must have left our dusters in the car. We always had to wear them because the roads were all dirt then.

In the photograph, Aunt Pleasantine was beautiful and young. And she was deceptively demure; the loose bonnet ribbons were a clue. Mary picked blueberries, waited to hear what Aunt Pleasantine would say about the divorce, and wondered what it would be like to wear a bonnet of violets.

Aunt Pleasantine said, "If James had chosen one girl, someone at least my equal or even superior to me, I believe I could have understood. But to have him taking up with anything in skirts and being so careless about being seen, it was too much for me."

"How awful. Bill is a born flirt, and I tease him about other women, but I truly think he's never"—Mary paused to select the verb—"made love to anyone else."

"James certainly did." Aunt Pleasantine smiled. "And so did I, when the divorce was final. After my self-imposed chastity during the last months of the marriage, it was especially good."

Mary laughed, while trying to think who the guy Aunt Pleasantine had slept with had been. That Al Somebody?

The field sloped up to pines, beeches, birches. A scrubby field, it seemed barren, but there was an abundant crop of blueberries this season and Mary didn't have to search. She'd picked more than two quarts. Enough? Blueberry pies, blueberry muffins. She would freeze some of the blueberries and be surprised by them all winter; in January she would put into her yogurt the blueberries from July.

Aunt Pleasantine said, "I've remembered the poem I was trying to remember last night when we were watching that circus on television." Looking at the woods, she recited:

> 'Twould ring the bells of Heaven
> The wildest peal for years,

If Parson lost his senses
And people came to theirs,
And he and they together
Knelt down with angry prayers
For tamed and shabby tigers,
And dancing dogs and bears,
And wretched, blind pit ponies,
And little hunted hares.

Mary shivered in the sun. "Oh, yes. Ralph Hodgson. He wrote 'Stupidity Street' too, didn't he? About selling larks for people to eat."

"I think I recall Parson wasn't a parson but a man named Parson, yet I'm not sure. You know what I mean."

"Gotcha," Mary said.

After a while Aunt Pleasantine said, "I have been very lucky in my life, but one of the luckiest things is that when I was in school we had to memorize poems. I take great pleasure in them now, although, of course, I didn't when I was made to learn them, spoiled silly and headstrong as I was. Much later, memorizing became a habit, but I remember best the poems I learned in school. Now I recite them when I can't sleep. I understand children don't memorize anymore?"

"No."

"A pity."

The pity is, Mary thought, that actually Aunt Pleasantine's life has been very difficult, and the difficulties haven't ceased, and what the hell am I going to do?

Aunt Pleasantine said, "Blueberry picking is on my list of things which make me feel peaceful, make me feel everything will be all right."

"What else is on the list?"

"Well, I suppose the first is watching snow coming down. The second is watching a glowing fireplace. And the third is watching ocean waves break on a beach. I've spent many hours doing these things, and to me it wasn't wasted time. Though I suppose the blueberry picking was the most useful. Do you bake muffins by your grandmother's recipe, the one with sour milk?"

"Yes. Are muffins okay for your diet?"

"I really think I can eat—and drink—anything now. That damn flu was so annoying. I felt like a wet washrag, and I had to eat baby food and I began to expect I would soon start to bang with my spoon on my high chair. The whole thing was particularly annoying because luckily I've inherited my father's stomach and until then I'd never even had indigestion. I'm fine now, Mary. The doctor told me I'd live to be a hundred. I said, 'God, I hope not.' "

Mary moved to a new bush, but the peace of picking was gone. She stood up and stretched. "Enough for one day. Would you mind a detour to the shopping mall? I ought to get some stuff but nothing vital if you don't want to postpone your nap any longer."

"I'm fine."

Mary carried the bucket of berries and the picnic cooler down the field to the dirt road and put them in her car, a white Saab. Then she went back. Aunt Pleasantine was folding the deck chair. Mary restrained herself from rushing to help and instead said, "Thank you."

"It's I who thanks you. In Florida I didn't dare dream I'd ever see a New Hampshire blueberry field again."

Mary took the chair, and she and Aunt Pleasantine walked slowly to the car. Mary couldn't believe how well Aunt Pleasantine moved for someone eighty-four years old. She helped Aunt Pleasantine into the passenger seat and walked around and put the chair in the back, tossed her straw hat in, and got into the driver's seat. She started the car and drove down the hill toward the farm where she had been born.

It was a hardscrabble farm. Its present owners, the Ames family, often repeated, as Father had, the saying about how New Hampshire earth grows rocks. Stone walls surrounded green fields still rocky after two centuries of being farmed. Looking at the grazing Guernseys and at the weather-beaten barn, Mary remembered the barn's dark smell and how Father had entertained her and her sister during milking time by squirting milk into the pink mouths of the barn cats. She'd sketched the barn and silo often. Nowadays the silo was empty because Mr. Ames stored in a field his mountain of fodder, covered with black plastic anchored with old tires. She looked at the farm pond Father had made, and she remembered the geese which had scared her when she was smaller than they. The farmhouse needed a fresh coat of white paint. Her bedroom had been at the back, so she couldn't see it from the road, but she could feel it: the eaves, the dolls, the easel and Brownie camera, the old wallpaper hidden by tacked-up drawings and paintings, the goddamn daydreams.

Taking off her hat, Aunt Pleasantine said, "I used to gallop you pickaback around that yard."

Mary didn't know this. She was always disconcerted that Aunt Pleasantine could remember her at an age before Mary could remember herself.

Aunt Pleasantine said, "You and I used to make Toll House cookies in that kitchen. I'm afraid you were so young you don't remember how you tried to find a face in every cookie."

"A face?"

"You tried to see if the chocolate chips made a face."

Mary drove past the farm. "I must have been a weird kid."

"You were a very cute towheaded tot, but sometimes you were rebellious. Your mother certainly did need help when your sister came along. I'm so glad I was able to help her for a while."

From towheaded tot to thirty-six-year-old blah blonde. Mary laughed and drove into town.

Aunt Pleasantine said, "Whenever you had to be punished, you were furious. Connie was another problem altogether. When her hands were slapped for such naughtiness as dumping over a flowerpot or getting into the woodbox, she would crouch on all fours and place her head carefully on the floor and sob as though her heart were broken. As your mother said, that nearly wrecked all discipline."

The city of Saffron Walden was an old mill and resort town on a large lake. At the far side of town a shopping mall had recently been built. Mary pulled into the parking lot. "Will you be okay in the car? I'll lock the doors."

"I could come with you, if you don't mind my snail's pace. Does this mall have benches? I could sit there while you do your shopping."

"Sure," Mary said, although she'd intended just to run in and out. Her usual shopping routine had got disrupted by Aunt Pleasantine's sudden arrival four days ago.

As they walked slowly toward the mall, Aunt Pleasantine said, "Malls interest me. I like to watch the people. And sometimes there are displays in the corridors. Do you have displays here?"

"Mostly cars and snowmobiles. And too often an electronic organ. Remember the summer after my junior year in high school when I refused to work another summer as a waitress? Mother must have mentioned it in a letter."

"You wanted a photography job at the newspaper, but you couldn't get one."

"I found a job writing copy at the radio station. We wrote most of the copy ourselves, but we got prepared scripts from companies, too, and one was an electronic organ commercial. The first sentence ran, 'Have you ever longed for an electronic organ?' The disc jockeys—all male—never could read it without breaking up."

Aunt Pleasantine was delighted.

Mary had decided that a madman must have designed this mall. It was the most hideous she'd ever seen. Garish colors. The building was bright yellow, with an enormous red sign on the long flat roof. The sign said SAFFRON WALDEN MALL, and already one of the letters, the *W*, had fallen off. The colors indoors were dizzying, stripes and zigzags of orange, pink, red.

Aunt Pleasantine said, "There *is* a display."

"And an electronic organ."

The woman at the organ was loudly and enthusiastically playing "Somewhere, My Love."

Aunt Pleasantine said, "May we look?"

"Sure."

They started down the corridor.

"Jesus Christ," Mary said. "It's a crafts display. In this joint?"

Down the corridor between the stores—a Purity Supreme supermarket, a Knickknack Nook gift shop, a CVS drugstore, a Junior Deb dress shop, a Zayre's Department Store, a His Boutique—there were displays of quaint crafts. Pottery predominated. Mary and Aunt Pleasantine walked along and looked at leatherwork, silver jewelry, pine furniture, weaving, and quilts.

Mary said, "What do they lack? Hand-dipped candles?"

"Over on that table."

"You're right."

"Oh, see!" Aunt Pleasantine said. "Such enterprising children!"

In the midst of the displays, a small girl and boy had their own concession, a cardboard carton on which was lettered FREE KITTENS. Adults and children were lifting out and cuddling kittens.

Aunt Pleasantine said, "I've always been glad that although I inherited my mother's love of music, I didn't inherit her love of cats."

"Neither did I inherit Mother's, but I ended up with a mother-in-law nicknamed Kitty. Is this bench okay?"

"Perfect." Aunt Pleasantine sat down on a circular bench. It was pink and enclosed a garden of plastic green plants.

"I won't be long," Mary said. "Anything I can get you?"

"If you should happen to go past detergents—" Aunt Pleasantine opened her pocketbook, took out her wallet, took out a dollar. "A small box of Ivory Flakes."

"But—"

"Only if you should happen past it, don't go out of your way, and tell me if it costs more than I've given you."

Bewildered, Mary shoved the dollar into her shoulder bag. She went from store to store, doing her odds-and-ends shopping. Bread, milk. Ivory Flakes. When she came out of the drugstore after buying hand cream and vitamin pills, the woman at the organ was playing "Your Cheating Heart." She bought buttons in Zayre's. Back out in the corridor, she heard the woman playing "Lady of Spain."

Mary paused and examined the quilts and then went on down the corridor to Aunt Pleasantine's bench. Aunt Pleasantine, looking alert and amused, said, "From the blueberry field to this. I have certainly lived a long life."

They walked to the car, and Mary drove around new clumps of housing developments and got onto an old farm road and took a shortcut over toward the lake.

"Odd," Aunt Pleasantine said. "I'm thinking of sleigh bells. Why should I be reminded of sleigh bells in July? I can't tell you how much I regret leaving those three straps of bells hanging on their pegs in the harness room of Papa's stable."

"Three?"

"Princess's. my grandmother's carriage horse. Gypsy's, a brown horse broken to both saddle and carriage. And my pony's, Diamond's, which were double-throated. I can't remember the style of the other two, only that they were melodious. How I regret the things I either left behind or sold or gave away when I sold the Kingsbridge house."

"I'm so sorry, Aunt Pleasie."

"No, *I'm* sorry, I didn't mean to sound gloomy. I must be needing my nap. Thank God I can at least remember the sleigh bells; at least I've got my faculties, such as they are."

Mary said, "Funny, I was never horse-crazy when I was a kid the way most girls seem to be. I rode Jed, but the whole thing was such a chore, getting the saddle on and everything and grooming him and shoveling shit."

"I was horse-crazy. And wasn't Connie?"

"Hell, yes, she rode Jed bareback. She rode cows bareback too."

They came to the bay. Aunt Pleasantine didn't say anything, but Mary guessed she must be again observing the changes. The icehouse was gone; it had contained ice cut from the lake and stored in sawdust, and this was where Mother had bought the ice for the icebox until Father could afford a refrigerator. There was a Pizza Hut here now, and a McDonald's had replaced the dairy bar where Aunt Pleasantine had once bought her an ice-cream cone. Motels between the old cabin colonies advertised swimming pools and rock bands and water beds; the old cabin colonies years ago had proudly advertised flush toilets and now simply announced rates. Mary drove past restaurants, souvenir shops, a miniature golf course, and onto the lake road.

Its most dangerous curves had been widened, and new camps had been built, yet it must seem to Aunt Pleasantine pretty much the same, twisting along the shore, crowded on both sides with camps under pines.

Mary turned off onto the dead-end road which stopped at her house at the end of the Point, and she drove up the driveway.

The green clapboard house was enormous, an old summer camp. The woods behind and beyond the house looked cool after the heat of the blueberry field, and so did the deep porches that surrounded the house on three sides. In front, a long green lawn descended to the lake. At the dock beside the little beach the sailboat was tied.

Mary knew she and Bill had been foolish to buy the place when they got married fourteen years ago. Two acres of lake property cost plenty, and they'd had to put an exhausting and expensive amount of work into repairing and insulating the house, but Bill loved to sail, and she, during her youth on the farm having envied summer people on the lake, had avidly wanted to live here. Bill, a boat salesman, worked for his father, who owned Emersons' Marina down the lake. His two brothers, younger than he, also worked there.

Aunt Pleasantine said, "A tranquil scene. A charming sailboat."

"Yes." Despite the many years she'd crewed for Bill, Mary had never conquered her nervousness about *The Nomad*'s small seventeen-foot size. But she liked the boat, its varnished mahogany woodwork, its blue hull.

Aunt Pleasantine asked, "Did you plant the flower beds?"

"The rosebushes, too." Mary helped her out of the car and thought: what a ridiculously big house. Aunt Pleasantine could live here and never bother us, really. The solution to Aunt Pleasantine's problem is simple. Money. The obstacle is her pride. Mary said, "Bill wants to take the boat down to the ocean sometime again this summer. Would you like to see your third favorite peaceful thing, ocean waves breaking on a beach?"

"Wonderful."

"We could find a place at the harbor for you to sit while we have a short sail. Or I could stay on shore with you while Bill goes out to the Isles of Shoals. Naturally you can stay here if you want and we'll get someone to come in—"

"Mary," Aunt Pleasantine said, "I would be deliriously happy to see the northern Atlantic Ocean again. The Atlantic off Flamingo Gardens simply is not the same. I would love to see the Isles of Shoals again." The words "Flamingo Gardens" made her glance back toward the mailbox, and Mary said, "I'll check the mail before we go in," and jogged down the driveway and opened the box.

The mail had come. There was the monthly mortgage bill and a postcard for Aunt Pleasantine from Connie. The postcard showed a sugaring-off scene. Connie lived in Vermont. There was nothing from Flamingo Gardens, Florida.

At the car Aunt Pleasantine read the postcard. "Connie says she's looking forward to the party. How kind of her to find time to drop me a card—with all those children of hers, she must be so busy!"

"I can't imagine how she copes." Carrying the shopping bags, Mary helped Aunt Pleasantine up the back steps. In the kitchen she set the bags on the wooden dropleaf table and took out the Ivory Flakes. "And here's your change, but honestly, Aunt Pleasantine, I've got plenty of detergent you can use—"

Aunt Pleasantine blushed, put the money in her pocketbook, and picked up the Ivory Flakes and said, "Celia Thaxter. I just remembered Celia Thaxter. 'One little sandpiper and I.' Do you by any chance have a copy of *Among the Isles of Shoals?*"

"Yes, Grandmother's copy, it's in here somewhere."

They went into the living room. When Mary and Bill bought the house, they had decided not to disguise it, they wanted to keep it as much a camp as possible. So the furniture was a hodgepodge, from the farmhouse and from secondhand stores. Big old sofas, old wickerwork chairs. Fringed cushions, rattan rug. The room was a real room in winter, but in summer they lived mostly outdoors or on the porches, and it was just a shelter for cold rainy days. The walls throughout the house were cluttered with Mary's paintings and photographs done over the years, the ones not good enough to sell, and in the living room were paintings of the lake and above the fireplace some of her sailboat photographs.

Mary rooted around in the bookcases. "Found it."

"Thank you." Aunt Pleasantine took the book, kissed Mary's cheek, and went off to her bedroom.

Mary waited, then went to the hallway and listened, making sure she'd got there safely. Offered her choice of rooms, Aunt Pleasantine had chosen a downstairs spare room because it was next to the downstairs bathroom and because the staircase to the upstairs spare rooms was narrow and steep. Those were the reasons she gave, but Mary suspected she mainly chose downstairs in order to leave private Mary and Bill's bedroom and Mary's workroom upstairs.

Used to living in other people's homes, Aunt Pleasantine had adapted quickly, an ideal houseguest. She could become invisible. She made her breakfasts. She stayed in her room a lot. When she had a drink before supper with Mary and Bill on the front porch, she always told one entertaining story and then was silent, invisible again. So far she had twice asked to eat supper in her room if it wasn't too much trouble. When she ate supper with Mary and Bill, she once more told an entertaining story. Yesterday she insisted on dusting her room herself.

Aunt Pleasantine traveled light. She had brought her clothes. On the spare room bureau she'd laid out her evidently cherished dresser set, which included a silver-backed mirror and a hair receiver. The set had been, she explained, her mother's. She had brought a hostess gift of little seashells. And that was that.

Mary went back to the car for the blueberries, picnic cooler, camera, hats, deck chair. In the kitchen she tossed away the picnic scraps and put away her purchases. She tipped some of the berries into a colander and sat down at the table with it, feeling tired. She wished Bill didn't work Saturdays, she wished he were home.

By the time Mary guessed that Aunt Pleasantine must have finished her nap, Mary had finished picking over the blueberries and had tray-frozen half of them on cookie sheets in the refrigerator freezer. Aunt Pleasantine always stayed in her room after her nap until she was invited to the porch for what she called "cocktails." Mary rolled out piecrust and pictured her sitting in the chintz-covered bedroom chair, reading *Among the Isles of Shoals* and remembering.

Mary made the pie, put it in the oven, and heard Bill's car in the driveway.

Bill came into the kitchen. "Hi."

"Hi."

They kissed.

He said, "Blueberries. Let me see your tongue, I'll bet it's purple. It is. How's Aunt Pleasantine?"

"Not so tensed up, but still—I don't know." Mary looked at him. His long dark hair curved smoothly. His beard didn't match his hair, it was reddish. He was her age. "Bill, I've been wondering. I mentioned a trip to the ocean, and Aunt Pleasantine was tickled. But could we take her out for a sail too, out to the Isles, or would it be dangerous for her?"

"Jesus, I hadn't thought of even taking her out on the lake. Wouldn't a sail scare her?"

"I doubt it. How was your day?"

"Boring."

Mary said, "She talked about her husband. Ex-husband. I don't remember ever hearing her say anything about him before. Getting divorced back then must have been one hell of a scandal."

"What I want to get her talking about is Florida. The Inland Waterway."

"How could she know about the Waterway?"

"She might."

"Shall I go tell her it's 'the cocktail hour'?"

"Okay, I'll get the drinks."

Mary went through the living room and down the hall to Aunt Pleasantine's room and knocked on the door. "Bill's home. We're going to have drinks, please join us if you'd like."

"Thank you."

Already a ritual, the invitation offered and accepted. Mary wanted to shout, "Damn it, you don't have to hide in there, we love you!"

In the living room Mary searched the record rack, trying to decide what to play during drinks. She and Bill disagreed about music. She was fond of Debussy; Bill said it sounded like Muzak. Bill preferred Bach; she said it could have been composed by a computer. Since Aunt Pleasantine's arrival, Mary had been playing Debussy because he was a favorite too of Aunt Pleasantine's. Mary flipped through the records. Bill deserved a change. Helen

Reddy? Leadbelly? George Carlin? Piaf? *Bert and I?* She sighed and put on Bach for Bill.

Aunt Pleasantine liked Cheezits. In the kitchen Mary poured some into a bowl and added it to the drinks tray, which Bill carried out to the front porch. She checked the pie, gathered up silverware, and joined Bill on the porch. Aunt Pleasantine was sitting in the fan-backed wicker chair, listening to Bill and watching the lake.

"—impressions of Florida," Bill said. "For instance, what surprised you most?"

"Christmas," Aunt Pleasantine said promptly. She sipped her vodka and tonic. "Christmas is crazy."

Mary began setting the red-painted wooden table. In summer they ate here on the screened porch. In winter they ate in the dining room, a glassed sunporch at one side of the house.

Bill said, "Christmas?"

"Yes," Aunt Pleasantine said. "I was astounded the first year, and I've never got over it. Every Christmas I cannot believe what I see. Candles and wreaths in *open* doors and windows! Green grass, flowering plants and shrubs. At Christmas! Utterly incredible. Christmas lights twinkling in orange and grapefruit trees! Crazy."

"What else surprised you?"

"All the little houses. Miles and miles of little white houses. Everything is white there. I'm exaggerating, of course, but even the eggs are white."

Mary sat down on the glider. She couldn't resist saying, to get Aunt Pleasantine's reaction, "But isn't there some black? For contrast?"

"Oh, yes. That reminds me, did I tell you about the nice colored boy who met me right at the curb at the airport and helped me into a wheelchair? He was a porter. He took care of my suitcase, he even got my ticket okayed, and then he parked me in the waiting room. Soon he wheeled in a gray-haired gentleman and parked him near me and left. The gentleman and I chatted. Eventually my boy came back again, and he put one hand on the handbar of my chair and the other on the gentleman's handbar and pushed us both through the airport. At one point we were stopped and frisked, because of skyjackings, you know. When we reached the plane, the gentleman grinned at me and said, 'Too bad we didn't each have a porter; then we could have staged a chariot race!' "

Mary and Bill laughed, and Aunt Pleasantine sipped her drink. She had told her cocktail-hour story. She ate a Cheezit.

The sailboat creaked against the dock.

The Bach in the living room made everything seem very organized and sane.

Bill said, "When I was a kid, I read a book about three kids and a dog taking their sailboat down the Inland Waterway, and ever since then I've wanted to do it, but something always interferes. Things like going to school and earning a living."

Mary said, "Maybe you've done it too often in your armchair. The dream has palled."

"If it's palled, that's because of the horror stories I've heard about the Waterway's pollution nowadays. Have you heard any, Aunt Pleasantine?"

Aunt Pleasantine looked alarmed at having been consulted. "Well. I'm sorry, but I did overhear a guest at a party complaining about seeing, among other things, a dead pig floating in it somewhere."

Mary couldn't decide if another horror story added to his collection depressed or satisfied Bill. He said to Aunt Pleasantine, "Would you like to go out to the Isles of Shoals for a picnic on Star Island? *Nomad* would be too uncomfortable, and I could borrow one of my brothers' stinkpots—"

"—powerboats," Mary translated.

"—but wouldn't a sail be more fun?"

Aunt Pleasantine was staring at him. "Yes."

"Okay. I'll borrow the twenty-two footer from the Hubcap King, his boat will be more comfortable for you. There's a head—a bathroom."

Mary said, "On ours there's a porcelain bedpan. Bill was so thrilled to find it in a secondhand store."

Bill said, "You've got to admit it has more class than the enamel chamber pot we had."

Aunt Pleasantine said slowly, "I never thought I'd picnic on Star Island again. The Hubcap King?"

"A friend," Mary said, "who lives at the ocean. He builds houses for a living, and he collects hubcaps and he sails." She stood up. "Supper is salmon salad. I've set a place for you, will you join us?"

"Thank you."

But Aunt Pleasantine looked uncertain, and Mary guessed that she was worrying about what suppertime story to tell. Mary said, "Maybe while we eat, you could tell Bill the history of your name. I told him long ago, but I can't tell it so well as you."

"It's a silly story, I'm not sure he'd—"

Bill said, "I'd like very much to hear it again."

"Then," Aunt Pleasantine said, "I shall tell it at supper."

Bill beamed at her, and suddenly she beamed back. Aunt Pleasantine had always appreciated a handsome man.

Mary said, "Excuse me," and went into the house to the kitchen. The pie was done. She loaded supper onto a large tray she had painted during her Tole Period (which had been brief, thank God) and carried the tray out to the porch table. Bill escorted Aunt Pleasantine to one of the red wooden chairs.

Aunt Pleasantine said, "I *thought* I smelled a blueberry pie baking."

"We'll have muffins tomorrow," Mary said. "Won't you join us for breakfast?"

"Will you have time to bake them before Bill leaves? Mary mentioned, Bill, that tomorrow is your Sunday at the Marina."

Bill said, "There'll be time."

"Oh. I've always been so grateful to Becky—Mary's grandmother—for passing along that muffin recipe to me." Aunt Pleasantine ate a bite of salad, put down her fork, and told her story. "When my father was a young man, before he'd married and I was born, he made a tour of Europe, as many young men did in those days. I understand young men are still making tours of Europe, but in my father's day I don't think they wore blue jeans and knapsacks. On the ship back to Boston, he met a nice French family. They had a little daughter named Pleasantine. The story goes that he was so enchanted with the beautiful little French girl that he resolved to name his own daughter after her if he married and had a daughter."

Aunt Pleasantine paused. "However," she said with obvious enjoyment. She paused again and sipped her iced coffee. "That's the official version. And later Papa met and married my mother and brought her home to Kingsbridge, New Hampshire, and a correct ten months after the marriage I was born and I was named Pleasantine. Papa told everyone about the little girl on the ship and about his resolution. But the relatives and all the people who knew Papa were highly suspicious of his tale. They took considerable delight in whispering that it was a damn sight more likely that the Pleasantine who enchanted him on the ship was not a beautiful little French girl but a beautiful *big* French girl."

Bill leaned back in his chair and laughed, and Mary felt bold enough to ask, "Did your mother know about the whispers?"

"You think the way I think. When I heard the unofficial version —from my drinking uncle, naturally—I asked if my mother had known. The question almost jolted poor Uncle into sobriety. He was so horrified at my asking it that I never got up the nerve to ask Papa or even Grandma—who was, by the way, my father's mother, not my mother's mother, who had earlier succumbed to TB too. So I don't know, Mary. I like to believe that if my mother overheard the whispers, she didn't mind. Papa's first Pleasantine, child or woman, had happened before his marriage and was only a memory."

Mary said, "Did your father remarry after—uh—"

"No. He didn't need a mother for me, you see, because Grandma moved into the house after my mother's death and Grandma took me in hand. Or she tried to."

"I used to figure Bill and I would have to name a daughter Pleasantine, we wouldn't be able to resist, but then, of course, we decided not to have kids. Yet in your family the name must have descended—" Mary stopped, remembering that neither of Aunt Pleasantine's daughters nor her granddaughter had been named after her. Or great-grands?

Aunt Pleasantine glanced at Mary, seemed about to reply, but she'd told her story and she was silent.

They ate.

To Mary's relief, Bill noticed the lawn and changed the subject. "Oh, Christ, I've got to mow the grass again."

Mary said, "If you'd show me how to use the power mower, I could do it," deliberately provoking an old argument which dated from the day Bill had forsaken his principles and bought a power mower to replace the worn-out push mower she'd used.

"No," he said, "I won't show you how, it's the sort of thing you're clumsy with, you'd mow your toes off. Remember how mad you used to get at just the push mower?"

"If you'd kept it sharpened—"

"Were you incapable of taking it to the sharpener's yourself?"

"Touché." Mary turned to Aunt Pleasantine. "May I ask a favor? If it wouldn't tire you too much, could I sketch you sometime? Sitting in that chair over there."

"Good heavens," Aunt Pleasantine said, "I can't imagine why you'd want to." Then she blushed, and Mary knew that she knew why Mary wanted to. Aunt Pleasantine was well aware of her facial bone structure. "When would you sketch me? I should go to a hairdresser's first, the packing and the plane flight made me cancel my last appointment."

"Your hair is just right." But Mary understood that trips to a hairdresser were an important part of Aunt Pleasantine's life, so she added, "Why don't I sketch you tomorrow, and then Monday I'll make an appointment for you—oh, hell."

"What's wrong?"

"The place we go to, two men own it and they mainly cut men's hair, women are a sideline, but they're the best haircutters in town, so I go there. Stylists, they call themselves. My only complaint is I have to read *Sports Illustrated* in the waiting room."

"I don't know any Saffron beauty shops," Aunt Pleasantine said. "When I was helping your mother out, I never went to one; she and I did our hair ourselves. A wartime sacrifice."

Mary said, "These guys don't do perms and stuff, they wouldn't be right for you. The beauty shop I used to go to before they opened has closed, and I've never been to any other. Let's see, I could ask—"

Bill said, "You could consult Kitty."

"Smart-ass," Mary said to him. "I'll ask Norma. Or Janice or Donna—"

Aunt Pleasantine said, "I don't want it to be a problem—"

"No problem." Mary sliced the pie. "Bill and I sometimes go to those guys together if our schedules coincide, and it always reminds me of that scene in *Tender Is the Night,* Nicole and Dick having their hair cut together. We're lucky I prefer Mr. Charles while Bill prefers Mr. Ronald."

"Flits," Bill said.

"Don't be prejudiced," Mary said.

Aunt Pleasantine seemed puzzled, then amused. "Deciding about a hairdo became a problem for me in my old age. I followed hairdressers' advice. But two years ago I was in a mall with the children and while they were shopping I studied all the old ladies in the place, and their hairdos were just like mine. Blue curls. We dames looked like elderly Shirley Temples. I immediately made a decision about my future style; I decided I would let my hair grow, I would leave it plain white, and I would have a French twist. I've never been sorry I made that decision."

Mary said, "It's very becoming."

Bill said, "It certainly is."

"It takes a long time, and it's hard on my arms, but I manage."

Twilight now. The halyards slapped. Soon bats would be swooping over the lake.

After Aunt Pleasantine had gone to bed, Bill shut off the TV, and he and Mary went out to the porch. Mary turned on the lamp, and they sat down and opened their books. Bill liked books about faraway places, and his latest discovery was Eric Newby's *A Short Walk in the Hindu Kush.* Mary could hardly wait for him to finish it so she could get her hands on it because she liked books about eccentric Englishmen doing insane things. But at the moment she was reading about flower arranging. She read in the lamplight and listened to the sailboat and the lake.

Bill said, "Did you mention money to her?"

"I can't think how to. She insisted on buying her own soap flakes. Awkward."

They read.

Mary said, "Maybe you should be the one. She pays attention when men tell her what to do, that's been her downfall. Maybe you could talk about money without embarrassing her."

They read.

Bill said, "I don't know her. I never met her until four days ago."

"Maybe she wouldn't be stubborn with you."

They closed their books.

Mary burst into tears. "She arrived here so—so open! One suitcase and no place to go."

"I can't understand her daughters."

"Where's the goddamn Kleenex!" Mary went over to a round metal table and grabbed a Kleenex and wiped her eyes. "Strain. I hadn't realized it's been such a strain."

"You're with her all day. You're used to being alone."

"But I've kept right on working since she's been here, she hasn't got in the way of the work, she isn't an interference. Is she?"

"Depends on how long she's staying."

"What if she stays for good? If we asked her to. If we could convince her to."

Bill said, "She's sharp as a tack now, but we could end up with a baby after all. A senile baby."

"If it came to that, we can afford a nursing home, can't we?"

"My grandmother died in a nursing home."

"Which grandmother?"

"The Emerson one. Grammy Em. Not the nursing home's fault that she died. Look, if you want to ask Aunt Pleasantine to stay here, it's okay with me. She hasn't said anything yet about any plans?"

"No."

"Habit might be the answer. Nothing is mentioned, she just stays on."

Mary said, "Aunt Pleasantine? She doesn't vegetate, she acts."

"At eighty-four?"

"She's here right now, isn't she? She acted."

"I'm going to get a drink. You too?"

"Thank you."

While Bill was indoors, Mary looked at the night lake. She tried to think about the humorous stories Grandmother and Aunt Pleasantine both told about their friendship, but she could think only of death.

She'd never known her father's parents, her father's father having died in his forties, as some farmers, worn out, had a tendency to do, and Father's mother having earlier died in childbirth.

She remembered her parents' deaths and the descriptions the private nurses had given of Mother's parents' deaths. If Aunt Pleasantine stayed on here, Mary would have to face death again. And she'd been a failure at facing it before.

Grandmother falling out of bed, vomiting on the bedroom rug, twisting in her flowered bedsheets. Grandfather wasting away. Father quick, a heart attack while shoveling snow. Mother turning yellow with cancer of the liver, lingering eight months. Mary remembered the helpless gesture of moistening Mother's dry lips with a wet washcloth. Memorial services. Crematoriums.

Mary looked at her wrists. For her, they were the first real sign of her age. No throat wrinkles yet, no gray hairs, only some eye crinkles, and her hands long ago had become working hands, she was used to that. She looked in the lamplight at the creases in her wrists.

Bill brought the drinks. "Kitty is on the prowl already. The old man says she wants us to bring Aunt Pleasantine over for supper anytime. I said Aunt Pleasantine has been sick and is still recuperating."

"Kitty will get us sooner or later."

"Yes, it's inevitable."

He opened his book, and she opened hers.

Aunt Pleasantine said, "I've noticed you don't smoke, but I can't remember when you wrote me that you and Bill had stopped. Oh, I'm sorry, I probably shouldn't be talking."

"No," Mary said, sketching, "talk doesn't bother me. We quit two years ago last month. I still have dreams about cigarettes, but Bill doesn't. I dream I'm at a party and there's a pack on a table and I automatically take a cig and light up."

"One evening twenty-five years after your grandmother had stopped smoking, she went into her living room and automatically took a pack of cigarettes down from the mantel where your grandfather always kept them. She'd lighted one before she realized what she was doing. She tossed it in the fireplace. For no reason she had done what she'd always done twenty-five years earlier, had a cigarette to relax when the day was over. Her example, by the way, made me stop, too."

ninety-one in Kingsbridge, New Hampshire."

Mary, waiting, sketched. A tree swallow flew into the birdhouse on a post at the end of the dock.

Aunt Pleasantine said, "I was delighted when our school friend Grace asked me to come stay with her. After all my travels, it was good to be back in my hometown."

You mean, Mary thought, to be back to die in your hometown. "How long did you live with Grace? I can't keep dates straight."

"Just a few months. She died in nineteen-seventy-two."

And returning from Grace's funeral to the house now owned by Grace's relatives, who were discussing its sale, Aunt Pleasantine had fallen on the icy sidewalk. Mary learned this from a letter written months later in Florida.

Aunt Pleasantine was apparently following the same line of thought. "Such a stupid fall. Most old fools like me break their hips when they fall. I had to be different and break my arm. Lucky, and very lucky it was my left and I'm right-handed, but annoying." She changed the subject. "The party you mentioned you're giving. I gather Connie's coming? With her family?"

"Yes, Connie and George and their gang."

"What sort of party will it be?"

Mary knew that Aunt Pleasantine liked parties. Her daughters seemed to be rather merry widows, and whenever they gave a party at their bungalow Aunt Pleasantine wrote a detailed description of it in her letters, which two years ago had suddenly begun to arrive from Florida monthly, in addition to the usual Christmas-card and birthday-card notes. Aunt Pleasantine observed the parties closely, the preparations, the decorations, the color scheme, the canapés, the flowers, the china, her daughters' hostess gowns, the behavior of the guests, and she described them all with relish.

Mary said, "This will be a We-Owe-Everybody Party. God, do we! We're slack about returning parties. I hope you'll join us, I think you'd enjoy it. Remember back when I was teaching art?

We've still got high-school-teacher friends from those days, and there'll be a lot of them here, and they're unbelievable at parties in the summer. They never stop talking, they talk a mile a minute. My theory is that this is caused by their being deprived of classroom captive audiences in the summer, and when they see people they go berserk. There'll be about thirty guests—friends, neighbors, Bill's customers. The party is August ninth, and it's just a coincidence it'll be the first anniversary of Nixon's leaving the White House—one date I *can* keep straight."

"What will you serve?" Aunt Pleasantine asked, not using the date as a chance to discuss her plans.

"A buffet out here on the porch. Dips, sandwiches and stuff, and drinks. Mainly drinks."

Aunt Pleasantine, who liked drinks, smiled. Then she said, "I was surprised when you resigned from your job."

"I know, it's hard to explain. I got fed up with administrative bullshit and teenagers, and we didn't need the money after we got the house done."

Money.

Aunt Pleasantine said, "I believe Clara Baldwin is still alive. I had a Christmas card from her last year, and I found her name still listed in your phone book."

Mary thought fast and remembered Clara. "She's the one you made friends with when you were helping Mother out with Connie and me."

"Yes. Clara had decided to give her granddaughter a baby bunny for Easter, and someone told her your father raised rabbits, so she came to the farm. Your parents were busy, so I took her to the hutches, and I happened to mention how I once had hired a magician for one of my daughters' birthday parties and how flabbergasted the children were when he pulled a real live bunny out of his hat and presented it to Elizabeth, who named it Snowball. After Easter, Clara phoned me and told me her granddaughter had named *her* bunny Vanilla, and Clara invited me to tea. We became friends."

"Why don't you phone her and arrange a visit? She could come here or I'll take you to her house."

Aunt Pleasantine was silent for a long time. "Thank you. Probably I'd better visit her at her house; she's mentioned in her Christmas cards that her arthritis has worsened, and I suspect it's even worse than she lets on."

Mary asked, "Is there anybody else you'd like to see?" before thinking—oh, God, is there anybody else alive?

"Well, there's a schoolmate of mine in Kingsbridge. She was in the same class your grandmother and I were. Her name is Lillian Crawford. We never got along, and I didn't visit her when I returned to Kingsbridge. She was jealous of me when we were girls. I've told you my father spoiled me rotten. I had my pony, I had the best clothes of anyone in school, I had parties for my friends. Papa was wealthy, but I just took that for granted. I must have been hateful. Becky, your grandmother, put up with me, bless her, but Lillian hated me and I don't blame her."

"Would you want to see her? I could drive you down sometime."

Another long silence.

Mary thought about Aunt Pleasantine's grandchildren, Chris and Dan and Jean. They lived out West, and apparently their homes bulged with children. No room for Aunt Pleasantine, and no money either.

"Perhaps," Aunt Pleasantine said. "Thank you, I'll think it over." Again she changed the subject. "Are there still bobhouses on the lake in the winter?"

"Oh, yes. And a few still go through the ice every winter. When snowmobiles go through the ice, we cheer."

"Do you remember ice-fishing with your father?"

"I certainly do. Damn near froze my ass off."

"And do you remember how he'd bring home fish that had frozen after being caught because the weather was so cold? He'd put them in the bathtub, and you and Connie and I watched them thaw out and swim around."

"Yellow perch."

"He got such enjoyment out of your enjoyment. Is that a car I hear or a boat?"

"A car." Mary set down her sketchpad. "Hey, it's Norma. I'll go meet her."

In the backyard Norma parked her Gremlin, whose bumper sticker said ADAM WAS A ROUGH DRAFT. She opened her door. "I wish to God the State of New Hampshire would stop telling us how to run our lives. I'm out of booze, and I've got unexpected company. Can I borrow a cup of gin?"

"Sure. Come in and meet Aunt Pleasantine."

Norma was a divorced woman in her forties who lived farther up the lake. "At least the state has finally allowed us to buy beer on Sundays—"

"After noon," Mary said.

"Generous of them. And tough for me that my guests don't drink beer. Jesus Christ, New Hampshire! Lotteries, dog tracks, horse racing, probably casinos next, but you can't buy booze on Sundays. Aunt who?"

"Not really an aunt, she's a sort of godmother. She's up from Florida, visiting. Who's your company?"

"Water-skiers. Amateur but plucky."

"Oh, shit."

"You said it. There ought to be such a thing as an unlisted address. Is there? People on the lake ought to get one every summer."

Indoors Mary led Norma through the house to the front porch. "Aunt Pleasantine, this is Norma Wentworth. Norma, this is Pleasantine Curtis."

Aunt Pleasantine said, "How do you do."

"Hi," Norma said. "Love your pantsuit."

"Thank you. It was a Christmas present from my daughters. I've always liked pink."

Mary said, "Norma teaches art, she came out of retirement to replace me. Norma, where do you have your hair done?"

"Irene's. Irene's Beauty Boudoir. Sorry, can't stay, gotta get home to make sure the company hasn't gotten killed."

In the kitchen Mary fetched a fifth of gin from a cupboard. "Will that be enough?"

"I devoutly hope so. How long is Aunt Pleasantine visiting?"

"We aren't sure."

"Oh. A problem?"

"No," Mary said firmly. "Is your vacation still going okay?"

Norma didn't really have a vacation. She worked summers as an arts counselor at the girls' camp on the lake. Her eighteen-year-old daughter, Ginger, was also a counselor there, and her sixteen-year-old son, Freddy, worked pumping gas at Emersons' Marina.

"Yes," Norma said, "it's okay."

Mary realized Norma used the same tone of voice as Bill had when he said his day yesterday was boring. Frustration, exhaustion, depression. Mary supposed she herself must have spoken that way the last years of her teaching.

Norma said, "Thanks, I'll pay you back," and went outdoors and drove off.

Mary took two sherries to the porch. "Do you approve of Norma's hair?"

"She's a walking advertisement. I'll make an appointment at Irene's tomorrow. A nice girl. She lives on the lake?"

"She got the house and the kids when she was divorced, but no whopping amount of child support. She works at the school and the girls' camp. She's managing."

"Divorced?"

"A few years ago." Mary sat down and picked up her sketchpad.

Aunt Pleasantine said, "Managing is very hard. Did you know that at one stage of my life I sold corsets?"

"Uh-huh."

"That was before I went to work for the Websters in nineteen-twenty-five."

"Mmm."

"Delicious sherry."

Mary sketched and waited.

Aunt Pleasantine said, "James was handsome. I wish I'd kept my photographs of him. I met him through Becky's brother, you know, your great-uncle, just as she met your grandfather. They were classmates at Harvard. James was so handsome and charming."

"What did he do after Harvard?"

"Nothing. I really don't think he married me simply for my money, but I've never been such a fool not to know the money was an attraction. He owned his family home, of course, down in Brandon."

Brandon was a swanky suburb of Boston, where Mary's grandmother too had moved after her marriage. Aunt Pleasantine and Grandmother were Kingsbridge girls transplanted.

Mary said, "I've got all the family photograph albums. Connie insisted I keep them all because she was afraid her kids would ruin them. I've only skimmed the older ones; a thorough study is a wintertime project that keeps being postponed. Think there might be a picture of James in them?"

"Your grandparents' albums? Probably."

"Want to have a look? I'll lug the whole bunch to your room and you can go through them if you want."

Aunt Pleasantine watched the lake for a while. "Thank you."

A half hour later Mary said, "I'm starved, are you?" She put aside the sketchpad. "I'm wondering about cucumber sandwiches. Can you eat cukes? These are supposed to be burpless."

"I love cucumbers. I'll go freshen up."

Aunt Pleasantine went off to her room.

Mary went into the kitchen. As she began making lunch, she thought about divorce. She could not imagine life without Bill. They had dated in high school and married after college. While he was in the Coast Guard, she'd lived here alone, waiting for him, teaching art at the high school. The winters in the house then had been very cold.

Aunt Pleasantine came into the kitchen. "You prepare cucumbers exactly as I do."

Mary looked at the cucumbers. Before slicing them, she had peeled strips, leaving some green skin, and she had run the tines of a fork down the white flesh. Just a pretty design.

Aunt Pleasantine said, "You learned that from your mother and grandmother. And your grandmother learned it from me, and I learned it from my grandmother. Please, let me fold the napkins."

Aunt Pleasantine made a Tuesday appointment at Irene's Beauty Boudoir and was happy she was able to get an early one so she wouldn't miss *Hollywood Squares* before lunch. Mary had gathered from Aunt Pleasantine's letters that she was a great fan of *Hollywood Squares,* and Mary had got a hint—Aunt Pleasantine could be maddeningly subtle—that her daughters allowed her to watch it only when they were in good moods. The morning after she arrived, Mary casually asked if she wanted to watch it, and she had looked delighted and said, "I adore Paul Lynde, don't you? He's so naughty!"

Mary parked near Irene's and helped Aunt Pleasantine out of the car. They contemplated the Boudoir.

Aunt Pleasantine said, "I can never understand why people create these things."

The Boudoir had a bakery on one side and a chiropractor's establishment on the other. The Boudoir was a Cape with Victorian additions, a combination Mary enjoyed, but to the everlasting shame of Irene or somebody, onto the front had been stuck a fake brick structure trimmed with aqua.

Indoors, there was also aqua. Women sat in a row under aqua dryers; women sitting in cubicles wore big plastic aqua bibs. The room reeked of shampoo and permanents.

Aunt Pleasantine said to the receptionist, "Pleasantine Curtis," and the receptionist said, "Just a few minutes."

Aunt Pleasantine sat down on a vinyl aqua sofa before a clear plastic table heaped with beauty and movie magazines. She surveyed the beige walls' pictures of hairdos.

Mary said, "Will you be okay here?"

"I'll be fine. I know exactly what I want done. Don't hurry."

So Mary went out to the car and drove up North Main Street to Jerry's place, The Watercolor, supposedly an art gallery but actually more a gift shop. It was the sort of gallery which had a Master Charge credit card sign. Jerry took her stuff on consignment. The Watercolor was a converted gas station; in the old bay were gifts, and the gallery was in the old office. The bay's door had been replaced by bow windows, and everything was colorful and chic, but Mary always found herself remembering a grease pit and the smell of gasoline.

Tourists browsed in the gift shop.

"Hi," Mary said to Sally. "Jerry here?"

"Yes. Did your aunt arrive?" Sally, Jerry's wife, was small, brunette, wiry, and despite having three children, one adopted, she ran the gift shop and made dolls which sold so fast she couldn't keep up with the demand. "I mean your aunt who isn't an aunt."

Nearby, a grandmotherly woman was trying to choose between a gingerbread man doll and a Red Riding Hood. On the counters were scented candles and wooden buckets of wooden spoons and glass jars of penny candy. Spices. Place mats. Salad bowls, children's books, souvenirs.

Mary said, "She arrived last week. We picked her up at Logan. She wanted to take some hedgehopper from Boston to here to spare us the trip, but we insisted."

"She sounds spry."

"She is."

The customer said, "Maybe neither. Maybe the snowman."

Sally looked at Mary resignedly and reached for the snowman doll.

"Or maybe one of the babies."

Mary said, "See you," and went into the gallery. "Any news?"

Jerry was fat and cheery and carefree. Mary never got over being amazed by the delicate pencil drawings of old houses he did. Sometimes he broke down and did covered bridges, and that was the only time his wares competed with Sally's dolls.

He said, "A couple of your Yacht Club regattas went. And the milkweed."

"Hooray."

Jerry scrawled a check. "If you want to bother making a few more regatta prints, I could probably move them."

"Okay. Thanks."

On the way back downtown, the car in front of her had a bumper sticker which said:

EAT BEANS
AMERICA NEEDS THE GAS

She drove past Irene's and found a parking space near the camera store. She did errands there and in the hardware store, glanced up at the bank's clock, and went into Woolworth's and sat down at the lunch counter and ordered an iced tea. Her friends were horrified that she still stopped here for a break, as she always had, instead of going to, say, the Dunkin' Donut.

This Woolworth's hadn't changed much since her childhood. It was dark. The wooden floor was crooked. There were hair ribbons and Crayolas and emery boards and pots of paste. She believed she could smell Tangee lipstick. She toyed with the tea, looking at the pictures of food on the wall behind the counter. They hadn't changed much either, but the prices certainly had. Green lemon-and-lime still burbled in a glass cooler.

She wondered how many little painted turtles Connie had bought here when she was a kid. And how many white paper boxes containing goldfish had Connie carried home?

Their mother liked categories. Mary figured Mother had got so confused by falling in love with Father and marrying him and moving to the farm, that from then on she clung to categories to simplify her life. Mother never hesitated about saying aloud what categories her daughters fitted into. "Mary is the smart one. Connie is the pretty one." "Mary-Mary-quite-contrary has a nasty disposition. Connie must have inherited her sweet disposition from my mother." "Mary is the artistic one. Connie is the tomboy." Good God, Mary thought, twirling her straw, it's a bit of a miracle that Connie and I survived that and remained friends.

The Woolworth pets which Connie brought home all died sooner or later, but this didn't stop Connie. Mary remembered a cat's discovering behind the refrigerator a turtle corpse fuzzy with dust.

As she drove back to Irene's, she wondered whether or not Aunt Pleasantine's daughters were friends. She joked with Connie about how if she and Connie ever decided to have face-lifts they'd do it together to give each other courage, but they'd never talked about living together someday, widows. Together again, childhood again.

At Irene's, Aunt Pleasantine was paying the receptionist.

Mary said, "But—"

"No." Aunt Pleasantine paid and tipped.

In the car she patted her coiffure.

"You look lovely," Mary said. "Did you like Irene's?"

"I'm very satisfied. Did you have a good morning, too?"

"Lucrative. Jerry sold two photographs and a painting."

"Wonderful."

They came to the lake road.

Aunt Pleasantine said, "Vanity. My great-aunts used to visit Grandma, and I remember one time when I was fourteen I was sitting in the living room while they went to the kitchen for Grandma to make tea—it was the maid's day off—and I heard my great-aunts say, 'Pleasantine certainly is a beauty,' and, 'You're going to have your hands full with suitors coming courting.' After they had left, I teased Grandma and asked what they'd said about me, and she said I would become vain if I heard, so I told her I *had* heard, and she said that I must not let it go to my head, or words to that effect. All very gently said, as always."

"Do you look like her?"

"It was generally concluded that I was a combination of both sides of the family. Oh—did I tell you that the assistant at Irene's who gave me my perm is a new bride? She described the apartment she and her husband have rented. They're buying a living-room set on time."

Mary parked in the driveway. She went down to the mailbox and found the mailbox empty.

"Not even an ad," she said to Aunt Pleasantine.

In the living room Mary turned on the TV. "Eleven-thirty. We're right on the dot."

"That housewife is nice. But the airline pilot is, too. I can't decide which one I want to win. I wish they both could win."

Mary brought sherries and sat with Aunt Pleasantine and watched *Hollywood Squares.* Paul Lynde was very funny; so was George Gobel. Neither contestant won the Secret Square prize which included the *World Book* encyclopedia, a Caribbean cruise ("five fun-filled weeks"), a shag carpet, a three-door frost-free refrigerator, and a million S&H Green Stamps.

Aunt Pleasantine said, "I always wonder if the winner has to lick all those stamps."

After lunch Aunt Pleasantine took her nap. Mary worked upstairs in the darkroom, then went downstairs and heard her getting ready for the visit to Clara Baldwin. Suddenly Mary knew shorts and old tie-dyed shirt were not presentable, and she went back up the steep staircase and in the bedroom took off her clothes and put on a jersey and skirt. She hurried downstairs.

Aunt Pleasantine came into the living room, wearing a wispy summer dress.

"Wow," Mary said, "you look gorgeous."

"I've got my best pantyhose on. I hope to God I don't get a run in them."

Aunt Pleasantine was very pale. Nerves? They drove into town.

Mary said, "Hey. Is this going to be too tiring for you? You've had a busy morning—"

"I'm fine. Do you remember where the Baldwin house is?"

"It's the one with the turrets, it's always fascinated me. I wish I could remember going there with you."

"You were very well-behaved during that visit, and you didn't touch anything."

"This time I'll see you in and go do errands."

Mary drove into the oldest part of town. The summer afternoon was lacy under the tall old trees. The houses seemed silent. Nobody walked along the sidewalks. Sunlight wavered.

Clara Baldwin lived in a great old shingled house amid big landscaped grounds. Mary drove carefully up the narrow drive, which was suitable for horses and carriages, and parked beneath the porte cochere.

Aunt Pleasantine said, "I'm so glad to see that Clara's been able to keep the place up."

For Christ's sake, Mary thought, how dumb can I get? This isn't only a social call. Aunt Pleasantine, companion and houseguest since her housekeeping and innkeeping days, is doing some reconnaissance.

Aunt Pleasantine rang the doorbell.

A large woman opened the door. "Mrs. Curtis? I'm the Mrs. Stafford who answered your phone call, I'm Mrs. Baldwin's companion. Come right in, she's expecting you." Mrs. Stafford's voice was loud, probably because of years of talking to deaf old ladies.

"Thank you," said Aunt Pleasantine, whose hearing was excellent.

Mrs. Stafford wore rhinestone eyeglasses, a large housedress, and wedgies. She led the way into the living room.

Clara, very arthritic, struggled up from an armchair. "Pleasantine!"

"Clara, my dear." They embraced. Aunt Pleasantine said, "You remember Mary, of course, Louisa and Arthur's older daughter, but I'm afraid she doesn't remember you because she was so young."

"How do you do," Mary said, discreetly studying the huge living room, trying to memorize the tiled fireplace and its summertime paper fan, the bay window's green velvet windowseat, the grand piano, the family photographs.

Clara said, "Good Lord, Mary, when Pleasantine brought you here, you were a toddler!"

Aunt Pleasantine said, "And now I'm the one who's unsteady on my pins," and she and Clara laughed.

Mrs. Stafford helped Clara into the armchair. "I'll get the tea." She left.

Mary said, "I'll be back in an hour."

Outdoors, Mary realized she didn't have any errands, she'd done them all this morning. But she had to kill the hour. Her camera was in the glove compartment of her car; she brought the camera with her everywhere. She could go indoors and ask permission to spend the time taking outside pictures of the house, yet she didn't want to interrupt the reunion. She could visit Bill. She drove to the lake, to Emersons' Marina.

It had grown from a boatyard to a marina, expanding as the boat business flourished and as new competitive marinas were built. The showroom had been enlarged, and instead of a few slips along the shore, there now were also slips in dredged canals. Multilevel winter storage berths were the latest addition. Mary got out of the car and looked at the people puttering with gleaming white cabin cruisers in the network of docks.

She entered the showroom. Boats always seemed so much bigger indoors. She walked around the displays, and she didn't see a salesman or a customer. She tapped on Bill's office door and went in. The office was empty. She checked the other offices and the stockroom, and they were empty, too. Near the door to the old inside slips she heard voices.

She opened the door and went down the steps to the dark slippery platform. Oily water slapped quietly against the pilings.

And then she saw William Emerson, her father-in-law, out beyond on the long dock in the sunlight. She heard splashing, shouting. She ran down the dock and saw Bill and his younger brother Paul and Norma's son, Freddy, all struggling in the water beside a capsized Sunfish sailboat. They were fully clothed, and they were trying to wrestle a bathing-suited teenage boy to the dock.

"Hi, William," Mary said. "Another rescue?"

"The damn young idiot tipped over coming in. Must be high on something, he apparently wants to go down with his ship."

Bill popped out of the water onto the dock and leaned over and grabbed the boy's armpits under his flailing arms as Paul and Freddy pushed him up.

"Fuck you!" the boy yelled. "Fuck you! Fuck you!"

Bill said, "It's the Harrison kid, are his folks still here?"

Mary said, "I saw them working on their boat just now."

"Hi," Bill said to her, noticing her.

"Your clothes are a mess," Mary said, but she was used to that. An occupational hazard.

The Harrison kid yelled, "Fuck you!"

Paul and Freddy dragged him off toward his parents' boat, and Bill, looking philosophical, dived back in and righted the little sailboat and tied it up.

William said, "Mary, did you come through the showroom? Any customers?"

"Nobody."

"Good, then maybe we're the only witnesses to this scene."

Bill picked up his wallet and watch which he'd put on the dock. "I'll go home and change." He and Mary walked with William up into the showroom and met Paul and Freddy.

Paul said, "That kid is ready for a rubber room. And are his folks embarrassed."

William said, "Go home and change. Bill and Paul, don't bother coming back this afternoon, I'll handle things."

Bill looked at Mary, his eyes saying: Patriarch. "Okay," he said aloud. A customer came in, and Mary and Bill and Paul and Freddy went outdoors to their cars.

Mary said to Paul, "How's Donna doing? Neck brace off yet?" Paul's wife Donna had skidded and rolled her Volkswagen over in a late snowstorm last spring. She'd been alone in the car, the kids had been home with a baby-sitter, she was the only one hurt. The family wondered why she was still wearing her neck brace. According to her doctor, no medical reasons remained. And there was no whiplash lawsuit. And it wasn't a flattering piece of apparel. Bill had once observed that Donna was the sort of person who had a Dixie Cup dispenser in her bathroom but it was always empty. Mary had tried to find a reason for the neck brace in this observation.

Paul said, "She says she still needs the brace," and got soggily into his car and drove off.

Bill said to Mary, "How come you're here?"

"I didn't have any errands to do while Aunt Pleasantine visited."

"Were your old ladies glad to see each other?"

"Very. Funny, I think of them as new friends, not old friends as Grandmother and Aunt Pleasantine were, but hell, they've known each other thirty-odd years, and that's a long time for even a Christmas-card friendship. You all right?"

"Oily. I wish people wouldn't tip over near the gas pumps."

"Where's Leonard?" He was Bill's other brother. "I didn't find him reading *Hustler* in the stockroom."

"No, he's on a house call. Sensitive negotiations with a doctor about trading up."

"I'll be home soon."

"Anything I can do about supper?"

"No," she said, "it's simple, cold ham and coleslaw."

"I could make the coleslaw."

"Thank you."

They smiled at each other, because they were pronouncing it cole-e-slaw. Mary remembered sitting beside Bill in Romantic Poets class in college and hearing the professor bellow his annual announcement, famous on campus: "The man's name is Samuel Taylor Coleridge. His last name is pronounced Coleridge. It is *not* pronounced Cole-e-ridge. Did you ever hear coleslaw pronounced cole-e-slaw?"

Mary drove back to the Baldwin house. Mrs. Stafford opened the door and said loudly, "They've been having quite a gabfest."

Mary went into the living room. "Hello."

Aunt Pleasantine looked tired. The teacups were empty. She rose. "Please, Clara, don't get up. Thank you, this has been such a treat."

While they said good-bye, Mary wandered away, feeling awkward. She looked at pictures and discovered one which resembled Aunt Pleasantine's automobile photograph. In Clara's the women wore veils and dusters.

Aunt Pleasantine was silent almost all the way home. Then, as Mary turned off onto the dead-end road, Aunt Pleasantine said, "Clara invited me to stay for a visit. I politely declined. Poor Clara, did you see how bad her arthritis is?"

Later, on the porch, while in the living room Piaf sang, *"Non, je ne regrette rien,"* Aunt Pleasantine's cocktail-hour story started out to be entertaining, but it changed midway. "Do you remember when I returned to Brandon to become Mrs. Goodhue's companion? You and Connie called her Mrs. Goody-Two-Shoes behind her back. Whenever your parents were in Brandon visiting your grandparents, your mother would come over to Mrs. Goodhue's to visit me, and sometimes she brought you and Connie along. We mostly visited in the kitchen. Such an enormous kitchen, full of fascinating things for a child. Once we lost Connie and eventually found her playing cave in a pantry cupboard. Sometimes Mrs. Goodhue invited you and Connie into the living room and gave you bonbons." Aunt Pleasantine sipped her drink. "You and Connie were so curious about the house that after Mrs. Goodhue died, when your mother visited me while I was closing up the house and looking for another job, I let you and Connie have the run of the place. You promised not to touch anything. We expected you to be gone for hours, but you were back in five minutes. Do you remember?"

Mary nodded. She and Connie had rushed up the wide curving staircase to explore the mysterious upstairs. In the first bedroom they had halted abruptly. A canopied four-poster, plump satiny chairs, gilt-framed paintings. And a smell of age. Mary and Connie had backed out of the room, necks prickling. Mrs. Goodhue was dead, was not in the house and never would be again, never offer them bonbons again. Never. They looked down the long carpeted hall at the fragile vases on thin tables. They turned and fled down the stairs back to the safety of Mother and Aunt Pleasantine.

"I remember," Mary said.

Aunt Pleasantine said, "You two were white as sheets, and we asked you what on earth was wrong. You, Mary, wouldn't say anything, but Connie said she had felt a ghost."

The Hubcap King's hair was a cloud of red curls, reminding Mary always of crazy poets, not a house contractor, sailor, and hubcap collector. He came out of his ranch house as they drove up the driveway.

Bill said, "I'll just get Hub's dinghy and we'll be on our way."

Mary said, "But I think he wants to show Aunt Pleasantine his hubcaps. Yes, look."

Hub pushed up the garage door to display his collection. Silver circles dazzled.

"Good heavens," Aunt Pleasantine said.

Mary said, "Would you like to get out and take a look? He's got more all through the house, in even the attic and cellar, but his feelings won't be hurt if you just look at the garage collection."

"I'd love to." Aunt Pleasantine was sitting in the passenger seat of Bill's Chrysler; they'd insisted, and she gave in, apologizing for making Mary sit in what she called the "mother-in-law seat" in back. She hadn't said a word as they zoomed along the turnpike to the ocean until Bill asked, as they approached the Kingsbridge exit, "Want to go through the town?" Then she said, "Thank you, no."

Three hundred years ago the settlement of Kingsbridge had been built on a tidal river. Since the Second World War it had spread across new bridges and now dominated the cities around it.

They had sped past.

Bill helped Aunt Pleasantine out of the car. She wore blue cotton slacks and a white blouse.

The Hubcap King, whose name was Francis Watson, said, "Teresa—the kids—Sundays. *Teresa!*" he bawled into the salty breeze, but Teresa didn't come out of the house.

Aunt Pleasantine said, "What an interesting hobby."

Hub led her and Mary down the aisles in the garage. There were hubcaps on long counters, there were hubcaps on the walls and ceiling. He'd already begun collecting when Mary and Bill met him in college, and by now his accumulation was astonishing. People with cars which had lost a hubcap came to him and pleaded with him to let them buy one, and if it was an ordinary hubcap he usually would. His precious ones he didn't sell.

Aunt Pleasantine stopped and touched a hubcap. "Do you remember your grandmother's Packard, Mary? And how your grandfather cleverly never learned how to drive so she had to do all the driving?"

"Which was terrifying."

"Her theory was, 'drive at 'em.' "

Hub, not distracted by superfluous reminiscences, said, "Where's the Packard now, does she still own it?"

"No," Mary said. "Years ago she traded it in for a Mercury with automatic shift."

"Oh. Too bad. Hey, here's Teresa."

Teresa came into the garage. Hub had met her after college when he hired her as his bookkeeper. She was blond and Dresden-china pretty. Mary never knew quite what to make of her and, when they all dined out together, was rather frightened of her. Teresa had a tendency to get belligerent in bars. One summer they were in the Buccaneer Lounge of the disreputable Seacoast Chowder House, and a policeman came in checking for minors; Teresa had grabbed him by his sleeve and yelled, "What the hell do you think you're doing in here harassing *us,* you fucking old drunk!" Mary had expected to be jailed instantly. On an earlier occasion Teresa had been arrested, drunk and disorderly and shouting wonderful insults at the cops. Hub was proud of her.

"Hi," she said to Aunt Pleasantine. "Isn't the collection great? Did Mary tell you there's lots more indoors?"

"It's—overwhelming."

Teresa said, "Hub ought to be in *The Guinness Book of World Records.*"

Hub tried to look modest. "Teresa is biased. I'll go give Bill a hand." He left.

Teresa said, "I've got a baby-sitter all arranged, so we'll be up for your party." Their children were younger than most of their contemporaries' because they'd waited to have kids. "The party isn't going to be dressy, is it?"

"Very informal. Wear anything, bring a bathing suit."

Aunt Pleasantine said, "The hubcaps are all so shiny. Polishing them must be a tremendous job."

"Hub doesn't mind," Teresa said. "When we got engaged, I told him I thought his collection was terrific but I refused to polish it. He said he didn't expect me to, he likes polishing. I'd better go in and see what the kids are doing. Sundays. I can't find anything on TV except God, and that doesn't keep them amused."

After Teresa left, Mary asked, "Had enough?"

"They get blinding, don't they. I've been looking for a Jaguar, but I can't see one."

"I'm sure he's got at least one somewhere."

"Do you remember Mrs. Goodhue's Jaguar? Not a sports model, of course. I used to chauffeur her around in it."

Outdoors, Bill and Hub had put the dinghy on the roof of the car and the oars in the back seat, and they were hunkering in the driveway discussing the economy. The dinghy was white fiberglass, larger than Bill's cockleshell and safer for Aunt Pleasantine in an emergency. Mary, looking at it, reflected that Bill's preference for small dangerous boats even included dinghies.

"—tract houses," Hub said, "cheap developments, I'm the first to admit mine are, but they're better than some. Some companies, they buy wood that's been cut down the day before, so the next ten years the homeowners have to listen to the green wood snap. I try to keep my standards, but if the economy doesn't turn around soon—"

"All set?" Bill said to Mary, standing up.

Aunt Pleasantine said, "Thank you for letting me see your collection."

Bill helped her into the car. "Watch out for the lash lines."

Teresa came to the front door with her younger son, and she and Hub waved as they drove off.

They drove up the narrow coast road. Aunt Pleasantine was silent, looking out the window at the ocean, looking in the direction of the ocean when it was hidden behind seawalls. The day was clear, and on the horizon across the blue water the Isles of Shoals seemed very close. Sea gulls drifted in the air, then plummeted.

Camps were crammed together, big old-fashioned cottages, shabby shacks, rusty trailers, and new houses with freshwater swimming pools beside the ocean. Most of the cars parked in the driveways had Massachusetts license plates.

Aunt Pleasantine said, "I told you, didn't I, how much I enjoy your pictures of this."

Mary had painted and photographed these scenes again and again, the ocean, the islands, the coast road, the beaches, the camps, the harbor. They sold fairly well. "I keep trying; maybe I'll get it right one of these days. Do you know the story of how Turner—he's my favorite—had himself lashed to a mast for four hours in a storm so he could observe it? He figured he'd either get killed or get it right. What he got was *Snowstorm—Steamboat off a Harbor's Mouth.*"

Bill said, "And the critics hated it. 'Soapsuds and whitewash.' "

"My problem is," Mary said, "whenever we've hit a storm, I'm so busy being scared and obeying orders that I don't have any chance to observe anything." She added a request she made often. "I wish you wouldn't yell your orders, Bill."

"I wish you'd listen," Bill said, the reply he always made. "Here we are."

The harbor was crowded on Sundays, but Bill found a parking space. The sea breeze through the car's open windows ruffled the wisps of Aunt Pleasantine's French twist. Aunt Pleasantine sniffed the air and said, "Beautiful."

It didn't exactly smell beautiful, Mary thought, because the lobster boat at one of the docks had just dumped its leftover bait overboard, and pieces of fish were floating in the water, stinking. But it certainly was an ocean smell, and she knew what Aunt Pleasantine meant. Sea gulls screamed.

Bill said, "Mary and I'll get things organized. Do you mind a short wait?"

"Not at all," Aunt Pleasantine said. "Amazing how little this harbor has changed. That general store was here when Becky and I used to come here."

Bill said, "Really? I knew it was old, but I didn't realize—" He stopped.

"We flirted with the sons of the owner."

Mary clambered out of the car and pulled the oars out of the back seat, and Bill began unlashing the dinghy.

The old store had weathered so many gales that its clapboards looked like driftwood. On the door of the new cinder-block addition was a sign:

NO BARE FEET
OR PETS
MEN MUST WEAR SHIRTS

"No bare pets?" Mary murmured as she always did when she noticed the sign.

Behind the store the modern restaurant named Davy Jones's Locker had opened for its Sunday buffet.

The harbor was small. Cottages and lobster shacks, a blur of pastel colors, curved around its shore. Two floating wooden ramps went down to two floating docks. One dock was heaped with lobster traps. On the other, a man and woman wearing crisp white Bermudas and red jerseys and white caps were loading a cabin cruiser named *Dreamboat.* Beyond the bait the many boats moored in the harbor were bright and clean, and over the water came voices.

Mary, helping Bill lift down the dinghy, said, "Don't you just love that couple's matching outfits?"

"Well, look at us."

They both were wearing torn-off Levi's shorts and faded blue shirts. Mary said, "At least our hats are different." His was a beat-up blue denim crew hat, hers was a red one faded to pink. "Heave ho," she said, and she and Bill lugged the dinghy down to the launching beach.

Nearby a sign on a litter bin said: DUMPING OF LARGE FURNITURE AND APPLIANCES PROHIBITED, and Mary imagined Massachusetts people arriving with trailer-loads of rump-sprung armchairs and broken washing machines which their garbage collectors had refused.

Bill rowed off, and she watched him. When he had first taken her to the lake's Yacht Club twenty years ago to teach her to sail, she'd been irritated by the slow pace of the whole thing. "Sailing," she'd said, "is mostly waiting." He'd said, "What's wrong with waiting?" and soon her impatience had ebbed. But today she felt it jangling again. He rowed out past moored boats, and she returned to the car for the gear and saw that Aunt Pleasantine had got out and was watching, too.

Aunt Pleasantine walked over to a pile of ancient lobster traps which were bejeweled with barnacles.

Mary said, "He'll be a while."

"When I was a girl, I went lobstering with a Kingsbridge boyfriend who had a few pots. Pulling them out of the water is very strenuous."

"You went unchaperoned?"

"Grandma thought I was spending the day at Becky's."

"I've never gone lobstering. Bill has."

Dreamboat moved off. Mary walked down the ramp to the dock and set down the gear. Bill had reached the spot where Hub's boat, the *Teresa II,* was moored. Mary walked back up to the car.

Aunt Pleasantine had put on her sunglasses and Oriental hat.

Mary said, "Guess I've got everything. If you want to freshen up, there's a rest room over there, kind of primitive—"

"I know, I've already visited it."

They walked toward the left-hand ramp.

Mary wished the Isles idea had never occurred to her. "Aunt Pleasie, if you're suddenly nervous about this outing, just say so and we'll cancel it."

"My God, Mary, this is fun! And we haven't even left dry land! Don't worry, I'm not nervous."

Mary, nearing the ramp, knew that she herself was the one who was nervous. Terrified. Scared to death about getting Aunt Pleasantine down to the dock safely. The tide had made the steep ramp even steeper. "We'll go slowly."

"I'm slow-motion. A tortoise. I'll get there."

Very slowly they went down the long ramp, Aunt Pleasantine gripping the rail and Mary's arm, pausing now and then, braced against the cleats. During the pauses she looked at the view. They reached the foot of the ramp, and Mary helped her step over the gap of water onto the dock. She'd got there.

"Good timing," Mary said, heart pounding. "Bill's on his way."

"Yes, I see him."

Mary breathed what she hoped were not too obvious deep inhalations and began to relax. "Don't worry about a borrowed boat. We know it, we've borrowed it before. And don't worry about sinking. I think Teresa must have every piece of Tupperware ever made, and the galley is so full of Tupperware that Bill says sinking is impossible."

Aunt Pleasantine smiled. Bill motored in to the dock. He helped Aunt Pleasantine into the boat and helped her put on a life jacket. Mary stowed away the gear and cast off, and they motored out of the harbor.

Mary said, "The wind's okay?"

"Ideal," Bill said.

Mary ran around obeying orders. The sails went up, flapping wildly, always exciting. Bill held the lines and settled in at the tiller, and Mary sat sideways, cross-legged, on the deck above the cabin. They sailed for the Isles of Shoals.

Mary said, "Do you want some sunscreen lotion, Aunt Pleasantine? I brought some."

"Thank you, but I think this hat will protect me."

Mary looked at her sitting there calmly, watching everything, and all at once Mary remembered one of Mother's childhood memories of Aunt Pleasantine before the divorce and the money loss, at a party at Grandmother and Grandfather's house. Mother said, "I was supposed to be sound asleep in bed, but I got up and peeked over the banister, and I saw Aunt Pleasantine sitting on the staircase being courted by four or five men."

Mary went down into the cabin and dug beers out of the cooler and found a Tupperware glass for Aunt Pleasantine.

On deck Aunt Pleasantine said, "Thank you," and the beer prompted a story. "James and I used to rent a summer cottage in Maine. We had many picnics and parties with friends and visiting firemen. I remember best a picnic far up the coast from our cottage. We were picnicking on a rocky piece of shore, and James decided he wanted to go swimming at a nearby hidden beach, but the rest of us—your grandparents were visiting us, Mary—weren't in the mood for a dip, so he went off alone. I suddenly realized James hadn't brought along a bathing suit. I couldn't resist. We sneaked over, and sure enough, there were his clothes piled on the beach, and he was swimming so far out he wouldn't see the raid. I gathered up his clothes, and we ran back and put them in the car. We continued our picnic. I recall that a flask was an important part of our picnics. We were merry. And soon we heard James. I'll never forget the sight of him creeping naked through the bushes, shouting, 'Pleasantine, give me back my clothes!' "

They enjoyed that, and Mary asked, "Did you give them back to him?"

"Eventually," Aunt Pleasantine said.

The Isles of Shoals loomed larger and larger. A huge old white hotel was mostly all that remained of the old summer resort. Before the resort period, fishermen had lived here.

The chain of rough gray islands held secrets, everything from flowers to murders.

Aunt Pleasantine recited the names of the islands. "Appledore. Smuttynose. Cedar. Star. White Island."

Moored off the islands today were sailboats and cabin cruisers. Mary saw Bill eye, as usual, a catamaran, and she wondered if someday he would buy one. People rowed dinghies into shore; other people fussed on their boats, getting lunch ready.

Bill had decided not to risk lowering Aunt Pleasantine into the dinghy except in an emergency, so Mary walked out to the bow and studied the dock at Star Island and waited to be yelled at. She was. Bill, loosening sails, gave orders, and she flung fenders over the side, and Bill motored up to the dock, and she jumped out and tied up.

"I'm trying to remember," Aunt Pleasantine said after Mary and Bill had helped her out of the boat, "how many years it's been since I was last here. It's hard to notice that you're doing something for the last time when you don't know you are."

Mary unloaded the picnic cooler and blanket. She always felt that on the Isles she should be wearing a long summer dress. Bill motored out and dropped anchor, then rowed the dinghy in and joined them as they were slowly climbing the path up the bleak island.

He said, "Was it in the Florida newspapers that a company tried to put an oil refinery in Durham and they planned to moor tankers off the Isles of Shoals?"

Aunt Pleasantine nodded. "The evening television news reported that Durham had voted it down, a small town versus a big company, and I silently gave a great whoop of joy."

"We're still betting the bastards will manage it somehow. And now we're worrying about a nuclear power plant being built in Seabrook."

"Are nuclear power plants dangerous or safe? The arguments confuse me."

Bill said, "Using a nuclear power plant is like jumping out of an airplane and trying to invent the parachute on the way down. Where's your favorite picnic spot?"

Aunt Pleasantine chose a view of the White Island lighthouse, and Bill helped her lower herself onto the picnic blanket. "What an elegant lunch," she said as Mary unpacked lobster salad rolls, a bottle of white wine, and wineglasses, and after Bill poured her some wine, she said, "Did I write you about the lobster party the children gave last year? I'm sure I must have. Oliver, who was

Hester's fiancé, you know, got the bright idea and luckily he could afford it. He had a shipment of live lobsters flown down from Boston. All the way from Boston. The children steamed them for the party, but I prefer a cold salad, which I had the next day. The children wore lovely outfits at the party, flowing hostess trousers."

Mary did remember the letter describing the party. Between the lines she'd read that Aunt Pleasantine hadn't been allowed to join in the eating of the lobsters, she'd had leftovers the next day. Punishment? An earlier paragraph mentioned her embarrassment about forgetting to pay for a box of Kleenex she'd asked her daughters to pick up for her while they were shopping; they'd reminded her they hadn't been reimbursed, and she'd joked in the letter about her age and loss of memory. The letter concluded, "Do you know this old adage? 'There are two ways of meeting difficulties. You either alter the difficulties or you alter yourself to meet them.' I think I have learned both how to change the difficulties and how to change myself. Looking back, I guess I've been learning how for the past sixty years."

Mary nibbled a potato chip and tried to come up with an answer.

Bill was saying, "Shoals. Didn't that company know what the word means? Did they ever open a chart of this? They planned to moor tankers off *shoals?*"

"Shocking," Aunt Pleasantine said. "Celia Thaxter could have told them about shipwrecks here. Large and small. Remember how she tells about their lighthouse boat coming into the lighthouse from a trip to Portsmouth for provisions? The breakers were so bad it capsized, and they lost everything except a roll of wire and a barrel of walnuts."

After the picnic, as they walked around the island, Mary remembered Mother's only childhood memory of Aunt Pleasantine and James's house in Brandon. "The Curtis house was a handsome house," Mother said, "but all I remember is a sunroom for birds of every kind."

They walked down to the dock. Mary and Aunt Pleasantine waited while Bill rowed out to the boat, and Aunt Pleasantine said, "Do you remember when I brought you and Connie to the ocean to give your parents a break? You must have been four, and Connie was one and a half. She was too young to understand where she was, that this was different from the lake, but you took my hand and marched right into the waves and you loved it."

"I think I remember."

Aunt Pleasantine watched Bill motor toward the dock. "The children served exotic canapés at the lobster party. Including caviar, which reminded me of the jar of caviar Al Dawson sent me once when I had a cold. He sent a dozen red roses, too. It was just before things went wrong. Dear Al, he didn't simply send roses, he sent caviar also."

The sail back to the mainland was more complicated than the sail out. The wind was tricky, and Bill had to do a lot of tacking. The boat heeled. None of this seemed to faze Aunt Pleasantine. She sat bracing herself, watching Bill and Mary work.

And after they'd returned the dinghy and oars to Hub and were driving home, she listened to Bill talk about money.

He said, "Social Security isn't enough. You can't live on it. I know we're not family, we're not blood relatives, but you and Mary's family have been so close you've got to let us help you."

In the back seat Mary waited.

Aunt Pleasantine didn't say anything.

Bill persevered. "Think it over. Don't dismiss it. My God, we've got plenty of room in our house."

Aunt Pleasantine patted her French twist. Mary saw her hand was trembling.

Bill said, "We admire your independence. If you'd rather live alone, if you think you'd be safe living alone, let us help you do that. There're some condominiums in Saffron with views of the lake, and we'd be nearby."

Silence.

Bill said, "The main thing is, what we don't want you to do is go back to Florida and take any more of that shit—I beg your pardon."

Aunt Pleasantine said quickly, "The children are going through a troubled time. I was underfoot. *De trop.* That's all."

So Mary knew now for certain Aunt Pleasantine had been on the verge of getting kicked out. Aunt Pleasantine had left first.

"You're very kind," Aunt Pleasantine said. "But." Then she used her age. She leaned her head back against the headrest, said, "Goodness, I must need my nap, such an exciting day," and she closed her eyes and appeared to doze.

Bill looked at Mary in the rearview mirror.

The next evening Connie phoned from Vermont while Mary was washing the supper dishes. Connie phoned when long-distance rates were cheap. Mary said into the kitchen extension, "Hi, how are you?"

"It's a madhouse, as usual. But how are *you,* how's Aunt Pleasantine, how are things going? Can you talk?"

"Yes, she's in her room reading until TV. Things are sort of settling down. She was happy to get your postcard. How are the kids?"

"Mary, don't ask."

Connie had two sets of twins. "Just," as she often remarked, "like the fucking Bobbseys." But Connie's twins were all boys. The older set was fifteen years old. When they were nine, Connie decided she wanted a daughter. She got another set of twin sons, now five years old. Her husband, George, was a small-town newspaper reporter, and his salary barely kept the family in shoes; Connie actually wore rubber shower sandals all the time.

Mary said, "Aunt Pleasantine spent today reading *Fanny Hill* on the porch. She spotted it in a bookcase and said she'd always wanted to read it. I glanced out at her every now and then. A sweet little old lady giggling fiendishly over *Fanny Hill.*"

"You'll have to lend her *The Story of O* next."

"That's an idea." Mary looked out the kitchen window. Twilight trees. "Yesterday Bill tried to get her to let us help her. She wouldn't answer."

"If only she were thirty years younger and we had space for her in our hovel, she could come here and help me with the kids the way she did for Mother, an excuse for room and board. We could maybe manage the expense. Maybe. Maybe. Have you got around to reading the TA books yet?"

"Not yet—"

In her spare time Connie was reading Transactional Analysis books. She'd suggested titles to Mary, and Mary had bought paperbacks of a couple, had read the first page of each, and, bored stiff, put them away. She felt unsisterly, disloyal, about this. Connie suffered deep depressions, something Mother had never been able to fit into the "sweet disposition" category. Mary hoped TA would help Connie; any port in a storm.

Connie said, "Do you know more about what happened in Florida? You said her phone call was incoherent? Have you made sense of it?"

"Most of the call was incoherent, asking if my standing invitation still stood because she needed a change of scenery. I only realized it was an emergency when she got specific about dates. She wanted to come in two days, she had the flight number, and Elizabeth would drive her to the airport. The rest was awfully vague, something about her having had the flu and something about Hester's boyfriend had died. I said of course the invitation still stood."

"Sounds like a mess."

"I'm positive her daughters were going to tell her to move out. But why and where?"

"I've got to hang up," Connie said. "The kids are fighting. I don't know which is worse, teenagers or preschoolers. The other day Dave and Keith were in the getaway car that picked up one of their buddies who streaked through a tourist trap."

"No!"

"Yes, we got a little visit from a cop. Thank God he found it funny, thank God the twins didn't do the streaking. And yesterday—this is the really bad news I didn't want to tell you—Bobby and Tommy were playing with a roll of paper towels I hadn't had a chance to put away, and they carefully flushed the entire roll into the toilet."

"Oh, hell."

"At least we never got around to tearing down the outhouse. We're using that now. Tomorrow the plumber will arrive. In his Cadillac. Give Aunt Pleasantine my love, see you at the party. Oh—be forewarned, Dave and Keith's appetites are still enormous, don't count them as regular guests, get in extra supplies. Christ, every time I go past the kitchen doorway all I can hear is the sound of munching."

During television Mary told Aunt Pleasantine about Connie's call and news.

Aunt Pleasantine said, "I saw two streakers this spring. I believe I forgot to write you that."

"Two?" Bill said.

"They were together. Oliver, Hester's fiancé, had taken us all out to dinner at a very fancy restaurant. He insisted I come along with him and Hester and Elizabeth and Elizabeth's beau, Ralph. It was Oliver's sixty-ninth birthday. We had seafood crepes and champagne. A fine meal, I thought, but Hester was dissatisfied with the service. Anyway, during coffee there was a sudden commotion in the lobby, and into the dining room dashed two streakers. They were passing a football back and forth. In the middle of the room they assumed a three-point football position, you know what I mean, legs spread, bent over with one hand touching the floor. Then waiters rushed at them, and they did a broken-field run out of the restaurant. I hope they got away safely. You ought to have heard the shrieks of the ladies in the place. I thought Hester and Elizabeth were going to faint. Oliver was angry. Ralph and I laughed and laughed."

After television, when Aunt Pleasantine had gone to bed, Mary went upstairs and searched the bedroom bookcases for Lynn Caine's *Widow.* She found it, went downstairs and out to the porch, where Bill in the lamplight was still in the Hindu Kush.

He glanced up. "I thought you bought that because you knew you should read it but you couldn't get up the guts."

"I did read it, last month."

He took the book from her and looked at the title. "Makes me feel like I'm already dead and gone."

"I read it in one afternoon, crying my eyes out." Mary walked to the porch railing. The lake was black, glimmering. "I couldn't ask then but I can now. I won't cry. There's a chapter Caine asks husbands to read. Would you? Not tonight, just sometime."

"Okay."

"Chapter Twenty-one, 'Contingency Day.' The point is, I've got to stop being an ostrich. We should sit down once a year and you'll bring me up to date on money. Life insurance and stuff."

"You've never wanted to hear about life insurance."

"I'm praying I'll croak before you do so I won't have to live without you. But statistics say my odds aren't too swell."

"If I croak first," Bill said, "you'll starve to death soon anyway because you can't open jars."

"If I don't starve, if I buy a jar opener to replace you, what then?"

"We're simple. No kids. I have a twenty-five-thousand-dollar policy. The Marina pays the premiums. Reread Jessica Mitford and buy me the cheapest pine coffin, find me the cheapest crematory, that'll be a battle with the undertakers, that'll keep you occupied. No memorial service. Don't waste any money on funeral crap."

"I didn't intend to. How about if I sail out and heave you overboard in a gunnysack?"

"You've read the wills, you know we're each other's executors. Everything we own goes to you when I die, and if the house isn't paid for by then, my death will pay it off, we've got mortgage insurance. My shares in the Marina go to you, and of course, our joint accounts. And my gas guzzler is a company car, your car and *Nomad* are paid for. No sweat. The Marina will support you. You won't have to earn your living with your paintbrush."

Mary snapped, "Don't be patronizing!"

"Sorry, didn't mean to be."

Mary walked down the long porch. She walked back. "What a horrible subject. Once a year is definitely all I can take of Contingency Day."

Bill pulled her onto his lap.

Moths bumped against the screens.

"Seeing Aunt Pleasie," Mary said. "Seeing her so helpless."

"Do you know why she never remarried?"

"Nobody in the family could ever figure it out. Everyone gossiped, especially about the husbands of people she worked for and a handyman or somebody at The Mountain Inn, but she never married any of them."

"How old was she when Dawson died?"

"In her thirties, I think. Grandmother said she'd planned to marry him after an interval after the divorce. She's so beautiful. If only she could have snared a millionaire."

"An unliberated wish, but practical."

"Hell," Mary said, "she was liberated for her time. She was sheltered before the divorce, but afterward she coped. Clerking in stores, running households, running that Inn, factory work during the War as well as helping Mother out, all her jobs. She supported herself and she supported her daughters until they were married."

"No alimony or child support?"

"I gather not. I don't know why."

"Want a drink?"

"Yes."

While Bill was indoors, Mary remembered cleaning out the farmhouse after Mother died. One day, when Connie and George were working downstairs and Bill was in the barn, she had collected her courage and set to work on her parents' bedroom closet. She made two piles of clothes: things for the Salvation Army and things Connie might be able to use. Some of Mother's clothes were Grandmother's, which Mother had saved after clearing out Grandmother's closet. Mary had never been able to understand how Mother could wear them. But maybe Connie could bring herself to make over Mother's somehow for the kids, as she had Father's. Mary lifted down hatboxes from the closet shelf. She opened the first one and almost leaped out of her skin. It wasn't a hatbox, it was a wigbox, and it contained the gray wig Mother had bought for special occasions before she became ill. Mary had fled downstairs and outdoors to the barn.

Bill brought the drinks.

"Thank you," Mary said, kicking off her leather thongs. "I think I'll go visit the dock."

She walked barefoot down the cool dark lawn. The sailboat creaked. She sat on the end of the dock and sipped her drink and, dabbling her toes in the water, wondered if she herself was a dabbler. "You won't have to earn your living with your paintbrush."

When she was a kid, she had imagined she would grow up to live a bohemian life in New York, doing innovative works which would eventually be recognized. She had instead grown up to sell paintings and photographs to tourists.

She heard girls' voices far away at the girls' camp up the lake. She thought of Norma, art teacher and arts counselor, and realized that she'd never asked Norma what she in her childhood had hoped to happen when she learned she was clever with a crayon.

Two days later Aunt Pleasantine, making her breakfast of tea and cinnamon toast in the kitchen, said, "I've been doing my exercises. I suppose I should be taking my daily walks. Is that a path into the woods?"

"Yes, to the end of the Point and then it loops back along the shore. I'll just change out of this bathing suit—"

'No, no. I'll be fine. I always take my walks alone; in fact, I've become very skillful at avoiding neighbors who want to join me."

"But if you should fall—"

"The children gave me a police whistle. I'll bring it with me into the woods. Please, Mary, do your work as usual."

So Mary went upstairs and quickly showered, and in her workroom she matted the new regatta prints for Jerry. The room was the sunniest room in the house. After a while she saw Aunt Pleasantine emerge from the woods and move slowly toward the pale little curve of beach beside the dock. Mary wondered if vanity was what made her not use a cane. Aunt Pleasantine sat down in a beach chair and looked at the morning lake.

Later, when Aunt Pleasantine came out of her room for *Hollywood Squares,* she was carrying a frayed photograph album. "I've found some pictures of James in one of your grandparents' albums."

Mary took the album and sat down.

Aunt Pleasantine said, "That's James."

"I'd've guessed. Good Lord, he *was* handsome!"

Aunt Pleasantine watched the show, and Mary studied the pictures. Brown snapshots, they'd all been taken at beach picnics, and everyone wore funny old-fashioned bathing suits.

During a commercial break Aunt Pleasantine said, "You know, I'm sure, that long ago the children and I spent a month on this lake with your grandparents, who had rented a camp for a month. The Websters had closed up their house that August and given me a vacation. Your mother and my girls were teenagers, and did they have a whirl!"

"Mother used to point out where the camp was. There's a motel now. Weren't you visiting them the summer Mother met Father?"

"Yes. In the winter I resigned and went to work for Mrs. Kimball, because Mrs. Webster heard unfounded rumors about me and Mr. Webster. Mrs. Kimball was a widow. Anyway, your father came to the camp delivering milk. Your mother and Hester and Elizabeth giggled about his being a milkman, a farmer, but he was so handsome Louisa couldn't resist him. Heavens, I wished I were twenty years younger, I'd have thrown my cap over the windmill, too."

"But Grandfather made them wait to get married."

"Your grandfather wanted Louisa to have at least one year of college before she decided. No doubt he was wise, but the situation was very difficult for Louisa and Arthur. Romance," said

Aunt Pleasantine, "is always very difficult."

During the next commercial she said, "Milk no longer tastes different in the spring. It used to taste different, and one knew the cows had been put out to pasture."

"I miss the glass bottles."

"I miss especially the little cream bottles."

Mary said, "It's amazing Mother adjusted to farm life. I gather she didn't know which end of a cow was which when she came here."

"It certainly amazed your grandparents. But your mother loved your father, and what made him happy made her happy. I'll never forget those sweltering summer days when we did the canning, both of us trying to keep an eye on you and Connie and the wood range *and* the canning kettles *and*—! Louisa wasn't just stocking up for winter. She was determined to pack perfect jars because she knew your father liked to go down cellar and look at the canning shelves. He thought shelves of canned vegetables and fruit were beautiful. Soon Louisa won canning prizes at the Fair."

"Yes."

At lunch Aunt Pleasantine said, "James was the most handsome man I ever knew. But did you notice his air of being mightily pleased with himself?"

"Um," Mary said.

"I never noticed it for the longest time."

They ate.

"Probably I didn't notice," Aunt Pleasantine said, "because I was so mightily pleased with *my*self."

"In those snapshots you don't look that way. You look—mischievous."

Later, when Aunt Pleasantine was invited to the porch for drinks, her cocktail-hour story was: "Mischievous. You're right, Mary. I remember one day I bought a gorgeous outfit in Boston.

When I got back to Brandon, I put on my new finery and arranged myself decoratively on the sofa to greet James when he came home from wherever he'd been. He came home, but he didn't notice my new clothes at all. He went off upstairs for a nap before dinner. I was crushed. But I got my revenge by sneaking upstairs with a pitcher of water and pouring the water into his new special deluxe shoes which he'd taken off and placed beside the wardrobe."

Mary said, "What a unique revenge!"

"I can't imagine now how I thought it up."

That evening, Mary and Bill and Aunt Pleasantine went to the Summer Playhouse and saw a summer-stock *My Fair Lady.* Aunt Pleasantine, excited, wore her wispy dress. The Playhouse was a huge converted barn. In the audience, people who weren't familiar with the Playhouse's problem ducked and cringed whenever bats zoomed down from the rafters. Some women squealed, disconcerting poor Henry Higgins. But Aunt Pleasantine didn't seem to notice the bats. She sat very straight on the hard wooden seat, her hands folded on her evening purse, and she seemed in a trance.

During the drive home toward the lake she said, "Miss Vera Miller was the most disagreeable person I ever worked for, but her yearly trips to England made me stay on until she died. I would have put up with the world's worst tyrant in order to see London once a year. Did I mention I saved the postcard you sent when you were there? And I was so glad you went on the *Queen Mary.*"

Bill said, "Mary insisted. She thinks it was named for her."

"I insisted," Mary said, "because I knew if I agreed to whatever the smaller ship was Bill wanted, he would keep conning me into something smaller and smaller and we'd end up trying to sail the Atlantic in *Nomad.*"

Bill said, "So what happens? Mary gets seasick. I think she must be the only person who ever got seasick on the *Queen Mary.* The damn ship was a floating city, Mary, it's impossible you felt any motion."

"In the shower," Mary said. "Just a few times in the shower."

Aunt Pleasantine said, "Oh, dear, I hope that didn't spoil your voyage."

"No, I popped Dramamine and was fine. Much better than Bill was when we got to London and visited the Tower. He took one look at the beheading spot, and I thought he was going to pass out."

"Grisly," Bill said.

Aunt Pleasantine said, "But so historic."

Mary said, "Bill waved cheerio to the beefeater guide and dragged me off to get a slug of Beefeater gin."

Bill turned onto the lake road. Some camps were dark. Some yellow windows showed backs of heads watching television, showed knotty pine and knickknacks.

Mary said, "How many yearly trips did you make to England? It was after you worked for Mrs. Goodhue, wasn't it?"

"Mrs. Goodhue died in nineteen-forty-nine, and I became Vera Miller's companion a few months later, in nineteen-fifty. I was fifty-nine then. Vera died in nineteen-fifty-seven. We went to England seven years, right up to her death. I must say, to her credit, she was a game old girl."

Mary, doing arithmetic, realized that in nineteen-fifty-seven Aunt Pleasantine was sixty-six, not exactly a spring chicken herself.

At home, in the kitchen, Bill said, "Won't you have a drink with us?"

Aunt Pleasantine glanced uncertainly at Mary, who said, "If you're like me, I get so keyed up by plays I can't go to bed immediately. Plays make me nervous because I'm afraid the actors will forget their lines."

"Thank you."

They all sat on the porch and watched the lake.

After a while, Bill hummed the chorus of "With a Little Bit of Luck."

And after a while, Aunt Pleasantine said, "Weren't the flowers on stage beautiful? I suppose they were fake, but they reminded me of the trip to the Lake District which Vera and I made one year. We visited Wordsworth's grave. It was springtime, and there was a light rain. The churchyard was deserted, but somebody had thrown a bouquet of wild daffodils on the grave."

Mary said, "I bet I can guess what poem you recited in bed that night."

"Actually, I recited it at the grave. To myself, of course, not aloud. Then we drove over to Dove Cottage."

A yahoo speedboat came smacking along the water toward the Point, and as it passed the camp they heard a man and woman laughing.

Mary looked at Bill.

"Yeah," he said, "Leonard's laugh. He's not with Janice, naturally. I wonder with whom?"

The boat roared on, and its lights vanished beyond the Point.

When Bill got home from work the next evening, he was furious.

Mary saw this at once, so she didn't greet him, didn't kiss him, and kept on boning chicken breasts. He slammed around the kitchen, made a drink, and, to her relief, strode outdoors and disappeared into the woods.

Bill's temper had taught her to control her own. Her childhood tantrums were a family legend. She'd banged her head on the floor; she held her breath and turned blue. When a grammar school bully threatened her or baby sister Connie, she beat him up, at insane risk to life and limb. She never felt the bullies' blows, and the next day she was always startled to discover bruises. Mother used to recite:

> There was a little girl who had a little curl
> Right in the middle of her forehead,
> And when she was good, she was very, very good
> And when she was bad, she was horrid.

In high school, Mary had fought Mother all the way. If arguments didn't work, she threw things. She could still recall the satisfaction of hurling a shoe at Mother and hitting her solidly in her solid stomach because Mother wouldn't let her go to a pajama party at the home of a girl Mother categorized as "cheap." Father helplessly attempted peacemaking, and Connie observed from the sidelines.

But those had been safe fights. She hadn't cared about the consequences. Fights with Bill, she'd learned, were dangerous. He might leave her forever. So she stopped fighting. She could nag and insinuate, but if she was really angry she fumed silently. And when he was in tonight's foul mood she kept silent, too, because just her speaking, just her asking him what was wrong, could spark an explosion.

She set the porch table. Bill walked up the lawn and went indoors. Soon he came downstairs in his swim trunks.

He said, "I'm going for a sail."

She nodded.

"You want to come along?"

She stared at him.

"Well, make up your mind, I'm not waiting."

She ran down the hall and knocked on Aunt Pleasantine's door and called, "Will you be okay if we take off for a sail?"

Aunt Pleasantine, holding an old photograph album, opened the door. "I'll be fine. Have fun."

"The drinks tray is in the kitchen, and if you get hungry—"

"Isn't there some way I can help out with supper?"

Mary hesitated, wondering whether or not Aunt Pleasantine

would want to or was able to. "I haven't cut up the string beans yet—"

"I'll cut them. Do you cut them the way your mother did?"

"Yes. Thank you."

"Run along."

The lake wasn't so crowded as it was on weekends, but it was noisy. The end of July; summer half over; everyone was playing feverishly. Speedboats roared around, towing water-skiers.

Yet despite the noise of the motorboats, *Nomad* and the other sailboats on the lake seemed serene, isolated in their slowness and silence.

Bill tacked past Duck Island. Mary held the jib line and remembered when most of the islands were empty and a childhood dream of hers had been to be a castaway. Now the islands were jammed with camps, ringed with docks.

She looked up at the white slants of sail and pictured her easel in her workroom. After breakfast this morning Aunt Pleasantine said, "I hope I didn't wake you or Bill last night. I couldn't sleep and the poems didn't do the trick so I turned on the radio you so kindly put in my room. I found the strangest program. I couldn't figure it out at first, but I gradually gathered that people from all over the country were calling in to a man in Boston to talk about things. They were all phoning a perfect stranger to tell him personal things."

"Yes," Mary had said, "it's a call-in talk show. Trouble is, it puts Bill to sleep but I get so interested I stay awake."

"Exactly," Aunt Pleasantine said. "I was fascinated. One woman went on and on about her canary. A man who worked in a gas station told how he'd been held up and robbed the night before last. His voice was still shaky. A striptease artist who had a cold and wasn't working called in and talked about her job. It doesn't involve just stripping, it also involves drinking champagne with customers. Real champagne, I wonder, or ginger ale? And someone in Chicago asked about the Freedom Trail in Boston, and then lots of callers talked about the Bicentennial, many of them using that term 'rip-off,' which I think I understand but probably don't. Some people sounded drunk. The host of the program never flagged, he took call after call. What a crazy job."

Bill sailed past Little Triangle Island and out into the widest part of the lake. This was named The Broads, a name considered extremely humorous by generations of Saffron Walden teenagers. The camps along the shore were distant now and hidden in woods.

The Broads could be dangerous during weather as calm as this evening, but Bill loosened the sails, dropped anchor, dived overboard, and swam.

When Mary had gone upstairs to her workroom today, she'd intended to start work on a painting of Aunt Pleasantine. A small canvas. Instead, she found herself stretching a huge canvas and starting a painting of the call-in talk show. Late-night people. Lonely people, drunks, insomniacs, night watchmen, cleaning women, policemen, bakers, widows. Telephone lines.

Bill climbed into the boat. "Brown study?"

She crawled forward and got a towel and handed it to him.

He said, "Did Aunt Pleasantine have a good day?"

She looked at him, gauging his mood. "Before her walk she complimented me again on the flower beds, and she said the herb garden smelled heavenly and how beautiful the bulb garden must be in the spring. She said she'd had a bulb garden at her Inn, mainly for her own enjoyment because only the very early guests saw it, and she mentioned Wordsworth's wild daffodils again. Shaggy little daffodils. And finally I got her drift. She wanted to work in the flower beds."

"The bending, though."

"I know, that's why I was so slow on the uptake, it didn't occur to me she could do it. I asked her if she'd like to and what she would need, and she said a claw and a cushion and a hat, so I got them and she sat on the lawn and spent most of the morning weeding."

"Sorry I was shitty."

He pulled up the anchor. His bare back was as dark as the boat's mahogany. He always apologized after a foul mood, but he hadn't ever before asked her to run away from it with him.

She said, "Thanks for the sail."

They tacked back toward the camp.

Bill said, "The old man is never going to ease up. He'll never retire. He'll have to be carried out of the boatyard feet first."

"Don't underestimate Kitty."

"She can con him into anything but retiring."

"She got him to take a vacation last winter."

"And he was so jumpy on the cruise I bet she'll never try it again. Why the fucking Christ can't he retire to Florida like everybody else!"

These tirades made Mary feel sick and helpless. She sat limp, and Bill sat brooding.

They neared their dock. Mary climbed onto the bow. "If William does retire, that'd just mean more work for you."

"In this case, more work might mean less ulcers. *God,* he was picky today!"

Mary jumped out and tied up.

Bill furled the sail. "But what the hell do I think I'm accomplishing anyway? What's a life of selling toys to fat cats? On a lake dying of pollution?"

Mary refrained from pointing out that *Nomad* was also a toy, with a polluting outboard motor. She walked up the lawn. Aunt Pleasantine was sitting on the porch, reading Jimmy Breslin's *How the Good Guys Finally Won.* Indoors, Mary discovered in the refrigerator a colander of string beans cut exactly into the same lengths Mother had always cut them.

She took the drinks tray to the porch. "Thank you, Aunt Pleasie."

"I enjoyed it. Keeps your hands busy while you remember things. The same as shelling peas."

Before Aunt Pleasantine started out on her walk the next morning, Mary switched off the vacuum cleaner in the living room and asked, "Okay if I vacuum your room now?"

"I wish you'd let me try—"

"Christ, no, I wouldn't let anybody wrestle with this damn thing, it's a vicious monster."

Aunt Pleasantine left, and Mary dragged the canister down the hall. Aunt Pleasantine's double bed was neatly made, the white chenille bedspread smooth, the blue eiderdown puff folded at the foot. Mary looked around. She wasn't going to snoop. Of course she wasn't. Of course she was. She had during the vacuuming last Friday, too. But still there was nothing to discover. Except for the photograph albums, the room looked the same as the day Aunt Pleasantine moved in. A spare room; a guest room. The furniture was a secondhand-store clutter of pine and maple. The cushion of the chintz chair was plumped up. Mary eyed objectively her paintings hung here, then plugged in the vacuum and vacuumed the room.

After she finished all the vacuuming, she hauled the canister back to the kitchen to the broom closet and, sweating, chugalugged a Diet Moxie. The phone rang.

Kitty said, "Mary, I've been so worried about your aunt's health ever since Bill told William she's recuperating from an illness. Do you need help? I was a candy striper, you know. I have faced bedpans."

Mary stalled. "Thanks, but we're doing fine. Sunshine and rest are the best medicine."

"I would have thought she could have gotten more sunshine in Florida."

Mary read the ingredients on the Moxie label. Carbonated water, caramel color, phosphoric acid, natural flavors, caffeine, saccharin. She wondered what the natural flavors were.

Kitty was saying, "Remember, you're all invited to dinner when your aunt feels up to an outing. I'm sure she'd enjoy seeing the house."

"I'm sure she would. Thanks for calling." Mary hung up and found Aunt Pleasantine, back from her walk, reading on the porch. "I'm going to take the regatta prints in to Jerry and then go do the Friday shopping. Would you like to come along?" She knew Aunt Pleasantine liked expeditions so much that last Friday she had skipped *Hollywood Squares* to go along.

Aunt Pleasantine closed her book. "I'd love to."

Mary brought her portfolio downstairs and put it in the car. They drove toward town, and Aunt Pleasantine looked out the window at the bay.

Mary said, "Are you finding Breslin's book interesting?"

"Very. The children voted for Nixon and they are extremely embarrassed. His name cannot be mentioned in the house and I've never been able to get any of the Watergate books. Do you know, when I first heard the word 'Watergate' I thought it was a Roman aqueduct."

A while later Aunt Pleasantine added, "I didn't register to vote when I moved to Florida because I didn't think I'd live long enough to make it worthwhile. Silly, eh?"

Mary cut over away from the bay toward North Main Street.

Aunt Pleasantine asked, "Does Jerry's shop sell postcards?"

"Racks and racks."

"I've been hoping to send postcards to the grandchildren. And great-grandchildren. Sometimes I find it odd that only Chris out of the grandchildren has ever visited New Hampshire; he climbed Mount Washington when he was a boy. None of the great-grandchildren has ever been here. But it isn't odd, not really. We all move about so much nowadays and mainly in a direction away from our roots. Does Jerry have postcards of the White Mountains as well as the lake?"

"Plenty."

At The Watercolor, Mary introduced Sally to Aunt Pleasantine in the gift shop and went into the gallery. Jerry was doing a pencil drawing of a covered bridge. When he did covered bridges he drank wine, the only way he could make covered bridges fun. Already the bottle of Rhine wine on his worktable was half empty.

Mary opened her portfolio. "I'll say it again. I *like* covered bridges. Here are the prints you asked for."

"Covered bridges are depressing, and I can't bear to be depressed."

"Your old houses ought to be depressing, too; they're getting torn down faster than covered bridges."

"Only because there are fewer bridges left. Have some wine."

Mary, a rather dirty glass in hand, roamed around the room. None of her paintings or photographs had sold. She looked at Norma's painting of a sorrowful puppy. Not even that had sold. She said, "Summer doldrums."

"Why do you think I'm drawing covered bridges? Don't worry,

things will pick up again, they always pick up."

"It's the heat. We need some rain." Mary roamed. "When you were a kid, did you know for certain you were going to do this?"

Leaning back, Jerry put down his pencil and picked up his glass. "I'll tell you exactly the moment I knew. I was in fourth grade, over in Sunderland. The Public Service Company of New Hampshire had a brainstorm, or at least its Sunderland branch did. It asked the elementary schools to help celebrate Thanksgiving and help Public Service sell its electricity by supplying Public Service with some kids who could draw. I guess Reddy Kilowatt can't draw. The brainstorm was to have kids stand in the Public Service showroom window, at easels, and draw inspiring Thanksgiving pictures. Pilgrims and turkeys and Indians. And in the background there'd be all the Public Service's electric stoves and refrigerators and stuff for sale. A kid from each grade in each school was chosen, and I was one of them. The other kids began planning and practicing what they'd draw, but I hadn't the slightest idea and could have cared less. Want some more wine? And then it was the day, and there I was in the showroom window. I was even wearing a tie. And all around me the kids were sketching away, and a crowd was collecting outside the window. But my sketchpad on my easel was blank. I picked up a crayon, and I did wild geese over a pond and I knew it was better than any of the other shit the other kids were doing. I was so sure that I only laughed when the teacher gave me hell for not using a 'Thanksgiving theme.' She said, 'You could at least have made them wild turkeys.' " Jerry bellowed with laughter. "Want some more wine?"

"I'd better get back to Aunt Pleasantine."

"Bring her in here. Maybe she'll buy something."

Out in the gift shop Aunt Pleasantine was buying postcards and looking at the dolls. "Sally, you must be so proud of these dolls, it must be a wrench to have to sell them."

"Not usually," Sally said, practical. "They keep us in the black.

Once in a great while, though, I do get attached to one, I remember something that happened while I was making it, I remember what I was thinking about when I sewed the apron ruffles or something. Is Jerry getting bombed?"

Mary said, "Moderately."

"Good, then he'll keep working." Sally gave Aunt Pleasantine a thin bag of postcards. "Glad to meet you, Mrs. Curtis." Sally went off to wait on a blue-eye-shadowed woman who was contemplating balls of scented soap.

Mary said, "Would you like to meet Jerry?"

"Very much."

After Jerry was introduced to her and she had admired his covered bridge and refused some wine, Aunt Pleasantine made a beeline across the room to a white painting. She read aloud the card. " '*Blizzard.* Mary Hutchins Emerson.' I knew it would be yours." She moved slowly around the room, looking at the pictures.

Mary arranged the regatta prints on a counter.

"Oh!" Aunt Pleasantine had stopped in front of one of Jerry's old houses. "This house. It's in Kingsbridge."

"That one?" Jerry said. "An early Kingsbridge house I did a year ago. Like it?"

Aunt Pleasantine didn't answer.

Jerry said, "I wonder if it's still standing. Look at the roofline, the place was ready to cave in."

Mary walked over to the drawing. The house was a sunken Cape in an overgrown garden.

Aunt Pleasantine said, "Lillian Crawford lives there."

"Right," Jerry said, "it's in private hands, or at least it was then. Maybe a historical society got smart and grabbed it when the old lady died."

"She died?" Aunt Pleasantine said.

"I'm assuming she did," Jerry said blithely, "because she sure didn't look like she was long for this world. I knocked on the door and rang the bell and knocked and rang and finally an old lady opened the door a crack and I asked permission and she slammed the door shut. She hadn't said yes, but she hadn't said no, so I sketched the house."

Mary said, "We could find out easily enough, Aunt Pleasantine."

Jerry poured himself more wine. "If you want to buy the drawing, I give discounts to all Mary's aunts."

"Thank you," Aunt Pleasantine said. "I'll consider it."

They said good-bye to Jerry and went back to the car. As they drove down North Main Street, Aunt Pleasantine said, "Becky, your grandmother, was friendly with Lillian and played at her house. The house is down on the river. I lived on a hill in a sea captain's house."

"Did you have a widow's walk?"

"Oh, yes. I was forbidden to go up out on it, but of course I did. Poor Grandma, coping with me." They reached Main Street. "Is that still the Post Office over there? Do you happen to need stamps, too?"

Mary interpreted this. "Yes," she said, although she didn't. She found a parking space and started to get out of the car.

"Wait, please." Aunt Pleasantine opened her pocketbook and counted out eighty cents. "Ten eight-cent postcard stamps."

The morning had become hotter. Mary walked along the sidewalk to the Post Office and up the long cement stairs. Her feet were sweaty and slimy in her sandals. The hazy sky was so pale a blue it was almost white.

She bought the stamps and lingered a few moments in the old cool lobby. She glanced at posters showing happy boys and girls in uniform who suggested furthering one's education in the service of one's country. Then she opened the door and heard the panic.

People were running along the sidewalk. People stood stock-still, staring. Mary dashed down the stairs, trying to see her car.

Her first instinct was that something had happened to Aunt Pleasantine—stupid stupid wrong, everyone was looking in the opposite direction. A girl ran out of the next-door hardware store and pushed past her, crying, "Oh, my God!" and Mary looked up and saw that the white sky was black with smoke.

Over the shouts she heard the fire alarm and the roar of the fire.

She ran for her camera.

Aunt Pleasantine was standing beside the Saab. "What's on fire?"

Mary unlocked the glove compartment and snatched her camera. "It's one of the mills, one of the abandoned ones. Kids, hippies, whatever, supposedly sleep there sometimes—Jesus fucking Christ, look at the flames!"

Into the billowing black smoke orange flames now shot from the arched windows of the enormous old brick textile mill.

Later Mary would be astonished that she had immediately thought as she stood there watching: Turner, *Burning of the Houses of Lords and Commons.*

Cars stopped in the middle of Main Street, and people leaped out. Crowds were rushing down the sidewalks, past the old stores with high wooden facades, past the stores remodeled with fake rock, the loud crowds were rushing and pushing toward the river and the mill. Fire engines' sirens sounded hysterical.

Aunt Pleasantine said, "People are so peculiar. Why aren't they running *away* from the fire? Those gas stations beside it must be dangerous. But I suppose if I could run, I'd be going that way, too."

"I've got to run at it. Are you okay?"

"Yes."

As Mary sprinted toward the fire, figuring angles, she noticed that the camera store was doing a lively business selling film. Amateurs. A fire engine had pulled up in front of Muirhead's Department Store and seemed to have troubles with the hydrant.

The heat from the fire was blistering. She heard men discussing what the firemen should do; she heard women worrying about victims. She took quick pictures of people and squeezed through the crowds and got to the bridge.

It was an old bridge of rusty iron gridwork. People stood crammed together on its sidewalks, so she had to run along the gridwork street. Underfoot, far below and very visible, a waterfall splashed and foamed. She hated heights, and this bridge was a star of her heights nightmares, but she looked straight ahead and ran as fast as she could and got across.

She ran on to the gas station nearest the mill. The only people here were the gas station owner, some foolhardy town loafers, and Philip Altman, a newspaper photographer. The hot smell of smoke choked her.

Philip said, "What the hell are the firemen doing?"

"Dubbing around, as far as I could make out. Is anybody in there?"

"Who knows? Bums, kids, who knows." Philip clicked pictures. "It was full of stored junk, mostly paper. A firetrap."

The heat shimmered. Mary could feel her skin burning like a sunburn. "The mill's a goner, isn't it?"

"Definitely."

Mary took pictures. The mill had been one of many on the green river below the white waterfall. Dark brick, the mills' handsome structures hid horrors. When Mary in her childhood first read Dickens she pictured these mills, and they remained her image of the Industrial Revolution. Most of Saffron Walden's mills had managed to keep producing something after New England's textile industry had moved South, but some had folded, and ten years ago this one put on a big sale in its mill-ends store and had closed. Mary remembered the hectic sale, the bright bolts of cloth, the smell of yard goods. She remembered in particular a flattering dress she had made from the cloth she had bought. After the sale the mill stood useless on the river. There'd been talk of turning it into apartments or offices, but nothing had come of that.

Philip yelled, "Look out!" and jumped back.

A high part of a brick wall slowly toppled into the river. The orange flames, freed, surged straight up to the black sky.

Mary sensed someone familiar. She turned, and Bill said, "Shouldn't you get back?"

She coughed smoke. "Can you hear the sirens at the Marina?"

"I heard them when I was heading there from an errand. Where's Aunt Pleasantine? At home?"

"At the car."

The gas station owner began lugging indoors his display of tires. Mary couldn't see any sense in this, but she took a picture of it. Fire engines screeched to a halt, and a ladder rose to face the fire.

"No," Bill said, "she isn't. I saw your car, that's why I came looking. The car was empty."

Another chunk of wall went. Mary dug in her shoulder bag for film and reloaded the camera. Atop the ladder a fireman aimed a hose at one orange window. She said, "Looks like the opposite of Gulliver's pissing on a Lilliputian fire." The flames roared higher. Other firemen began hosing down the roofs of nearby stores and houses.

Bill said, "Hand lines won't work. Yes, see, they're going to use deluge guns, and some of the pumpers will pump right out of the river. Mary, for Christ's sake, come back at least as far as the bridge."

But Mary stayed and he did, too. The explosions of water knocked holes in the brick walls. She saw the flames inside the walls and wondered how long the fire might have smoldered in some lost place before this conflagration. Spontaneous combustion? Or had a cigarette dropped from sleeping fingers? Or? More walls fell. She reloaded her camera again. Now the mill looked like Second World War footage of bombing raids.

Philip said, "Guess I'll get some shots from the other side."

Mary said, "See you at the party," and Bill said to her, "The fire's going to go on all day and probably all night. How long are you planning to stay? Aunt Pleasantine—"

Mary guiltily remembered Aunt Pleasantine. "She wasn't in the car?"

"We'll find her."

Mary was glad to have his hand to hold as they crossed the vertigo bridge.

The city had recently repainted its downtown benches. No longer dark brown, the wooden slats were now striped red, white, and blue in honor of the coming Bicentennial. Aunt Pleasantine sat on the library bench. She was listening to a plump woman who clutched a shopping bag.

Mary said, "I'm sorry, I got carried away—"

"But I hope you got some fine photographs. Bill, how nice to see you. Was anybody hurt?"

Bill said, "Probably we won't know until tomorrow's news." He turned to Mary. "The traffic is awful. If the side street beside the Post Office isn't blocked, take that and I'll meet you at the other end and lead you out."

"The errands," Mary said. "I haven't—"

"Can't you do them tomorrow when the traffic is cleared up?"

"I suppose so."

Aunt Pleasantine, "You're all sooty, Mary."

Mary looked down at herself. She hadn't noticed.

Aunt Pleasantine said good-bye to the woman and, as she walked with Mary to the Saab, said, "It's just like a war or any emergency, this fire. Strangers talking to strangers. That woman told me the hardest thing about widowhood was forcing yourself to eat proper meals. The first year she couldn't bring herself to make a meal for only one person, so she either didn't eat or she just snacked. She became ill, of course. Now she's taking care of herself again, but the meals do get dull because she can't buy those little individual cans and packages of food, they're too expensive. She has to buy the large economy size and eat the same thing day after day."

Mary managed to maneuver the Saab past parked cars in the Post Office side street. Smoke was rolling and rolling over downtown. She followed Bill's car around traffic jams and into a labyrinth of alleys and side streets. On the sagging porches of the shabby houses whose front yards were strips of sparse grass invaded by asphalt, old women and men stood peering toward the fire.

Aunt Pleasantine mused, "I went to work for Mrs. Goodhue in nineteen-forty-four. This June I remembered something I'd almost forgotten. I remembered how on D-Day when the church bells in town began to ring, Mrs. Goodhue and I headed for the Unitarian church to a prayer meeting. It was the only time I ever went to church with bare legs. I was painting my legs a light tan in those days. Becky came running across the Common to the meeting, too. In the church I saw that other women were wearing morning housedresses, they hadn't taken the time to change either, but I felt sure I was the only one with bare legs. I was dreadfully embarrassed until I realized that on D-Day nobody cared."

When they reached the lake road, Bill's car directionals blinked, and he motioned Mary to pull in with him to The Whistle Stop, a drive-in restaurant made out of an old railroad station. There used to be a railroad line along the southern shore of the lake. Trains brought families up from Boston to stay at cottages and hotels, the husbands spending the weekend and then taking the train back to Boston. Most of the track was ripped up now. In the track that did remain, weeds grew.

Bill leaned out his window. "Want some lunch? You could go on to the Marina and get cleaned up and show Aunt Pleasantine the place. I'll bring lunch."

Mary looked questioningly at Aunt Pleasantine, who said, "Whatever you'd like is fine with me."

"Okay." Mary drove back out onto the road.

Aunt Pleasantine asked, "This won't interrupt Bill's work?"

"He loves interruptions." Mary drove along the lake to the Marina and parked. White boats, blue water. Green islands. The bulk of mountains beyond.

Aunt Pleasantine said, "Will the Marina be Bill's? Eventually?"

"Well, he's the oldest, he has more shares. A family business, complicated, I don't understand it." Another question for another Contingency Day.

"There are so many masts."

"A recent sight. Just a few years ago it was almost all powerboats, and everyone thought Bill and other sailboat owners were insane."

"You mentioned Bill was the Yacht Club Commodore?"

"A while back. He never wants *that* job again."

They went into the showroom. Norma's son, Freddy, was polishing a cabin cruiser's chrome. Mary introduced him to Aunt Pleasantine and looked for William. "Any Emersons here?"

"Everybody's at the fire," Freddy said enviously. "Except Leonard, he's in the stockroom. We heard it on the radio. Bill was off somewhere, probably he's at the fire too."

"Aunt Pleasantine, do you want to freshen up?"

"No, go ahead."

In the rest room Mary scrubbed her face and arms and legs with wet paper towels. The towels turned gray. She tried not to think of people trapped in the mill. Suffocating from smoke. Burning to death. When you burned, your hair burned; your corpse was charred and bald. She combed soot from her hair and went back out to the showroom.

Freddy was giving Aunt Pleasantine a tour of the boats, telling her the prices, enjoying Aunt Pleasantine's gasps of amazement.

Mary went into the stockroom. Leonard lolled in a rubber raft and flipped pages of *Playboy.*

Mary said, "Hi. How's Janice?"

Leonard jumped. He was a year and a half younger than Bill. Although he didn't wear a beard, he looked disconcertingly like Bill. Paul, the youngest, took after the other side of the family and spared people more confusion. Leonard said, "Is the old man back yet from the fire?"

"No, but Bill is almost. How are the kids?"

"Fine."

"Come meet Aunt Pleasantine."

"I'm here," said Aunt Pleasantine in the doorway. "What a fascinating place."

Leonard thrust his *Playboy* under the raft and stood up.

Aunt Pleasantine moved carefully through the jumble of stock supplies, observing everything. Propellers, life jackets, outboard motors, deck chairs, running lights, ring buoys, drink coasters, drive shafts, anchors, sneakers, plastic fenders, line, compasses, shackles, boat ladders, fire extinguishers, and lake charts. She looked at the shelves of paint and polish. "Do you supply limes, too?"

Leonard didn't get the joke. "We don't sell food, it's messy." He glanced at the door. "Oh. Hi."

Bill said, "I'll handle things now, go have some lunch."

Leonard left.

Bill stopped in his office for beer stored in his little refrigerator, and he and Mary helped Aunt Pleasantine down the steps to the old slips. Bill moved deck chairs to the shaded end of the long dock. Aunt Pleasantine sat down and looked at the view. Mary, delving into The Whistle Stop bags and spreading out Bill's selection, hoped to God that Aunt Pleasantine's digestion really had returned to normal and that in its normal state it was as hardy as she claimed. Bill had chosen The Whistle Stop's famous foot-long hot dogs. With the works.

Aunt Pleasantine said, "I must have mentioned Blanche McGrath in my letters."

"Um," Mary said. "A neighbor in Florida?"

"Four houses up the street. She and I met when we were taking our constitutionals. We eyed each other warily, nodded, and went on our ways. We both were afraid the other would ask to walk together, and both of us preferred to totter along on our own. We learned about that later, of course, and laughed. In the meantime, for months, we nodded and passed."

"Then how did you become friends?"

"One day she stopped me and introduced herself. She said she'd noticed my daughters went shopping on Fridays. This was about nine-thirty on a Friday morning, and the children always left about ten. Blanche had a daughter-in-law in another part of the city, and the daughter-in-law usually took her shopping, but that day the daughter-in-law was ill and Blanche's son was working, and Blanche had run out of some important pills. So I asked her to come to the house. I introduced her to the children and we all went shopping and Blanche got her prescription refilled. I went along as a buffer, so the children wouldn't feel obliged to entertain her but I enjoyed her very much, and we were friends from then on. Such good friends, in fact, that we continued to take our constitutionals separately. I visited her occasionally at her bungalow. The children said she wasn't a lady, but I thought she was. You know what I mean."

Bill and Mary said, "Yes," and sipped beer and waited.

"Gradually we cooked up a scheme. I confided to her I felt like an albatross around the neck of the children, and she said she was lonely living alone. We added up her Social Security and mine—she had some sort of pension, too, because another son had been killed in the War—and we worked on our budgets and discovered we could manage if I moved in with her. Her husband's insurance had paid off the house. It seemed like a dream come true. My only worry was how to tell the children. I knew it would be a relief to them, but it would also be an embarrassment. They care what people say. Oh look, a sea gull. I'd forgotten how they fly up the rivers so far inland."

The sea gull perched on a gas pump at the end of the dock.

"Blanche and I had got everything planned, and I was steeling myself to tell the children and face a scene. I had even secretly begun packing."

Aunt Pleasantine paused for a long time.

Then she said, "Naturally I didn't write you any of this."

Mary said, "All I can remember is your mentioning her garden."

"Somehow talking things over doesn't seem as bad as seeing the same things in writing. Delicious hot dogs, Bill. I'm glad the railroad station is still in existence. I remember getting off the train there, happy about the lake."

"It was closed for years." Mary looked into the water at a brilliant red Coke can in the sand.

Aunt Pleasantine's voice became brisk. "Blanche's house burned down one night. She got out alive. It burned flat. The fire was nothing like the fire downtown today, but it was terrible. I brought her in her nightgown to our house. She called her son while we watched the fire engines. She went to live with her son and daughter-in-law. She was too tired to start over again, and they were planning to move anyway, so they chose a house with room for her. She phoned me and told me about it. She said, 'The new house is in a new development, twenty-five houses going up, they cost thirty thousand dollars, some cost more. Wall-to-wall carpets on all floors, three bedrooms, two baths. Joe Junior is giving me a TV. A comfortable chair I'll have to buy new because mine was burned. Wasn't that a mess? Not one chair saved. I'm getting my full amount of insurance. Cost me eight hundred and fifty dollars to have the ruins hauled away. I expect I've sold the land for more than Joe paid for both the house and land. I lost my handbag in the fire, too, there was thirty dollars in it, but I saved a metal safe which had a hundred and fifty dollars in it. I'll have to eat with Dolores and Joe Junior, but they go out to dinner twice a week. You know how I feel the cold, and Dolores is always hot, but I'll have an electric heater in my room. It's not pleasant living together, either for them or for me, and Dolores is so damn fussy over little things. Maybe it'll work out. There will be an electric stove and dishwasher.' "

Bill asked, "Did it work out?"

"As well as can be expected," Aunt Pleasantine said. "One should never live with one's children."

After a while, she added, "I remember the first time Blanche and I talked, standing on the sidewalk discussing her pill emergency. She said, 'Most of all, I miss being able to drive.' I agreed."

After lunch, when they went back into the showroom, they met William and Paul returning from the fire. Mary introduced them to Aunt Pleasantine and hoped William was too keyed up by the thrill of the fire to notice that Aunt Pleasantine was not an invalid.

Home, at the camp, Aunt Pleasantine took her nap. Mary began developing the pictures.

During cocktails, while in the living room Helen Reddy sang about love's being free and easy, Aunt Pleasantine said, "I liked to drive, but having someone drive you around was sometimes better because you could see more. Russell Peterson, the skier who worked for me at the Inn, had a knack with cars, and he loved to go for drives. Whenever we got a spare moment, we explored the White Mountains."

Bill said, "I'm taking Sunday off because of the races, but I think I can arrange to take Tuesday off, too. Want to drive up and see your Inn?"

"Is it still there?"

"Yes," Mary said. "I've pointed it out to Bill."

"How can you remember it, that was before you—no, I left it a year after Connie was born."

"Mother and Father showed it to us."

"It hasn't burned? I never heard it had, but old hotels and inns are so apt to burn down."

"It was there last time we drove through."

Bill said, "Let's plan on Tuesday."

The morning news reported that an unidentified man had died in the mill fire.

"Wino," Bill said and left for work.

A gray morning. Rain began. Mary was only mildly surprised when Aunt Pleasantine decided to stay at the camp instead of do errands with Mary.

Mary said, "Anything I can pick up for you?"

"If it wouldn't be a bother—I'm out of dental floss."

Mary had an extra package of dental floss in the bathroom supplies closet, but she was getting the hang of this. "No bother. Waxed or unwaxed?"

"Unwaxed." Aunt Pleasantine gave her two dollars. "Thank you. Tell me if it costs more."

"I think I'd better shop the white sales today, too. Bill put his foot through a sheet last night, reminding me I skipped last year's sales and January's. Anything you need?"

"Thank you, but I can't think of anything."

Not to need linen of one's own. "If I'm late, help yourself to whatever you want for lunch."

The gray lake shivered in the rain.

Mary drove into town to the new Industrial Park. It was not a park; it was an eyesore. Some of the flat cinder-block buildings on the expanse of parking lot had attempted to beautify themselves with bubble-glass windows and turquoise tiles. She parked near the newspaper office building. Before the Park was built, the newspaper office, on a downtown side street, had been a crooked wooden building overlooking the river. She remembered cluttered rolltop desks and the exciting smell of ink.

She went into the new building. Clinical. She dropped off some free-lance photographs, returned to the car, and drove downtown, thinking about Connie's husband George's newspaper office, much like Saffron's old one. George's hadn't changed.

She parked near the mill. A fire engine was still there, firemen keeping watch. All of the mill's third floor was gone, and the rest of the building was black and wrecked. She took some pictures through the rain.

In Muirhead's Department Store, Mary chose sheets and pillowcases. She was at the cash register charging them when she heard Bill's mother talking to a clerk in another aisle. Mary snatched up her purchases and tried to escape, but she was too late. She had been sighted over the stacks of jacquard towels.

Kitty cried, "Mary!"

And Mary halted in her tracks.

Kitty scooted around the towels. "What a wonderful coincidence! Your aunt—" She saw that Mary was alone.

"Aunt Pleasantine stayed home, Kitty. I know she'll be sorry she missed meeting you."

Kitty pouted.

Mary looked down at her delicately frosted short brown waves, her Revlon face, her tanned taut figure in a white jersey decorated with big buttercups whose yellow petals matched the yellow of her double-knit slacks, an outfit protected by a clear plastic raincoat which matched her furled clear plastic umbrella.

Kitty said, "I'm sorry, too. But I'm glad to hear she's recovered. William says she must have been a raving beauty—"

So the fire hadn't distracted William from Aunt Pleasantine.

"—and I gather you picnicked on Whistle Stop food, so she can eat out now. You must bring her to see the house. We'll have a barbecue. Shall we plan on tonight?"

"That soon? In this weather?"

"You know as well as I do the patio is covered. Anyway, the rain is supposed to stop by midafternoon."

Kitty fingered a towel, jangling her grandmother charm bracelet to which Mary and Bill had not contributed.

Okay. The inevitable. Mary yielded. "What time would you like us?"

"Sevenish. William will make shish kebabs." Kitty loathed cooking. In the winter she gave dinner parties only at restaurants. In the summer William became a barbecue chef. Kitty kept presenting him with Christmas and birthday gifts of chef's hats and funny aprons.

"Fine," Mary said, and fled.

At the mall Mary went into the dizzy-colored corridor to a pay phone and phoned Bill. "It's happened. I got Kitty-cornered."

"We knew we couldn't put her off forever. When?"

"Tonight. She pounced."

"Might as well get it over with. Warn Aunt Pleasantine about her, huh?"

"Yes. Good-bye."

There was a bulletin board beside the phone. People had thumbtacked up little ads, some neatly written, some scrawled on scraps. A McCulloch chain saw was for sale, and a 1958 Ford two-ton dump truck ("Cab needs body work"), a 1972 trailer which was 12′ × 65′ and partly furnished and could be seen anytime, three registered German shepherds seven months old, a 1961 "antique" Polaris snowmobile, a very reliable baby-sitting service ("Will look after children in my home"), a .58 caliber muzzleloader "like new," a maple dinette table, four studded snow tires, and an altered billy goat. In one corner a card written in childish penmanship read, "FOR SALE—Wedding dress and veil size 10, $50. Vacuum cleaner all rebuilt, $35. Call after 6 P.M."

Speculating about that one, Mary walked down the corridor. A banner saying SENIOR CITIZENS BAKE SALE festooned a long table where Saran-wrapped breads and cookies and cakes were displayed. Women sat behind the tables, knitting, chatting. The woman at the electronic organ played "Tie a Yellow Ribbon Round the Old Oak Tree." Mary hesitated, then bought for twenty-five cents an issue of *The Senior Citizens Newsletter.* It was subtitled "Places to Visit and Things to Do in the Granite State." She walked past old people sitting on pink benches. Along the corridor, mothers pushed shopping carts, juggling babies, dragging children.

At Purity Supreme, Mary yanked a shopping cart free of its nest and did the week's grocery shopping. Then she shopped at the CVS drugstore, and then on her way out of the mall she stopped again at the Senior Citizens' table, noticing something else, a stack of mimeographed sheets, free. She took one and glanced at it while she guided her shopping cart around people. It was an ad for the fall semester of the Saffron Walden Public Schools' Adult Education Program. Courses offered were Rug Braiding, Creative Writing, Bread Baking—she bumped into someone and waited until she'd got outdoors to her car and unloaded paper bags before she finished reading it. Chair Caning, Beginning Macramé, Knitting, Body Building, Beginning Crochet, Fund Raising Through Crafts, Bread Dough Ceramics, Weaving, Advanced Macramé, Advanced Crochet, and Transcendental Meditation. Which would she choose if she didn't have the painting and photography? Painters, someone had observed, lived much longer than writers. Which would Aunt Pleasantine choose? Adult Education. Mary stuffed the ad into the Saab's litter bag.

She drove out of town, past farms, to The Market Basket. The Nelsons were perhaps the only really solvent farmers in the area. Years ago they had opened a roadside vegetable stand beside their family farm, and the stand had grown and grown, stretching through added-on sheds, until it became the most important part of the farm. Rebuilt now, it was slickly rustic. Summer people adored it. And Mr. and Mrs. Nelson knew how to handle summer people, learning their names, asking after children and grandchildren, discussing each vegetable carefully selected. Mary enjoyed watching them work. Aunt Pleasantine had got the summer-people welcome-mat treatment last Friday.

Mary went in, waved to Mrs. Nelson, and began loading up. Despite the rain, the place was busy. The clean wooden bins were full of still-life produce. She chose lettuce, tomatoes, peppers, scallions, cucumbers, carrots, and an eggplant. The lettuce leaves were crisp and wet. The eggplant glowed purple. Even the clinging dirt on the carrots looked clean. Summer people were anxiously asking Mrs. Nelson when the first corn would be ready, and Mrs. Nelson was saying, "Any day now." Wooden shelves held little jars of jellies and jams, with old-fashioned labels. Mary, remembering Mother's making grape jelly from the backyard arbor, grabbed a jar of supposedly homemade grape jelly.

This year the Nelsons had added on a small greenhouse from which they sold bedding plants and houseplants. Mary wandered in to find out what a greenhouse felt like in the rain. It felt underwater green. Impulsively, she bought a weird cactus.

When she got home, she discovered Aunt Pleasantine watching an old movie on TV. "Hi, Aunt Pleasie, is it a good one? I'll put the shopping away and get us a sherry."

Aunt Pleasantine came out to the kitchen. "I'm so used to *Hollywood Squares* before lunch here, I miss not seeing them Saturdays and Sundays, and I turned on the TV just to see what's on. Was that all right? I forgot to ask you."

"Huh?"

"The children are afraid I'll break the television if I turn it on and adjust it. What an interesting cactus."

"I couldn't resist, may I put it in your room? Every room should have a plant—remember Mother's saying that? Do anything you want with the TV, Aunt Pleasantine. Bill has been known to kick it."

"The movie is awful. Everything else is cartoons." Aunt Pleasantine went back to the living room and clicked off the television.

Mary, putting groceries away, said, "I met Bill's mother at the white sales and she invited us over for supper tonight."

Aunt Pleasantine returned to the kitchen. "How nice. Bill looks like his father except his eyes, and I've wondered if he and Leonard inherited their eyes from their mother. It'll be fun to meet her. I've wondered about Paul, too. All such handsome men! Who does Paul look like?"

"Kitty's father. Uh—Aunt Pleasantine, Kitty can be very exhausting. If you get tired this evening, don't be polite, tell us you want to leave, use your age—that is—"

Aunt Pleasantine gave her an amused glance.

Hastily, Mary went on, "What I mean is, Kitty wears me out in nothing flat, and I don't want her to wear you out."

"She won't. I've had a great deal of practice."

Mary looked at her.

Aunt Pleasantine said, "If I may borrow your iron this afternoon, I'll press a dress for the occasion."

"Sure. Oh, that newsletter thing, I don't know if it's worthwhile, but—"

"Thank you." Aunt Pleasantine took it into the living room.

Mary finished the groceries and carried the cactus and dental floss and seventy-one-cents change to Aunt Pleasantine's room. Coming back, she noticed Aunt Pleasantine was wearing a soft coral cardigan over her blouse and slacks.

Mary said, "It's got chilly. I'll build a fire."

Aunt Pleasantine, reading the newsletter, became invisible in an armchair, but Mary sensed she wasn't missing anything about the preparations. Mary crumpled newspaper in the fireplace, laid kindling and logs, and struck a match. A domestic fire, not frightening. Aunt Pleasantine looked up from the newsletter at the second item on her peaceful list.

Mary brought sherries, then carried Grandmother's Martha Washington sewing stand over to a chair near the fireplace, sat down, and began finishing the handwork on the sundress she was making for the party.

Aunt Pleasantine burst out laughing. "Games! There's an article in here about senior citizen bus tours and games to play on the bus! Like children in a car."

"Oh, shit, I'm sorry—"

"No, Mary, it's funny as hell." Aunt Pleasantine read on. "There are relay races which involve passing an object such as a hankie or a wrapped—*wrapped,* mind you—candy bar to the back of the bus and around to the front. There are guessing games. They don't suggest guessing which animal you're going to see next, a dog or a cow or whatever, as we used to play with you and Connie when we went from the farm into town."

Mary got up and poked at the fire.

Aunt Pleasantine said, "In Kingsbridge I had a little Italian marble fireplace in my bedroom."

"You used it?"

"We used all the fireplaces downstairs and in our bedrooms. During the war—the First War, I was living in Brandon with James then—Papa did install a Franklin stove in the living room. I often wonder what happened to those fireplaces when the house was torn down. I hope someone saved the marble. I remember reading by my fireplace on winter afternoons."

"Why did you sell the house?"

"Al Dawson's death disclosed the true state of my finances, and I had no choice."

"You lost everything?"

"I sold some things to friends, my sofa to your grandparents, for instance, I hid other things in your grandparents' attic, and I pawned what I could."

"You were living in the Kingsbridge house then?"

"Yes. It's so complicated. When Papa died, he left me the house, all his property. That was in nineteen-twenty, and I was twenty-nine years old. Papa died the same year I met Al. Before Papa died, James and I were living on the money my mother left me. Blue-chip stocks—bonds—money! Confusing! I should have made myself understand it."

"Were you still married to James when you met Al?"

"I think the combination of Papa's death and my meeting Al helped me decide to divorce James. James's behavior was getting more and more blatant. I had a detective trail him, but that wasn't really necessary, everyone was talking. I told James I'd give him another chance, but if once again my friends began telling me about seeing him carrying on, I'd start proceedings without further warning. And when he didn't mend his ways, I did. I wasn't heartbroken anymore, but my pride was hurt. I divorced James in nineteen-twenty-one. We'd been married only eleven years. Hester was ten years old, and Elizabeth was eight."

"Did you get child support?"

"No, I didn't ask for alimony or anything because I never expected to be without plenty of money. I gave him visiting rights to see the children, but then he sold the Brandon house and moved to San Francisco. He sent them Christmas presents for a while."

"What did he do in San Francisco?"

"Remarried," Aunt Pleasantine said, "and continued his life of leisure. I moved back to the Kingsbridge house, which I had rented to a family after Papa's death. I went often to Boston to see Al, to have dinner and go to a play. Sometimes he visited me in Kingsbridge."

Later, drying the lunch dishes, Aunt Pleasantine said, "That Al. He knew the best speakeasies in all of Boston."

Aunt Pleasantine took her nap, and Mary worked on the late-night talk-show painting. The rain stopped; the sun came out. At Kitty's command? The afternoon warmed up, and Mary decided she'd worked enough, changed into a bathing suit, went downstairs and outdoors and dived off the dock, and swam.

Floating on her back, she recalled what Kitty had said years ago about Mary and Bill's putting their money into fixing up the camp and putting off having kids. Kitty said, "If you wait until you can afford to have children, there won't be anyone weeping over your grave."

Mary still thought this the oddest remark she'd ever heard.

She swam home. Walking through the house, toweling off, she saw Aunt Pleasantine in the laundry room arranging a dress on the ironing board. "Aunt Pleasie, I wish you'd let me do your ironing—"

Aunt Pleasantine sidestepped as nimbly as she had whenever Mary offered to iron. "Your washing machine suddenly reminded me how delighted your mother was when your grandparents insisted on buying her a washing machine after you were born. Because of your diapers and everything. She was especially pleased they had found a spinner type instead of a wringer, because she feared you might someday catch your arm in the wringer. That had happened to a neighbor's child. Spinners were dangerous, too, of course."

"She never let us go near it when it was spinning."

"You don't remember, but neither did I let you."

Mary went upstairs and showered and chose a sundress. Bill arrived, looking resigned. He looked better after a shower. He took the drinks tray out to the porch. In the living room Mary saw Aunt Pleasantine coming along the hall from her room.

Wearing a freshly pressed dress the color of peach ice cream, Aunt Pleasantine was ready for anything.

During drinks she said, "The cactus seems happy on that windowsill. It makes me think of the grandchildren and their families. So hard to imagine the climate. I try to keep track of their weather, and I've mentally composed many a letter to many a TV weatherman: 'Dear Sir, Please move your shoulder because you are blocking New Mexico and Arizona, where my grandchildren live.' "

They drove down the lake past the Marina and up the west shore. People were loudly mowing lawns. Mary remembered childhood summer evenings on the farm. No television then, nothing to do during the long twilights but sit on the back steps and read or draw and listen to Connie in the barnyard playing her secret games with the animals. There had seemed to be forever ahead in the dusk until Mother announced bedtime.

Bill turned right and drove across a causeway to Quarry Island. The Emersons had built a house here, the most fashionable island, twenty years ago. Expensive estates showed only glimpses of their backs to the loop of road. Hedges were high. Bill drove up the driveway to the hilltop and parked and said, "Kitty's Folly."

Aunt Pleasantine said, "Oh, my."

The house had shocked Saffron Walden in 1955. Built on several levels down the lake side of the hill, it was mostly glass. Mother had often wondered aloud what Kitty Emerson must have paid for all the floor-length drapes. Townsfolk had called it a goldfish bowl. But now everyone was used to it and to its imitations around the lake; now it seemed dated.

Kitty, however, still thought it sensational, and she rushed out and bore Aunt Pleasantine off for a tour.

Bill said, "I'll go see if the old man needs a hand."

"Deserter," Mary said.

Bill went down the lawn toward the patio near the beach. Mary, carrying the Gloriosa daisies she'd picked at the last minute, went into the house to the kitchen.

She'd known this house for twenty years, but she always was afraid of getting lost in it because the floor plan made no sense to her, and Kitty kept confusing her even more by constantly rearranging the rooms. The dining room had once been the informal living room; the old dining room was now the TV room. The den became a solarium. Bedrooms changed as sons left. The Ping-Pong table was peripatetic. And although Kitty hated cooking and had never managed to shift the kitchen, she did redecorate it occasionally. Mary opened a cupboard, took down a vase for the flowers, and looked nervously up at the ceiling, at the gleaming and unused copper pots and pans hanging from fake beams, Kitty's latest idea. Mary expected to get knocked unconscious by a falling copper kettle one day. The latest kitchen wallpaper was Blue Onion.

She heard Aunt Pleasantine's voice in Kitty's sitting room. "No, I wanted to name my daughter after my mother, who died when I was five, so we named her Hester. And then when another daughter came along, I wanted to name her after my grandmother, who brought me up. But my husband wanted to name her after *his* mother, so we named her Elizabeth. These pictures must be of Leonard's children."

"Yes. There's little Leonard in his Little League uniform."

"Splendid photography."

Kitty said, "Mary is clever."

And cheaper, Mary thought, arranging flowers, than a photographer outside the family would be.

Aunt Pleasantine said, "Are these Paul's?"

"The baby is fifteen months and a joy. Her middle name is

Katherine. Her first is Jennifer, and I'm afraid I fail to understand why that name is so popular nowadays. *Love Story* was very depressing."

Mary giggled. Kitty disliked being only a middle name.

"She's sweet," Aunt Pleasantine said.

Kitty said, "The group photographs of my sons' families are ones Mary did for Christmas cards. That's Janice, Leonard's wife, and Donna, Paul's."

Mary wondered if Donna would be wearing her neck brace in this year's Christmas photograph. Mary dreaded the annual nerve-racking sessions at Donna's and Janice's, the kids restless and noisy, the husbands bossy and bored, Donna disorganized, Janice apologetic.

Kitty said, "The kitchen's in here—oh, hello, Mary, this is where you went to. I know William would be grateful if you washed the cherry tomatoes. I'll take Pleasantine down to the patio."

As they left, Aunt Pleasantine said, "Artists have such a knack with flowers."

Mary, scrubbing tomatoes, wished she'd met Bill earlier so she could have known the house where he'd lived during his childhood. He had described it, but she wanted to see it herself. On South Main Street, near the Episcopal Church, it and other houses had been bought up and torn down when the A&P expanded from a grocery store to a supermarket. "Our backyard," Bill would say, pointing, "was over there. Part of the parking lot now." The house had been brown and comfortably ugly. Kidded about reading so much, Bill had made a hideout in the attic, and there he read books like *Captains Courageous* and *The Trade Wind.* He kept a cache of comic books there, too, and a metal toolbox which contained a hammer, a map of Indonesia, a Lone Ranger ring, a fingerprinting pad, and a stack of cardboard lists of Straight Arrow Injun-uities that had been shelves in Shredded Wheat boxes.

Mary carried the bowl of tomatoes down to the patio. Aunt Pleasantine and Kitty were sitting in filigreed white iron lawn chairs, sipping drinks.

Kitty said, "There you are. Pleasantine was just telling us about your planned trip to the mountains. Bill, I'm sure Mary is thirsty."

Heat wavered above the elaborate barbecue grill. William's apron said GALLEY SLAVE.

Bill mixed Mary a Tom Collins. The highball glasses had bright numbers on them so everyone knew which glass was whose. Holding her emerald No. 5 glass, Mary sat down in a chair near Aunt Pleasantine.

William said, "Thanks for doing those tomatoes."

Bill walked around the patio. He studied pots of petunias.

Kitty was saying, "Your inn must have been nice, but I suppose the work must have been tedious, and you must have been relieved to sell it and retire."

"Not exactly," Aunt Pleasantine said. "I went bankrupt."

Kitty stared at her as if she'd admitted she had leprosy.

Aunt Pleasantine said, "I have a tendency to go bankrupt."

Kitty said, "Bill, please light somewhere. I'm sure if you knew how annoying it is, you wouldn't pace."

"The War happened," Aunt Pleasantine said. "I wasn't alone; many other inns had troubles, too. No, the work was sometimes tiring, but never dull. I laugh and laugh when I remember some of the guests. And the help! One afternoon a waitress who had gone mad came at me with a kitchen knife."

Bill stopped pacing. "What did you do?"

"I told her, 'Give me that knife and leave immediately.' She was so surprised she surrendered the knife and ran."

In the bleached blue sky the stars were white. The wakes of busy Saturday-night boats kept the lake rocking.

William skewered a chunk of beef. "You went bankrupt more than once?"

"Dear," Kitty said, "I'm sure it's an unhappy subject for Pleasantine. Let's talk about something cheerier. You're living in Florida with your daughters? Are there grandchildren? Great-grandchildren? I want to take Leonard and Paul's children down to Disneyworld, but William is too fidgety on vacations. Maybe, though, by the time Mary and Bill present us with grandchildren William will have mellowed and we can make the trip." Kitty fished in her red No. 1 highball glass for a bit of ice. "But needless to say, we aren't getting any younger and neither is Mary."

Mary looked quickly at Bill, willing him to keep his temper.

Aunt Pleasantine said, "Bankruptcy is a shock, but very educational. You learn what things are precious to you, at the moment and, with regret, later. Before the Inn, I went bankrupt in nineteen-twenty-three. I've always thought I'd probably have lost everything in the twenty-nine Crash anyway, so I just got it over with earlier. Bill, are you still bartending?"

"Sure." Bill took her empty glass, he took Kitty's and Mary's, and as he walked toward the bottles on the white iron table, and as Mary relaxed, Bill said, "Sorry, Kitty. We didn't consider Disneyworld five years ago when I had a vasectomy."

Mary's heart pounded. Okay, she thought, it's said at last. And now the shit will hit the fan.

"Nonsense," Kitty said. "I know you've never ever considered vacationing in Disneyworld. When you think of Florida, you think of your Inland Waterway."

William had stopped turning a shish kebab on the grill. He spun around. "You goddamn fool. You had your balls cut off."

"*What?*" Kitty screamed.

Aunt Pleasantine said, "Oh, no, it's not that drastic. I've read it's a simple operation."

"Five years ago?" William said. "You never told us? You went ahead without consulting us?"

"Did *what?*" Kitty screamed.

"*Why?*" William shouted.

Bill said, "Mary had been on the Pill too long, and her doctor didn't want her trying an IUD."

"A what?" Kitty said.

Mary looked at Aunt Pleasantine, who seemed fascinated.

Kitty ran over to Bill at the table and clutched his wrist. "You aren't going to have children ever?"

"Never."

"Ever?"

"Never." Bill said to Mary, "In a moment this is going to be Gilbert and Sullivan."

Kitty said, "But you're the oldest. You're my—"

Mary thought, if Kitty calls him her Firstborn, he will murder her.

"—my Firstborn," Kitty wailed.

William said, "You stupid kids. Don't you care what people think? They've been talking enough as is, and when you're in your forties they'll say one of you is sterile."

Bill laughed.

And William, from whom Bill had inherited his temper, exploded. "You burn my ass!" he roared. "You burn my ass!"

"Ah," Bill said, "but you're the one burning the shish kebabs. Sorry about this, Aunt Pleasie. We'll get something to eat at home."

"Fuck the shish kebabs!" William flung them across the patio flagstones, and they skidded greasily into the petunias.

Bill helped Aunt Pleasantine out of her chair. Kitty began sobbing. Mary followed Bill and Aunt Pleasantine up the long lawn to the hilltop.

At home, Aunt Pleasantine went directly to her room.

Mary asked Bill, "A sandwich? A salad?"

"Nothing. My gut's churning. So's yours, I know. Make something for Aunt Pleasantine. Where can we go tonight, let's get out of here, Kitty's bound to start phoning."

"A sail?"

"No. Nothing to do with boats."

Mary rummaged around the living room for the newspaper, found it. "A couple of skin flicks are at the drive-in."

"Okay."

"Want us to go alone or should I ask Aunt Pleasantine if she'd like to come? If she stays here, she'll have to ignore the phone or cope with Kitty."

"Ask her."

Mary took Aunt Pleasantine a supper tray and asked her.

"Oh, no," Aunt Pleasantine said. "I'll stay here, you two go ahead."

"If Kitty is true to form, she might not just phone, she might come over. Enough is enough, she'd tire you out."

Aunt Pleasantine reconsidered. "Are skin flicks what pornographic films are called? I've never seen one."

She went with Mary and Bill. She insisted on sitting in the back seat, and Mary agreed, figuring Aunt Pleasantine could doze off in privacy there.

The drive-in theater, which had been built in the early 1950s, was shabby now. Potholed asphalt. Crooked speaker stanchions. But, thanks to X ratings, it survived. It was stubborn; whenever the cops closed it down, it somehow soon reopened. Tonight's movies were *The Fruits of Love* and *Milady's Maid,* and the rows were full of cars.

Bill had brought booze. Aunt Pleasantine accepted a drink. On the huge screen a girl was being seduced, and Mary suddenly doubted that Aunt Pleasantine would doze off. Mary thought of the high school nights here with Bill. Then, the movies had been stuff like Tarzan reruns, Martin and Lewis reruns, and the fucking had occurred in the cars, not on the screen.

Mary herself dozed off. She awoke to the intermission floodlights and to Bill's saying, "I'll stop at the Social Security office Monday and find out."

"Thank you." Aunt Pleasantine's voice sounded both embarrassed and relieved.

"I think they'll change your address and send your checks here, but I don't know what they can do about the one not forwarded. Do you want to phone your daughters?"

"No, no. The girls have simply overlooked it, and I don't want to bother them. That movie was hilarious. I suppose in the next one the actors will wear period costumes—at least for a while."

"Anything I can get you at what Mary calls the salmonella snack bar?"

"Thank you, no."

Aunt Pleasantine was right about the next movie, and Mary dozed off again. When she awoke, noblemen were applauding a girl in black stockings who was squatting on a wine bottle. "Christ," Mary said, yawning, stretching, "the obligatory wine-bottle scene."

"Sleepyhead." Bill looked at the dashboard clock. "It's after midnight. Kitty won't phone this late. Ready to leave?"

Mary said, "Aunt Pleasantine?"

"Whenever you are."

They drove back toward town, past used-car lots, secondhand stores, old-fashioned gas stations abandoned since the oil embargo, and sandy expanses of trailer sales lots. Over the entrance to a new car wash, a sparkling sign said:

TUNNEL OF LOVE
KISS YOUR HONEY UNDER THE WAX ARCH

They drove through the dark downtown and out to the weekend lake and home.

Mary, unlocking the back door, saw by the glow of the kitchen light a piece of paper tucked under the door. "Good thing we left." She handed the note to Bill. "How much you want to bet Kitty says we're selfish? Aunt Pleasantine, would you like a drink or something to eat?"

"No, thank you. And thank you for the evening." Aunt Pleasantine went off to her room.

Bill crumpled the note without reading it and chucked it at the wastebasket. Mary took it out. Kitty had scribbled, on the back of a Cabana Boutique receipt which must have been part of her pocketbook or glove-compartment clutter, "Dearest Mary and Bill, I've never known any couple who chose not to have children. It's unnatural and selfish. William says those operations are sometimes reversible, and I beg you to change your minds. Lovingly, Kitty."

Mary said, "We're selfish *and* unnatural. Poor thing, would she feel better if she learned that nowadays none-is-fun is fashionable? She could tell everyone we were ahead of our time."

"Who gives a shit," Bill said.

Upstairs Mary said, "Did Aunt Pleasantine ask you to have her Social Security address changed to here?"

"Temporarily. She emphasized the 'temporarily.' She's been fretting because her damn daughters haven't forwarded her check. Why couldn't she have said something sooner?"

"Pride."

They went to sleep. Mary had a new nightmare about heights. Not one involving a bridge, and not the one in which she had to walk a tightrope over the roofs of Saffron Walden's downtown. In this new nightmare, she was spread-eagled flat on her stomach on the wing of a jet plane that sped through high white atmosphere, and she was trying to fix something wrong with the wing and trying not to look down and trying trying trying not to fall into space.

Windy weather disturbed Mary. The next day a hot wind slapped waves against the dock and up the beach. That afternoon Mary walked through the woods to the end of the Point. The trees were louder than the lake. Sitting on a rock, she sketched branches.

Bill, a judge at today's Yacht Club races, had spent the morning at the Club setting out markers. When he came home for lunch, he saw the phone off the hook. Mary said, "It kept ringing. I couldn't stand it. I've never done such a thing before in my life." He said, "But she hasn't shown up here yet?" "Not yet." "Did Aunt Pleasantine change her mind about coming to the Club?" "No," Mary said, "she's deep in her book. And I still don't want to leave her here alone in case Kitty—" Bill said, "I think Aunt Pleasantine can take care of herself," and after lunch, as he went to his car, he added, "You mustn't be her baby-sitter, you know," and drove off.

Mary flipped shut the sketchpad and decided to join Bill at the Club. She walked back to the camp and tapped on Aunt Pleasantine's door.

"Aunt Pleasie, I've changed my mind about the Club. Have you? I'm going over."

"Thank you, but I'd rather stay." Aunt Pleasantine had finished the Breslin book and begun *All the President's Men.* "I hope the weather isn't spoiling Bill's races."

"If Kitty arrives, bar the door."

Driving up the east shore, Mary resolved not to worry.

Tall pines shaded the clubhouse, already camouflaged with dark brown shingles and dark green roof. Mary parked among the many cars. The trees were quieter here in this cove, and as she walked past the clubhouse she heard voices talking and a phonograph singing. In the sun on the blond beach a confusion of kids played noisily. Women, oiled and tanned, lay sunbathing, watching, Mary supposed, through their blank sunglasses, the children and the races. Mary dodged a Frisbee and walked down the dock, looked at the sailboats careening around the lake, located the committee boat where Bill would be with the other judges, and then she looked at the dock.

The inanimate objects she feuded with included vacuum cleaners, Coke machines, toilet-paper spindles, and charts and road maps which wouldn't fold back to where they'd started, but she'd never hated any inanimate object the way she'd hated this dock twenty years ago when Bill was teaching her to sail. A few years later in college she met a guy who got so mad at his obstinate car he took it out to a field and shot it, and she completely understood how he felt and wished she had shot dead that fucking Yacht Club dock. What she'd done instead was overshoot it. Always. Bill's boat then was a little catboat named *Zephyr,* and she didn't hate the boat, she could handle it out on the lake, but the moment she neared the dock she began to tremble. The people on shore seemed a vast audience. "Please, Bill," she'd say, "you dock her." "Concentrate," he'd say, "and forget anybody's watching." The most memorable docking of the *Zephyr* came when Mary rammed a dinghy which a man and woman were stepping into. The man and woman were very fat, and, yelling, flailing, they made enormous splashes in the lake. As they surfaced and began treading water, Mary, horror-struck, recognized them: the high school principal and his wife.

She walked back and dodged another Frisbee, and under the pines she sat down at a picnic table. Far up the lake there were tiny yellow pinwheels that whirled busily along the water—paddles of the girls in kayaks who were returning to the girls' camp from an expedition. She looked at the sailboats and opened her sketchpad. Behind her some women were starting early hibachi suppers on other picnic tables, and some men were playing horseshoes.

Plus sailing, she'd learned horseshoes here, and diving, and how grown-ups behaved when drunk. She remembered one evening William had come by the Club in a boat to pick up Kitty and friends for a party. The party was already under way in the clubhouse, and Mary and Bill had been observing it covertly while playing cards. Mary had hoped she looked jaded rather than spellbound, and she was completely unprepared for Kitty's reaction to William's knocking on the ladies' room door and calling, "Aren't you ready?" "No!" Kitty replied from inside. William said, "Not yet?" Kitty threw open the door. She wore white Bermudas and a flesh-colored bra, and she was brandishing a safety razor. She yelled, "Leave me alone, goddamnit, I'm shaving my armpits!" Everyone, including William, laughed. Bill shrugged at Mary. Mary nearly died of embarrassment, but later she realized that now she knew that Bill knew about leg and armpit shaving. She'd found out earlier that he knew about bras.

Grown-up and braless, Mary sketched sailboats coming home and wondered if the Commodore was sober enough to present the trophies.

She wished herself back in early July, before Aunt Pleasantine's arrival. Ashamed of the wish, she flipped to a fresh page and did a sketch of Aunt Pleasantine and the gray-haired gentleman having a chariot race through an airport. Aunt Pleasantine would enjoy the cartoon.

Horseshoes clanged.

When the committee boat docked, its loudspeaker was accidentally left on, and everybody at the Club who cared to listen could hear the quarrels and challenges of protesting contestants. Terrible deeds had been done; so-and-so on port tack had crossed so-and-so on starboard tack, et cetera, et cetera. The weather, some said, was too windy and the races should have been canceled. "Cowards!" others said. Booze in the clubhouse didn't soothe tempers. The Commodore, looking distinguished and nautical and drunk as a lord, managed to present the trophies with the help of stage whispers from Bill. Fisticuffs seemed imminent among several skippers at the bar. Bill grabbed Mary and said, "Let's scram."

Outdoors, the beach children were shivering now, irritable, wrapped in towels. A golden retriever ran around woofing, and a poodle began yapping. Hamburgers got black on hibachis.

Bill said, "What a bunch of assholes. I'll never judge another race."

"Hah," Mary said. "How many times have I heard that?"

She walked with him across pine needles toward their cars.

He said, "Why did you change your mind?"

"Your remark about baby-sitting, of course. Bill, did you ever visit Grammy Em in her nursing home? Where was it?"

"I went once. The Maples. Big old place on Maple Street."

"Oh. I remember, and it got torn down."

"And the Dairy Queen was built." Bill kicked at a forgotten

beachball. "The old man and Kitty visited Grammy Em there fairly regularly, I guess, but they only made me go with them that once. Leonard and Paul got out of going because they were too young. I was in junior high."

"Awful?"

"I expect it could have been worse. She had a room to herself. The nurses fawned—though God knows what they did when visitors weren't around. She seemed comfortable. She kept mixing up the old man with his brothers. She was vague about Kitty. She didn't recognize me at all, which bothered me more than I admitted. Grammy Em's house used to be near our old house; I must have told you how when I was a kid I'd ride my bike over and she'd give me hermits."

"I thought brownies."

"No, hermits."

Mary got into the Saab and drove home. As she swung up the dead-end road, she saw Kitty's car parked in the driveway.

Mary braked so hard her seat belt hurt, and then she unhooked the belt and jumped out and ran back to Bill's car behind her. She thought: I will keep my temper.

She said, "Kitty is pestering Aunt Pleasantine."

Bill got out of his car.

Mary said, "If we go in the house, Kitty will start lecturing us. I'm thirty-six years old, and I don't have to take any shit from any mother."

"Okay," Bill said. "Let's run away."

Which unclenched her fists and stopped her shaking. "Sure. To the Hindu Kush?"

They walked up the driveway.

Bill put his arm across her shoulders. "I know what. We'll distract Kitty's attention by letting slip that Leonard is playing around with half the ladies of the lake and the whole town is feeling sorry for his wife. Poor Janice, everyone is saying."

"Tempting."

Bill burst into song.

A capital ship for an ocean trip
    Was *The Walloping Window-blind*—
No gale that blew dismayed her crew
    Or troubled the captain's mind.
The man at the wheel was taught to feel
    Contempt for the wildest blow,
And it often appeared, when the weather had cleared,
    That he'd been in his bunk below.

They went up the back steps into the kitchen. The drinks tray was missing from its place behind the chopping board.

Bill bellowed:

The captain sat in a commodore's hat
    And dined, in a royal way,
On toasted pigs and pickles and figs
    And gummery bread, each day.

Mary walked through the living room to the porch and found Kitty saying to Aunt Pleasantine, "I am so mad I could spit! Well, Mary, there you are. Why on earth is Bill making that racket?"

"He's keeping his temper."

Aunt Pleasantine said, "I offered Kitty some refreshment."

"Fine." Mary went over to the tray and began pouring herself a vodka and tonic, and Bill came yo-ho-hoing out to the porch.

Kitty said, "You took the phone off the hook. Don't deny this, I saw it with my own eyes. I hung it up."

Aunt Pleasantine looked helplessly at Mary, and Mary understood she hadn't been able to move fast enough to replace the receiver when she realized Kitty had arrived.

Kitty said, "Do stop clowning, Bill, I'm trying to talk."

Mary watched a tree swallow go whizzing past *Nomad*'s mast.

Bill said, "I'll stop clowning if you'll drop the subject of kids and never mention it again."

The telephone rang.

"There," Kitty said. "See? People besides me have been calling you today. Aren't you going to answer it?"

Mary went out to the kitchen and answered it.

Connie said from Vermont, "Jesus, you certainly are a difficult person to get hold of. Out all last night and all today, and weekend rates are cheapest."

"I'm sorry. How's your toilet?"

"The plumber came, and he and George hunkered. I wasn't allowed to participate, naturally. The plumber said he'd send somebody the next day to dig up the leach field, but the fucker didn't, and when he did send a helper the day after, the guy just brought his backhoe on a truck, parked the backhoe in the middle of the lawn, and drove off."

"Aha," Mary said, remembering the men she and Bill had hired when they were fixing up the camp. "The old backhoe-on-the-front-lawn trick. Makes you think they're going to return immediately and go to work."

"Why didn't you *warn* me! He hasn't come back *yet!* The leach field runs under the iris bed, and like a goddamn fool I took him at his word about when he'd be here, and I dug up the bed—"

"You dug up *all those irises?*"

Mary heard Bill singing another verse.

"All those irises," Connie said. "Busted my ass. And Dave and Keith made themselves scarce the entire morning I was digging and lugging, while Bobby and Tommy got underfoot. My iris bed has been sitting in two wheelbarrows for five days." Connie's voice gave a little yipping gulp.

Mary said, "Oh God, I'm so sorry."

"All day long every day I wonder if I should set them back in and dig them up again when—*if*—the fucker ever shows up, I go round and round wondering which would be more harmful. They look so sad it breaks my heart."

"They're supposed to be dug up periodically and reorganized—"

"But not then left to sit in wheelbarrows for days! They break my heart, and George doesn't understand why. He never notices the gardens, and he thinks I shouldn't waste my time weeding when I could be baking bread. He doesn't notice *anything* about me. All he wants is a cook and a cunt."

Bill now was loudly inquiring, in song, about what will we do with a drunken sailor.

Connie was sobbing now.

Mary said, "Um, well, maybe you'd better set them back in, these guys take ages."

"And in the meantime we're still using the outhouse! Six people! The flies and the stink—Mary, I am ready for the loony bin."

"Want to come here earlier than the party? Spend some time and have a rest, and we'll laugh about how when you tear down or move the outhouse you can plant hollyhocks."

"You know I can't get away. The kids and the gardens. The veg garden's gone mad, I'm canning and freezing, and, anyway, it took all my energy to talk George into coming to the party a day early for a tiny vacation. The plumber was quick enough with his estimate. About four hundred dollars, and I'll bet George really had to kiss his ass to get him to let us pay in installments. It was either that or remortgage the house. George thinks this is all my fault because I didn't keep an eye on Bobby and Tommy and the roll of paper towels. Four hundred bucks is all my fault!"

Mary heard Kitty shouting over Bill's singing. Mary and Connie had silently agreed never to mention a loan to help Connie and George out, but she felt she had to say, "Look, owe us instead of the bastard plumber."

"I'm not calling to *beg!*"

Connie hung up.

Mary listened to the dial tone and Kitty screeching, "Your father is so furious it's a wonder he didn't fire you on the spot!" She looked at the back door. Escape. She hung up the phone and went into the living room and saw Aunt Pleasantine coming in from the porch.

"Sorry," Mary said, sick of the word.

Aunt Pleasantine said, "I hoped to be a buffer, but I wasn't, so I excused myself." She started down the hall to her room, then turned and came back.

Mary followed her onto the porch, where Bill was still pacing and singing, and Kitty was shouting, "Children are the cement that holds a marriage together!"

Aunt Pleasantine said into the din, "Kitty, Bill is very helpfully trying to drown you out with song, but perhaps you don't realize that he no longer does since you've raised your voice. I gathered that you and William care what people think. At the moment, people can probably hear you clear across the lake."

Bill laughed and dropped his voice to a hum, but Kitty had already shut up.

Aunt Pleasantine said, "Voices carry over water."

Kitty seized her straw purse, which matched her straw sandals. "Well. You've joined them. I would have thought you had more sense."

Aunt Pleasantine, age eighty-four, looked at her.

Kitty stormed out through the house, pausing only to throw the receiver off the kitchen phone.

During *Hollywood Squares* on Monday, a contestant made a lucky guess and won the Secret Square, which included a color TV, a Berkline recliner, a microwave oven, and an Elgin watch. Aunt Pleasantine won the Square, too, having blurted, "Sir Walter Scott, of course!" even before Peter Marshall, the Master of the Hollywood Squares, had listed the multiple-choice answers to "Who wrote the Waverley novels?" Whenever she won a Secret Square, she carefully considered her prizes, and today she said, "I don't understand microwave ovens, do you? I'd surely be electrocuted if I'd really won. Isn't it strange that recliners are always so ugly. James gave me a beautiful watch when we were first married. I gave it to Al to pawn when he had his troubles and needed every cent he could lay his hands on."

"I stopped owning watches after I forgot and washed dishes wearing my last one."

During the next commercial break Aunt Pleasantine said, "I hope things aren't too awkward between *père* and *fils* at the Marina today."

"Bill didn't go in. He decided to go down to Lake Sunapee to appraise a boat. That'll kill most of the day, and he'll stop at the Social Security office on his way home."

"The phone hasn't rung."

"Kitty is sulking. But she'll strike again."

They ate lunch on the porch. A hornet crawled up the screen, and Aunt Pleasantine said, "I remember discovering one afternoon at the farm that you were playing with a hornet. I noticed it all too late, just as it finally stung you. You were angry."

"I wonder why I can't nowadays swat them."

After a while Aunt Pleasantine said, "Papa was an avid reader of the Waverley novels. He read them over and over, and Grandma told me that when my mother was alive he read them aloud to her. He and my mother used to act in the plays which were so often a part of the social life then, and my mother played the piano when friends visited. I think they were a loving couple, and I gather the only things he objected to were the ways she treated the maid and the cat. My mother insisted on seeing to it that the food was just right, so the maid didn't have to do anything except wait on table and clean up. And when they dined, my mother would save half her meal for the cat and put it near the fireplace to keep it warm for the cat. I'm told Papa would say, 'Hester, sit down!' She would pay no attention to him—Grandma said she never did—and go her own sweet way."

"Do you remember her?"

"Very hazily. I remember the end, though, clearly. Her consumption was suspected when Papa met her, and all of Papa's family except Grandma made a hell of a row about his marrying her. When she was dying, Papa had nurses around the clock for her. I wasn't allowed in the room, but I eavesdropped on the nurses and learned she was remembering their courtship and talking about 'Mr. Howe is coming to see me.' Howe is my maiden name, you know. And Papa sat all alone downstairs in the evenings reading his Waverley novels, but God knows what he was thinking."

After lunch Mary went back to work on the painting and then went for a swim. When she returned, she found Aunt Pleasantine reading on the porch. Aunt Pleasantine said, "I hope you had a good swim."

"Don't forget, if you ever want to take a swim—"

"I'm still debating. The sand is so smooth I thought I might sometime go wading." Suddenly Aunt Pleasantine put aside her book. "No time like the present."

"I'll—"

"Please, let me attempt it by myself. You'll hear me holler if I need you."

So Mary puttered in the house, glancing out the living room windows. Aunt Pleasantine had rolled up her slacks, and she waded slowly ankle-deep along the shore of the beach.

Mary, reassured, went into the kitchen and started supper. Aunt Pleasantine eventually came indoors and reported, "That was fun!" and looked at the kitchen phone.

"Still silent." Mary diced an onion. "Bill and I used to assume we'd have a couple of kids when the house was done. But when the house was done, we realized we didn't want any. Simple as that, yet we knew Bill's folks would go bananas."

"They're not Catholic?"

"Nope. Lapsed Congregationalists. We didn't tell them, and we didn't tell Mother and Father either because Mother would have had a fit. Women are supposed to give birth, that's their category."

"I'm so glad a girl today can make a choice. She doesn't have to risk her life if she gets married. We never thought of it in such plain terms then, but that's what it amounted to. Your father's mother. In childbirth. You dice an onion, Mary, just as your mother and grandmother did and I do."

Mary said, "I actually once had a doctor—male, of course—tell me I was selfish not to have kids."

"He was a fool." Aunt Pleasantine went to her room.

Mary went upstairs and changed out of her bathing suit into a shirt and shorts. As she returned to the kitchen, she heard Bill's car. He came in, and he too looked at the phone.

Mary mixed meat loaf. "Kitty's still sulking. How was your day?"

"Anything's better than being around the old man. And I found out some stuff for Aunt Pleasantine."

"Want to go tell her it's 'the cocktail hour'? My hands are too hamburgy to knock."

He carried the drinks tray off. Mary packed the meat loaf into a loaf pan, put it in the oven, washed her hands, scooped out some tomatoes and dumped in some cottage cheese and chives and stuck them in the refrigerator, and went into the living room and put on a record, and joined Bill and Aunt Pleasantine on the porch in time to hear most of Aunt Pleasantine's cocktail-hour story.

"And so, to make a short story longer, James and I and the wedding participants finished the wedding rehearsal, and the men went their separate way, and we girls piled into my car to drive up to my house where Grandma had planned a little party for the bridesmaids and the maid of honor—who was Becky, you know. And you know our house was at the very top of that steep Kingsbridge hill. Unfortunately, halfway up the hill the chain drive broke and we started rolling backwards. Faster and faster."

In the living room Leadbelly was singing about how Washington, D.C., was a bourgeois town.

Aunt Pleasantine said, "I did the only thing I could think of. I swung the steering wheel and backed into the pole of a streetlamp. This certainly stopped the car but it knocked the streetlamp over, and we were jounced around considerably and I bumped my head. Your grandmother must have told you this story, Mary."

Mary nodded.

"It was a beautiful wedding," Aunt Pleasantine said. "Everyone said it was the most elegant wedding ever held in Kingsbridge. The only flaw was that the bride had a black eye."

They laughed, and Aunt Pleasantine ate a Cheezit.

> Me and my sweet wife Martha was standing upstairs.
> I heard a white man say I don't want no niggers
> up there.
> Lord, he was a bourgeois man!
> Hoo! In a bourgeois town.
> I got the bourgeois blues, I'm gonna
> Spread the news all around.

Bill said, "I stopped at the Social Security office this afternoon, Aunt Pleasantine. The trouble is, you left Florida in such a hurry you didn't fill out an application form to have your checks forwarded. You've got to phone your daughters and tell them to forward them, and in the meantime, for God's sake, let us give you a hand until this red tape gets straightened out."

"That's very kind of you, but—"

Mary tried to catch Bill's eye, to remind him Aunt Pleasantine listened to men; then Mary realized he was using just this trick.

"Aunt Pleasantine," he said, "don't you know how much you embarrass me when I discover you're buying your own soap flakes and stamps? You're our guest."

Aunt Pleasantine blushed.

"But hey," Bill said, "I learned lots of other things at that office. Goddamn government, you've got to pry information out of them. Have you ever heard of Supplemental Security Income?"

"No."

"You may be eligible. It's not a pot of gold, but it'll help you. I've got all the stuff, and if you feel up to it after supper we could do some studying."

Aunt Pleasantine said, "If it doesn't interfere with your plans."

"It doesn't."

Leadbelly sang, "Looky, looky yonder!"

And after supper was cleared off the porch table, Bill spread the bewildering pamphlets out and sat down beside Aunt Pleasantine and began to explain. Mary went into the kitchen and washed dishes. Supplemental Security Income. How on earth did they invent these terms? She heard a car, felt a spurt of panic about Kitty but then saw it was Norma Wentworth's Gremlin, and she opened the back door.

Norma dashed across the driveway. "Is Freddy here?"

"Freddy? No."

"Leonard said he didn't show up at work today. Where's Bill?"

"The porch. But Bill didn't go to the Marina today either—"

Norma, not listening, ran out to the porch. Mary followed.

Bill had turned on a lamp. He and Aunt Pleasantine looked up from the pamphlets.

Norma said, "Have you seen Freddy?"

"What?"

"You know about Leonard and me, don't you."

After a pause, Bill said, "Not about you in particular. I mean—I'm sorry—I mean I—"

"Leonard told me Freddy worked yesterday. Freddy didn't come home after work last night. I thought he'd stayed over at a friend's and forgotten to phone as usual." Norma was shaking. "He didn't go to work today, and he hasn't come home this evening."

Bill stood up. "Your daughter got any ideas?"

"Ginger? She keeps telling me to hang loose. Leonard says it's too early to call the cops."

"Where's Leonard?"

"He went home to supper." Norma's voice quavered. "Freddy hasn't drowned. His swimming things are on the porch, the boat is at the dock, he can't have drowned. But his car is gone. The one he saved up for since he was fourteen. What he's done is—what he's done is he's run away."

Mary said, "I'll get you a drink."

Howling horribly, Norma fell into a chair. Mary raced to the kitchen for brandy, found only B&B, which didn't seem right, seized scotch, and ran back to the porch. Aunt Pleasantine was holding Norma's hunched shoulders while Norma shook and dry-retched.

Bill paced. "That fucking Leonard."

"Literally." Mary sloshed scotch into an unwashed supper iced-coffee glass, the first glass she'd grabbed.

"That fucking Leonard. He probably made some wisecrack to Freddy. What was Norma's husband's name? Stan? Should we get hold of him? Maybe the kid went there."

Norma's head came up. "Stan is out in Oregon now. Freddy wouldn't drive to Oregon. He couldn't. His car couldn't make it, and he hasn't enough money for such a trip—"

Hitchhiking loomed in Mary's mind, and she saw that everyone else had immediately thought the same.

Bill started into the house.

Mary said, "Where are you going?"

"Leonard's."

"No. Janice will be there."

"Poor Janice. And little Leonard and all the little blessings. I'm going there."

Mary said, "You realize, don't you, that you're acting like your mother?"

Bill snapped, "And I'm sure you realize that sometimes you act like yours did?"

Mary lost her temper. "Oh, blow it out your ass!"

Aunt Pleasantine said to Norma, who was gulping scotch, "My

ex-husband moved to the West Coast, too, after our divorce. I wanted to write him whenever there were troubles with the children because I thought that since they were half him, he could help me understand the half I couldn't. You know what I mean. But I never did write or phone. My pride."

Norma said, "I won't phone that bastard. If Freddy wants Stan, he's welcome to him."

Bill was staring at Mary.

"Go ahead," Mary said, "go ahead, big brother, and beat up middle brother. Act like your father, too. Patriarch. Go ahead."

Beyond the lamplight and the screens, the lawn was black green. The lake had faded.

Norma said, "He didn't even leave a note." Slowly she hauled herself out of the chair. "Maybe he'll phone."

Mary said, "Maybe Ginger's already had a call by now."

"Ginger is so wrapped up in planning her college wardrobe she wouldn't hear an atomic blast, much less a phone." Norma walked back through the house. Mary followed. Norma went out the kitchen door, and Mary saw, as the car's interior light came on when Norma got in, that she was crying again. Norma backed the car around and drove off.

Bill was using the living-room phone. "Hi, Donna, this is Bill. Paul there?"

Mary saw Aunt Pleasantine on the porch, neatly stacking the pamphlets.

Bill said, "Paul. I understand Freddy didn't show up today." He listened. "Terrific. Just terrific. The kid's apparently run away." He listened some more. "I don't give a shit what we tell the old man. Let Leonard explain. Let Leonard hire another kid to pump gas. I'm going to Whitingham tomorrow."

He hung up.

Mary looked at him.

He said, "Paul says Freddy came into the stockroom in the midst of Leonard's saying to Paul that with Norma Wentworth he had to tie a board across his ass to keep from falling in."

"Gallant Leonard."

"I won't kill him. The hell with it."

Aunt Pleasantine carried the pamphlets into the living room. She'd probably overheard Bill's phone call. "If I could take these to my room, I'll study them so I can maybe be more intelligent if you've got time to go over them with me some other evening."

"Fine," Bill said, and Mary said, "I'm sorry things have been frantic. I wanted you to relax here and be calm."

"Mary," Aunt Pleasantine said, "I have done more *real* living here in almost three weeks than I did in Flamingo Gardens for three years."

Bill said, "Thought we could eat out tomorrow on our way home."

"Lovely." Aunt Pleasantine went to her room.

Bill said, "At The Yankee Doodle, I suppose."

Mary said, "I'm afraid it's the best, yes."

They looked at each other.

Bill said, "Want a drink?"

"Not particularly."

"Then I guess we might as well go upstairs and fuck."

"You're so romantic," Mary said, but she laughed and forgot the remaining unwashed dishes and went upstairs with him.

Whitingham was an old resort town in the White Mountains. It was a hay fever resort. On its outskirts a weather-beaten sign said:

WELCOME TO WHITINGHAM
THE PUREST AIR ANYWHERE

"Good heavens," Aunt Pleasantine said. She hadn't spoken during the trip up. "That sign was here when I was here."

The town was so high and flat it seemed the top of the world. Mary always felt that if she ventured away from Main Street, she'd tumble off the edge. Main Street was wide and straight, a boulevard between the ornate hotels which hadn't yet been burned or torn down. Summer people in shorts walked along the sidewalks and dawdled in front of shops.

Aunt Pleasantine asked, "Is it still mostly Jewish?"

"I don't know," Bill said.

The huge hotels were white. On the shadowy porches a few people sat reading newspapers. On one of the green lawns a group of children played. Teenagers lounged around. A woman was sketching a wedding-cake gazebo.

Aunt Pleasantine said, "That's the reason I decided to buy here. When I started looking for a cabin colony or an inn on a lake or in the mountains, I learned about the gentleman's agreement. Ridiculous. I may have no business sense, yet even I realized such foolishness was a waste of business. When I discovered I wouldn't have to cope with the problem here, I bought The Mountain Inn. Oh—the motel over there is where The Four Winds was. It was Whitingham's biggest hotel. They had concerts on the piazza."

People and golf carts moved across the golf course. Mary couldn't remember seeing anyone playing tennis here before, but the tennis craze had reached Whitingham, the old courts were repaired, and people were dashing back and forth swinging rackets.

Bill said, "The town's busier in the winter nowadays, since they expanded the ski area."

"Really? I wish Russell Peterson could know this. He was a skiing pioneer."

At the end of Main Street the feeling of flatness disappeared. Bill turned off onto a narrow road which twisted higher through the pines.

The Mountain Inn was a simple house. A square white Colonial wrapped in porches.

Bill stopped the car at the foot of the driveway.

Aunt Pleasantine said, "There's no sign. Is it open?"

A sudden sound of hammering came from the barn.

Bill drove up and parked in front of the Inn. He walked around and opened Aunt Pleasantine's door and helped her out. She was wearing her pink pantsuit.

Mary stood and looked at the view.

"There's only one car," Aunt Pleasantine said. "It must be a private house now."

"No harm in asking," Bill said.

Pale mountains as high as clouds.

Aunt Pleasantine said, "When I bought this place I was afraid I wouldn't get any work done because I'd spend all my time looking at the view. But to my amazement I gradually got used to it—except in autumn, I never get used to New England autumns. Over there is where we played croquet. You can see where the flower beds were."

The lawn needed mowing. They went up the walk to the front door, and Bill rang the doorbell, then knocked. No answer. "Let's see who's hammering." They walked across the gravel drive to the barn. He called, "Hello?"

The hammering stopped, and they stepped into the gloom. Far at the back, a young man in faded Levi's was nailing up a shelf. "Hi. Sorry, we're not open. The place is a ski club now."

Bill said, "We just stopped because Mrs. Curtis ran the Inn—when?"

"From nineteen-thirty-five," Aunt Pleasantine said, "to nineteen-forty-two. Which was, I expect, before this young man was a gleam in his father's eye. What's a ski club?"

The young man, wiping his hands on his bandanna, came toward them. "Nick Evans," he said, and shook hands. "You owned it then? Wait, I'll find Sue, she'll want to hear—" He ran outdoors.

Aunt Pleasantine said, "In the summertime Russell used to tinker with our car here and do repairs for guests."

Bill examined shelves and bins. "Evans must be making storage space for ski gear."

"Russell kept his skis here, and so did I and what few guests we had in the wintertime. Idiot that I was, I wanted to close the Inn and go to Florida and work there winters. I'd know better now, and I thank God that Russell liked to ski so much he talked me into staying."

Bill said, "You skied?"

"I was forty-four when we came here, and I said he couldn't teach an old dog new tricks." Aunt Pleasantine looked very demure. "Amongst others, he taught me to ski. He ski-jumped also, which terrified me, but I tried it—not, of course, on the sixty-meter as he did, but on the baby jump. Every time I see a picture of that new airplane, the Concorde, I'm reminded of Russell ski-jumping."

Nick returned with a freckled girl who wore her brown hair in a thick braid. "This is Sue."

Sue said, "The doorbell doesn't work, I was in the pantry."

Aunt Pleasantine said, "Nobody in the back of the house could hear the doorbell until my handyman finally rigged up a special system from the front door to the kitchen. It was so loud it always scared me out of my wits."

Sue said, "Would you like to see the house?"

"Great idea," Bill said before Aunt Pleasantine could answer.

They walked up the lawn through the long grass. Rosebushes had gone wild.

Inside the house, flies buzzed in naked windows. The living room was empty except for two broken chairs pulled up to the big fireplace. The dining room was empty. Cobwebs. Mildewed wallpaper.

Nick said, "Our club is just a bunch of skiers trying to save a buck. We've been looking around for a house, and we bought this in April. It'd been closed for years, and we're trying to get it in decent shape by ski season. I'm the president. That means I do most of the repair work."

"Where do you live?" Aunt Pleasantine asked.

"Freeman, Mass. I'm into remedial reading."

"Excuse me?"

Sue said, "He teaches, we're on vacation."

And, obviously, they were camping in the kitchen. Sleeping bags hadn't been rolled up, and supplies spilled out of cartons and suitcases and knapsacks. The kitchen was large. A serving counter ran down one side, and where Mary imagined bustle and food, and waitresses and cooks shouting back and forth, there were only two coffee mugs, a jar of freeze-dried Maxwell House coffee, a jar of Cremora, and two plastic spoons. On a paper plate, a half-eaten doughnut oozed its tiny jelly heart.

"We've got mice," Sue said. "I'm setting mousetraps in the pantry, Nick is too squeamish to do it."

Aunt Pleasantine looked at the kitchen. "My cook drank, and I often had to take over when he was incapacitated, but I never could bring myself to fire him. He could be so brilliant. Saturday nights were buffets, and he made the buffet table a work of art. Chicken salad shaped like a chicken, you know. His finale was always a flaming dessert, and the guests always applauded."

Sue asked, "How did you happen to buy this?"

"I was a housekeeper for a Mrs. Kimball, a very kind woman who left me a great deal of money when she died. Enough to invest in the Inn. Despite the Depression, it was a thriving business then, though much more modest than the hotels."

Mary said, "Mother always talked about your dining room."

"The cranberry glass," Aunt Pleasantine said. "Everyone liked the cranberry glass. Mrs. Kimball was so generous. I suppose she saw when I cleaned her cranberry collection that I loved the pieces, so she left them to me as well as the money. She'd outlived her children. Your mother was pregnant with you the last summer she came up from Saffron. She was too busy afterward to visit, but sometimes in the off-season I drove down to visit your family. When the roads weren't too icy. Russell minded the store."

Mary, catching implications, guessed that Aunt Pleasantine left Russell here during those visits because Mother's category for him was "gigolo." Mary remembered Mother's describing the cranberry collection. A fairy-tale illustration. A great array, a dazzling treasure. When the morning sun had struck the dining-room windows, the cranberry glass glittered behind glass in china cabinets all around the dining room, sharp and bright. Red and crystal. In the evenings the room was ruby.

Aunt Pleasantine said, "Your poor mother. I served lamb that last evening, and she threw up."

Sue asked, "Do you want to see the upstairs?"

"It's going to be a dormitory," Nick said. "Our sleeping quarters."

"Thank you," Aunt Pleasantine said, "but we've already taken too much of your time. I hope you have excellent skiing this winter."

Outdoors Mary photographed the Inn and the view. Bill stopped in Whitingham so she could get a few pictures of the hotels.

Aunt Pleasantine emerged from a reverie. She smiled. "Did Nick not use Sue's last name when he introduced her because they aren't married or is that just my dirty mind?"

Midway down the mountain, she added, "Russell and I had many a laugh about what everyone was saying behind our backs."

As they drove on through the White Mountains, Mary tried to think of a tactful way to ask. "Do you—um—know where Russell is now?"

"Not, I expect, anywhere near Saint Peter and the Pearly Gates."

Bill pulled into the parking lot of The Yankee Doodle, a big old house painted a Williamsburg red.

Aunt Pleasantine said, "This was a private house in my day."

Mary said, "The food's good if you can put up with the decor."

They went in. Eagles hovered on the wallpaper. The waitresses wore mobcaps and long dresses, and the busboy wore a tricorn and a vaguely Revolutionary uniform. In the center of each round white tablecloth stood a miniature Betsy Ross flag.

Aunt Pleasantine came back from freshening up. "Do they specialize in roast beef? I see they have a standing roast of beef over there."

"Yes." Bill pulled out her chair for her. "And the rare is really rare."

Aunt Pleasantine sat down and sipped her martini and picked up her menu. The cover of the menu was a facsimile of the Declaration of Independence.

Mary looked around the room. All the people here were older than she and Bill were. As usual. Bill had theorized this was because people with kids stopped at fast-food chains, not having time for a leisurely lunch. Mary looked at the couples at the tables and tried to imagine herself and Bill, years hence, sitting here together. Or perhaps she'd be here without Bill. Perhaps she'd be here with widowed friends, like that gang of blue-haired old ladies at the next table. Perhaps she'd be brought here by one of Connie's visiting sons who was dutifully giving his ancient aunt an outing.

Aunt Pleasantine finished reading the menu. "Russell enlisted right after we entered the War. He was thirty-six years old, and I still don't understand why they took him. I did understand why he enlisted; it was impossible for him to stay away from such an adventure, although he and military life were incompatible. He once briefly went AWOL. I never knew the cause of that, but I'm sure it was worthwhile and fun to him."

The waitress said, "Are you ready to order?"

"Aunt Pleasantine?" Bill said.

"The cold roast beef platter, please."

Mary and Bill ordered. When the waitress left, Aunt Pleasantine said, "I noticed there are three steps down to the kitchen. Those long skirts must be dangerous for the waitresses. Later, Russell's ship was hit by a Japanese suicide plane. Kamikaze. He was badly injured, badly burned, and he spent a long time in hospitals. Luckily, he married a nurse who was devoted to him.

He was mentally injured, too. He visited me once at Vera Miller's, and a low plane went over the house and he ran screaming outdoors and hid in the hydrangeas."

Mary said, "Why didn't you marry him before the War?"

"I was too old for him. Fourteen years. It didn't matter to us then, but it would have mattered later. His wife wrote me when he died in nineteen-seventy-two. He'd left her years before, but they kept in touch, and she was notified." Aunt Pleasantine looked at the platter of beef on display. "I do enjoy a good cut of beef, and I've always wondered if I inherited this. Did I ever mention that I'm remotely related, through my mother's side of the family, to the Houghtons of Houghton Tower?"

Mary and Bill glanced at each other. Had Aunt Pleasantine suddenly gone round the bend?

She said, "I've told you how disagreeable Vera Miller was. But I'll be everlastingly grateful to her for the detour she insisted on the time we went up from London to the Lake District. She was just as curious as I was, but still it was kind of her. I've told you she was an Anglophile. Once, making conversation, I mentioned the Houghton Tower connection and she became all ears."

At the next table, the blue ladies were giving a waitress the third degree about dessert.

"Apple pie? Is it homemade or store-bought?"

"Is the cheesecake fresh or frozen?"

"I want vanilla ice cream with chocolate syrup if you're positive it isn't French vanilla ice cream. Or would I rather have maple syrup?"

Aunt Pleasantine said, "And on our trip up, Vera asked me to repeat the story, this time reading it out of a guidebook I'd bought. It goes something like this. Lancashire is the seat of the Houghton—they spelled it without the *u*—family. In the reign of James the First, Sir Richard Houghton was honored by a visit from His Majesty. Sir Richard Houghton rode out of Houghton Tower down an avenue draped with purple velvet, and he and his entourage met the King's coach and escorted His Majesty to the Tower. There were three days of—well, merrymaking is what they called it."

"A bash?" Bill asked.

"A high old time, I should think. During the merrymaking a new word was added to the English language. At one meal the servants brought a magnificent loin of beef to the table. The King was so delighted with it that he drew out his sword and knighted the loin. Thus: sirloin."

Mary said, "For Christ's sake."

"The dictionary has a much duller version of the origin of the word; I prefer this one. Houghton is a pretty hamlet. The Tower does rather tower over it. The guidebook called the Tower a sixteenth-century manorial house. It's big and gray. We pottered around and looked at the coat of arms and the crenellated defense walls and the outer and inner courtyards and, of course, the banqueting hall where the loin was knighted. 'I dub thee Sir Loin!' " Aunt Pleasantine beamed. "Isn't that the silliest and best kind of family history to know? An ancestor who's not famous as a hero but famous as a host?"

That evening, Mary phoned Norma. "Any word?"

"No. If you want to come over, I'll pay you back the gin I borrowed." Norma's voice sounded hoarse from crying, and drunk.

"Okay."

Mary thought she ought to bring something along—for bereavement?—and so, feeling foolish, she brought a bunch of alyssum. She drove up the lake.

Norma's house, a cube squeezed between a large old-fashioned camp and a lengthy ranch-style one named Trail's End, was white, and its blue shutters had cutout anchors. Mary parked behind the Gremlin and went down the flagstone walk and knocked on the screen door.

"Norma? It's Mary."

"I'm in the kitchen."

Mary stepped into the living room and smelled paint. House or wall paint, not palette paint. The living room was carefully decorated with squashy bright imitation-leather furniture; chairs were scarlet poufs, the sofa a purple cloud. For contrast, the lamps and little tables were chrome mushrooms. The walls displayed Norma's paintings of sad large-eyed children and animals.

Mary followed the fresh paint smell into the kitchen and found Norma squatting on the floor and stirring a gallon of brown paint.

Mary said awkwardly, "I brought these," and put the alyssum on the table.

Norma didn't notice them. "The unopened bottle is the repayment. Join me from the opened bottle, I set out a glass for you. I'm getting smashed and doing what I should've done right after the divorce."

"Which is?" Mary found tonic in the refrigerator.

"This." Norma dipped a paintbrush into the gallon of paint. She stood up and slapped brown paint across a kitchen cupboard.

All the cupboards and cabinets were yellow, and they had been autographed by guests during the Wentworths' parties. The day after each party Norma retraced with a narrow red paintbrush the new guests' penciled scrawls, preserving the autographs presumably forever, like Hollywood stars' footprints in cement. Depending on the guests' degrees of sobriety, the scrawls ranged from simple signatures to such witticisms as:

> She was only a tobacco auctioneer's daughter,
> But oh, what a Chesterfield!

Norma's brush stroke wiped out that one.

She said, "I thought I was so fucking original when I decided to decorate the kitchen this way."

"Where's Ginger?"

"Spending the night at camp." Norma painted out the next-door neighbors' signatures. "I'm past the crying stage now."

"Why haven't you called the police?"

"What can they do about one more runaway teenager? I went to work today, I got through the day. Pine cone sculptures, a real challenge." Norma dipped her brush. "I'm past the crying stage now, but I'm into the guilts. Which, let me tell you, is just about as much fun as the crying."

Mary said, "How many kids are there at Saffron High now? Eight hundred? Eight hundred teenagers, Norma, and you and I have coped with the fuckers day in, day out, and we both know there's absolutely no reason for you to feel guilty about what any dumb-ass kid does."

"Easy for you to say. Different when the kid's your own." Norma's brush painted out Saffron High's Social Studies Department's signatures, including one wag's drawing of a globe which located Zsa Zsa Gabor in Hungary, Napoleon in Russia, the Beatles in England, and Christopher Columbus lost.

Mary gulped gin and tonic.

More signatures disappeared under brown paint, and:

> There was a young girl from Oak Knoll
> Who thought it exceedingly droll,
> At a masquerade ball
> Dressed in nothing at all
> To back in as a Parker House roll.

That was Bill's contribution, somehow recalled despite several scotches.

Mary said, "When you were little, did you decide to be a painter?"

"I wanted to be a fashion designer. Strapless gowns for high society. Then I just wanted to get married and have babies. Luckily, while I was hunting for a husband, I majored in art. Luckily? Why did I say luckily?"

A peace symbol disappeared, and the phone in the living room rang.

Norma dropped the paintbrush. She ran to the phone. In the kitchen, Mary listened.

"Freddy? Oh, Stan, it's you. He's there. Oh, thank God."

Mary looked at the cupboards. She found:

Marvelous artichokes! What *is* your mysterious marinade?

Janice Emerson

"Not even to Boston?"

Mary found the cartoon she'd dashed off and Norma later had gone over in red. It was of Norma and Stan exhaustedly surveying the debris of an ended party: spilled bottles and ashtrays, overturned lamps—

"Can I talk to him? Just ask, tell him I'll understand if he doesn't want to."

MHE, the cartoon was signed, *July 1964.*

"Okay. It's enough to know he's safe. Thanks for calling."

Mary heard Norma hang up. She looked at the kitchen clock. Norma stayed, apparently without moving, for four minutes in the living room beside the phone.

Then Norma strode into the kitchen. "I sure am learning there are stages. I'm over the crying. Now I'm over feeling guilty. Now I am angry. I am very very angry." She grabbed the paintbrush and painted out:

Q. Why do Frenchmen have wheels?
A. To beat the sea gulls to the dump.

Ray Brunelle

Ray was Saffron High's boys' gym coach.

Norma said, "Freddy got to Portland."

"Oregon, I take it, not Maine."

"His car conked out somewhere before Boston, and he phoned Stan collect, and Stan wired him the money to get a bus to Boston and a plane to Portland."

"Quite an adventure for a sixteen-year-old."

"Ungrateful little bugger. Selfish little creep. He's nothing but an ego with hair."

"At least he didn't hitchhike."

Norma ferociously slapped paint onto the cupboards, onto the cabinets.

Mary watched her cartoon vanish. "Do you want to come stay at our house tonight?"

"This paint is called Chocolate Velvet. Think it goes okay with the old Fern Green, or should I repaint the walls, too?"

"Shouldn't you phone Ginger and tell her Freddy's safe?"

Norma didn't reply and, painting, ignored Mary.

After a time Mary said, "Thanks for the drink," took the unopened fifth, and drove away.

At home Bill was watching television alone in the living room.

Mary said, "Freddy flew to Oregon. Stan just phoned Norma."

"Freddy planning to stay?"

"I don't know. Where's Aunt Pleasantine?"

"In her room. After you left, she phoned her daughters. I tactfully went down to the boat, so I don't know what she said, but I know it was a short call because she soon came down to the dock and told me the 'girls' had overlooked her check and would forward it and the next ones. Temporarily. Then she said the operator had phoned back, as she'd asked, and told her the price of the call, and she'd left the money on the telephone table and there would be no argument about that. Rigid with dignity. I saluted and said, 'Yessir,' but she didn't laugh. She's been in her room ever since."

"Reading those pamphlets?"

"I suppose."

"The checks. The next *ones?* Or the next *one?*"

"I thought she said ones. I could be wrong. Ones means months."

"Norma is having a fit."

"Leonard there?"

"No."

"Did you tell Norma what Freddy heard Leonard say?"

"Of course not."

Bill said, "Leonard's scared now. He's had a fright that'd make any hard-on keel over."

"Won't he even call her and ask if she's heard from Freddy?"

"I doubt it."

"Leonard and Norma are both invited to the party. And Janice."

"Interesting to see who shows up or begs off."

They watched television. Aunt Pleasantine stayed in her room. They read on the porch; Mary was in the Hindu Kush at last. Then they went upstairs to bed.

Mary had her school nightmare. Sometimes the nightmare took place in college, sometimes in high school. Sometimes the class she forgot to go to for an entire year and the homework she forgot to do was math, sometimes Latin or any subject, and sometimes the teachers were familiar, sometimes strangers. Always, however, there was panic. The sweating terror when she remembered she'd forgotten. She would flunk!

She tore herself awake. An art history teacher had been raging at her for not coming to class. She listened to Bill's breathing. She and Bill slept naked, tangled together like puppies. If he were sleeping lightly, she would say, as usual, "The school nightmare. Remind me I don't have to go to school ever again," and he would mumble, "You don't have to go to school ever again," and, comforted, she would fall back asleep.

Tonight he was sound asleep. She looked past him at the numbers on the clock radio: 3:46. When she was a kid, she had been slow to learn how to tell time. Connie could tell time before Mary could, confusing another of Mother's categories. This digital clock, which Bill bought a few years ago, continued to bewilder her; past the half hour, she had to do subtraction. 3:46. Fourteen minutes to four? She considered listening to the call-in talk show, but she'd been avoiding it since she started the painting. She tried Aunt Pleasantine's method. Silently she recited some *Child's Garden of Verses.* Then she recited poems her high school senior English teacher had made the class memorize. He was a Catholic and some of his choices seemed rather peculiar. She and Bill wondered if Saffron Walden's senior English classes had been the only public high school classes in the world who had to memorize "Lead, Kindly Light." She recited as much of "Ozymandias" as she could recall—and then she panicked. The nightmare awake. She hadn't done her homework, she couldn't remember the last lines, she would flunk!

She got out of bed and put on her summer bathrobe. She went into the workroom. Glimpsing her desk calendar, she realized that a year ago yesterday Nixon had admitted taking part in the Watergate cover-up and had released the Supreme-Court-ordered tapes. A deathwatch feeling. In two days he'd resign, and three mornings from now she'd watched him make that crazy farewell speech to his staff and leave the White House. Bill had stayed home to see the speech but got disgusted and went to work. A year ago. She looked at her talk-show painting, and, suddenly so discouraged she felt sick, she left the room and went down the steep staircase.

Herbs must be harvested in early morning. She'd learned that from Mother. She went out the back door. The green lawn was gray with dew, and she walked across the wet grass through opaque light which blended the shore and the lake. A breeze rattled the giant white birch's ragged paper bark.

At the herb garden she knelt. The herbs were ready for drying. The basil had got ahead of her and begun to blossom. She glanced up. Aunt Pleasantine was sitting on the porch, looking at the lake.

At four A.M.? How often did Aunt Pleasantine sit here, as well as recite poems and listen to the show?

"Good morning," Mary said. "The herbs are ready. I guess I won't wait until the dew is gone."

"Would you like some help?"

"Love some."

Aunt Pleasantine opened the screen door and came down the porch steps. Her bathrobe was the pink of the rosebushes.

Thyme, marjoram, sage, basil, rosemary, mint, summer savory. Mary and Aunt Pleasantine began pulling the plants up, putting them in little piles.

All at once Aunt Pleasantine laughed. "I'll never understand Elizabeth. For years she's claimed she won't remarry unless she finds a man who is very rich and will spend the nights elsewhere. She doesn't want a husband around at night again."

Mary crushed and sniffed a leaf of mint. "But Hester didn't set such qualifications?"

"Well, quite sensibly Hester wanted a well-to-do man, which Oliver certainly was. She and her late husband, Stephen, had had hard times for so many years. Stephen lacked spunk."

"And Elizabeth's late husband?"

"The trouble with Carl was that he was addicted to pistachio nuts. He carried little bags of them in his pockets and kept tossing pistachio nuts into his mouth as he talked, and he left shells everywhere."

"Did he do this at bedtime, too?"

"I've often wondered."

Mary straightened up. "I'll fetch baskets. Where did Hester's husband and Elizabeth's work?"

"Stephen was in Filene's menswear department. Carl worked many places, he called it job-hopping, and his last job, before he retired and he and Elizabeth moved to Florida, was in Cleveland, Ohio. I've never understood what he did in those factories, and Elizabeth was never interested enough to find out anything more than the amount of his paycheck."

Sunlight now seeped through the haze. The lake and lawn

seemed to steam. From the garage Mary brought the two flat garden baskets which had been Mother's.

Aunt Pleasantine said, "Louisa's."

"Connie has the vegetable baskets."

They moved the piles of herbs to the baskets.

Aunt Pleasantine said, "When Hester's fiancé, Oliver, asked her to marry him, he produced his dead wife's Christmas card list so Hester could use it to send out wedding announcements. I never liked him. He had one long eyebrow instead of two. You know. I never liked him, but that didn't deter me from enjoying his treats."

"His death must have been a blow to Hester."

"The real blow came a few minutes earlier, when he jilted her."

"He what?"

Carrying the baskets, they walked slowly up the lawn. The hems of their bathrobes were soaking wet.

Aunt Pleasantine said, "How was Norma?"

"Strung out. Freddy's with Stan, he got there safely."

"Thank God for that."

They walked past the birch.

Aunt Pleasantine said, "I noticed you don't have any caraway in your garden."

"I don't bother, Bill hates caraway. Connie gives me some of hers for myself."

"How I look forward to meeting her and her family. How I wish I were spry enough to help her out with her brood."

Mary said, "She wishes you could, too," hoping this sounded complimentary instead of tactless.

"I could still be a watchdog, but I couldn't move quickly enough in an emergency. And if her children are anything like she was! Whenever you were missing, Mary, we knew you'd just wandered off, but we couldn't imagine what Connie might be doing. I wasn't prepared for her escapades because when my children were very young I had help who took care of them, and

I heard only about the big emergencies, not the small. I'll never forget the dash I made when I saw Connie fall into the pigpen."

Mary put the baskets on the kitchen counter. "Would you like herb tea or regular?"

Every morning Aunt Pleasantine enjoyed two cups of Red Rose tea with her toast. She used the same teabag twice, as Mary years ago had done to save money. This morning Aunt Pleasantine said, "Grandma always said thyme tea is especially good for what ails you."

Mary looked sharply at her.

Aunt Pleasantine opened the silverware drawer. "I saw you have Becky's tea strainer."

Mary rounded up sieves, the colander, the salad basket, and filled the sink with water. She washed thyme and took it outdoors in a sieve to drain in the dooryard shade. She squinted at the lake. The haze had burned off, and today would be hot and blue.

When she came back in, Aunt Pleasantine was putting the tea kettle on the stove. Mary washed summer savory. Aunt Pleasantine arranged cups and saucers on the dropleaf table. The room seemed to Mary a double exposure, a triple exposure, this lake kitchen over the farm kitchen over Grandmother's kitchen in Brandon. Aunt Pleasantine was setting out cups and saucers in a kitchen with Becky and Louisa and Mary. The tea strainer's silver bowl, worn and bent, fitted beautifully onto a teacup; its slender ebony handle always felt cool.

"My Social Security," Aunt Pleasantine said, "is ninety-four dollars and forty cents a month."

Mary rinsed the summer savory, but she didn't leave to put it outdoors. Instead, she refilled the sink and washed marjoram and waited.

And after a while Aunt Pleasantine sat down in a wooden chair. "Out of that check I pay the children ten dollars a week for room and board, leaving me at the end of the month with fifty dollars and forty cents. Out of this I make my Blue-Cross-Blue-Shield payments and buy such incidentals as clothes, Kleenex, hairdos, toilet paper, and Ivory Flakes. In September, when I have my teeth cleaned, some of this extra pays the dentist's bill, and I give thanks I inherited Papa's teeth. When he died, every tooth in his head was his own, and so will mine be. The grandchildren send Christmas and birthday presents of money, which is a great help to my budget."

"Blue Cross? Can't you get Medicare or Medicaid or whatever?"

"My flu doctor's receptionist asked that. It hadn't occurred to me I was eligible. So confusing. I asked the children, who said Medicare and Medicaid are Welfare and for heaven's sake not to ask Oliver or Ralph how to apply, they'd think we are paupers. I agreed I hadn't sunk that low."

"It's not a disgrace. I'll ask Bill about it."

Aunt Pleasantine went outdoors and brought in some sprigs of thyme. She stripped off enough leaves for two cups of tea. "Bill was both wrong and right about Social Security, you see, because I *can* live on it, but only if I live where my room and board payment is so small it is really just a token gesture. For fifteen years after Vera Miller died I pooled my Social Security with other old women's. I lived with four of them in all, counting that short spell with Grace in Kingsbridge. But they all had houses paid for by their husbands' mortgage insurance, and, although my pittance was welcome, I was really once more a companion, not a boarder. I'd hoped to find another such place after Grace's death, but my hopes weren't high because such arrangements get fewer as one gets older. I suppose in a way I was relieved when I fell. I knew I couldn't burden anybody except the children with an old woman with an arm in a cast."

Mary felt dizzy from the effort of trying to guess what Aunt Pleasantine was implying. Was Aunt Pleasantine offering her forty bucks a month for room and board?

Aunt Pleasantine arranged thyme leaves in the silver strainer.

She poured boiling water over them into a cup.

The tea steeped, and Mary washed sage.

"Ralph suits Elizabeth somewhat." Aunt Pleasantine brought Mary the first cup of tea. "Elizabeth has always loved dancing, and he takes her out dancing almost every evening, brings her back, has a nightcap, and then he goes home. He isn't rich—I wonder if *he's* on Medicare—but he isn't around during the night either." She put fresh leaves in the strainer and made herself a cup. "Elizabeth says he's only interested in dancing. Why that makes her happy I'll never know."

"Is he single, divorced, or—"

"He's a widower. His wife was shot by burglars in their trailer. He came home from work one day and found her dying and the color television set gone."

"My God."

"Elizabeth still hopes to meet a rich Ralph at one of the dances, but in the meantime he's a suitable escort. And he's an excellent cook, too. He learned to cook after his wife's death. He went through his wife's recipe file and learned to make the things he'd liked best which she'd made for him. Although he doesn't have much money, he may yet win Elizabeth's heart either through his dancing or the bran rolls he brings to brunch."

The tea looked delicate, but it was strong as hell. "Why did Oliver jilt Hester?"

"Me," Aunt Pleasantine said.

Upstairs the toilet flushed.

Aunt Pleasantine glanced at the clock. "I must go do my exercises." She gulped her tea and hurried away.

Bill was up early because he wanted a sail and swim before work. Mary went with him. They anchored off Little Triangle and swam.

"Jesus," Bill grunted as he pulled himself back into the boat, "I've got to get a ladder for this motherfucker, I'm too old to clamber."

Mary handed him a towel. "What *is* Medicare? Or Medicaid?"

"Medicure, for all I know."

"We ought to know. We might need it someday, too."

"I'll find out. More pamphlets full of jargon."

When they returned to the house, Aunt Pleasantine was still in her room.

Mary poured Grapenuts. "You keep calm around Leonard and William."

"Let's hope they're as smart as I was and have both remembered boats to appraise. Far far away."

After he left, Mary went up to her workroom and faced the painting. An hour later she recalled the draining herbs and went downstairs. If Aunt Pleasantine had come out to the kitchen and made her cinnamon toast, there was no sign of it. Mary carried the herbs from the dooryard to the porch and saw Aunt Pleasantine emerging from the woods. She'd taken her walk. Mary brought a ball of string and sat at the red porch table and began tying herbs into bunches.

Aunt Pleasantine opened the screen door.

Mary said, "They've drained enough."

Aunt Pleasantine sat down at the table. Her hands were small and competent, the oval nails a natural pink. Mary wondered when, if ever, she had resigned herself to the brown age spots. Aunt Pleasantine tied rosemary and said, "During their discussions of the marriage, Oliver and Hester and Elizabeth naturally had to discuss what to do with me. There were many many discussions. The children and Oliver would sit in the Florida room and spin plans in lowered voices."

"Elizabeth joined the discussions? Was it going to be a *ménage à trois?*"

"That was the most discussed idea. The problem was that the third person Oliver wanted in his *ménage* was not Elizabeth but me. Needless to say, I eavesdropped shamelessly on all this."

"Did Oliver have a house?"

"Since his wife's death he had lived in a bachelor apartment in one of those modern apartment buildings—what's the word?"

"Condominiums?"

"I always think I'll either make a mistake and say condoms or I'll get an extra syllable into it the way I do with megalopolis. Oliver planned to buy a house, and he and Hester looked at a number of them. The discussions began to be heated. Oliver circled and circled, trying to avoid saying point-blank that taking on a second wife was enough of a project without also taking on a second sister-in-law. Oliver was a practical man, and I know he figured my stay with him and Hester would be briefer than Elizabeth's might be. Elizabeth, of course, wanted to live with them in order to get in on the little luxuries, but she couldn't come right out and say this. They discussed bedrooms. Hester wanted one of her own, so if we all lived together there would have to be four bedrooms. Oliver said he couldn't afford a large four-bedroom house, which probably was a lie but it let him maneuver. They discussed my living six months a year with Elizabeth in the bungalow and six months a year with Hester and Oliver."

"What did *you* want to do?"

"I'm used to the bungalow now. My room. Familiar territory. I was used to the routine, what's allowed and not allowed, and if Elizabeth continued to go off dancing with Ralph I'd have the bungalow to myself most evenings. But living in Oliver's house would be a new adventure. It was silly of me to try to decide, because it was not my decision. The children and Oliver discussed and discussed. Nerves were strained. And then I was stupid and got the flu. When I'd recovered enough to resume eavesdropping, Hester and Elizabeth were talking about nursing homes. Your grandmother taught me to put rosemary in chicken stew, do you do that, too?"

"A nursing home just for during your flu or a permanent one?"

"Permanent. Oliver wouldn't hear of it. And one evening he laid down the law. He said this was his final word. He would buy a three-bedroom house, and I would live with him and Hester year-round. Fireworks ensued. Hester said she didn't see why she should be saddled with me while Elizabeth got away scot-free. Elizabeth said she didn't see why Oliver wouldn't accept the sensible solution, a nursing home. At this point I didn't have to eavesdrop because they were talking at the top of their lungs. Even when I went into the bathroom and threw up, I didn't miss a word. Hester and Elizabeth said they had hated me from the day I divorced James. They said nobody else's mother was a divorcée then. And what they hated about me even more than the divorce, they said, was my losing my money."

Mary looked up from the marjoram.

Aunt Pleasantine was crying, but the tears were not to be noticed. Her hands kept working. "I always knew how it twisted in them, being the housekeeper's daughters, never having the toys and clothes they wanted. Once when Hester was thirteen years old, she said she wished my pony were still alive so she could kill it. I stopped telling stories about my pony. Elizabeth and Hester said to Oliver that they'd dismissed me from their minds the minute they each got married. This is my fault. I caused this. But I never knew how totally they hated me."

Aunt Pleasantine looked too resolute to touch. Mary started tying the basil.

"Hester shouted at Oliver that he was in love with me instead of with her. I couldn't believe my ears. I was in my room, and I began laughing, smothering it with my pillow. Hester said I'd once lived in sin with a younger man and no doubt would be capable of doing that again in my eighties. I fell to pieces laughing. Silently. Oliver left in a rage. I stayed in my room the rest of the night, and I didn't come out for breakfast. It's a nice room, as I've told you. The children subscribe to a newspaper and many ladies' magazines, which they pass along to me, and I do some reading and sewing and crossword puzzles and daydreaming. That morning I went over my finances. Over and over. But there hadn't been any miraculous mistake in my arithmetic. I couldn't live on my own. I thought of phoning Blanche McGrath, the friend whose house burned down, to see if she knew of someone who could use my meager room and board, but I didn't want to bother her with my problems when she had so many of her own, and I didn't want the children to overhear, and I didn't know when I'd be alone to phone. I couldn't ask Oliver or Ralph. Just as I was beginning to realize I'd lost my supper and hadn't eaten any breakfast, Oliver arrived at the bungalow. There wasn't another discussion in the Florida room. He stood in the front doorway. I peeked out from my room, and I thought he looked ill. He told Hester the marriage was off. Hester screamed for Elizabeth, who came out of the kitchen carrying the goldfish food. Oliver didn't listen to Hester's protests. He said he was too old and tired for this sort of thing, and he turned and left. The children were stunned. They stared at each other, and then they began talking wildly, and they didn't notice there was no sound of his car leaving. I was puzzled. Then I was worried, and I came out of my room and walked past the girls and went outdoors to the front yard. Oliver had collapsed near the carport. We called an ambulance, but Oliver died on the way to the hospital. Heart attack. There, the herbs are done. Where do you hang them to dry?"

"The attic."

"Just as Becky and Louisa did." Aunt Pleasantine sat back and blotted her eyes with a Kleenex. "I thought I might ask Long Distance if Lillian Crawford is still listed in Kingsbridge."

Mary came down from the attic in time for *Hollywood Squares* and fetched sherries.

"Smetana!" Aunt Pleasantine said, again blurting out the answer to the Secret Square before the Master could read the multiple-choice answers to the question "Who composed *The Bartered Bride?*" The contestant guessed wrong and lost, but Aunt Pleasantine won a rotisserie grill, a Honda motorcycle, a Frigidaire trash compactor, a His 'n' Hers archery set, and a mink coat which had been hammily modeled by Joan Rivers.

"I had some lovely furs long ago," Aunt Pleasantine said, thinking over her prizes. "But I don't suppose nowadays I could bring myself to wear that mink. If it were fake fur I could, but I guess I know too much now to wear real fur, endangered or otherwise." She looked, however, wistful.

Mary said, "I bought my latest winter coat on sale, and it was so cheap I figured the fur trim was fake. But when I got home I discovered a little tag in a pocket which said the trim was Australian opossum. Have you ever heard of Australian opossums? Neither had I. So what happens? The very next night I was flipping TV channels and I hit *Wild Kingdom* or one of those nature shows, and what was the narrator discussing? Marsupials. And there in a tree was a cute little creature called an Australian opossum. So I had to tear off the trim. Um, is Lillian Crawford still listed?"

"Yes. I phoned the number, but nobody answered. I'll try again later."

"I just remembered I'd better get my hair cut before the party. How often do you have yours done? Do you want to make an appointment at Irene's for, say, Friday?"

"Fine."

After the show they made their appointments, and during lunch Mary went over with Aunt Pleasantine the list of party food. "What am I forgetting?"

"You said Connie and her family are coming early, Friday evening."

"Christ, that's right, and the older twins are a ravenous horde, what'll I feed them for supper? Hot dogs." Mary scribbled that on the list. "Hot dogs and junk food. If I forgot Friday's supper, what else have I forgotten?"

"Were you planning a dessert at the party buffet?"

"Christ. Dessert. I've never ever remembered dessert at a party. Would a bowl of fruit do?"

"Yes, and I could make a lemon bisque, my so-called specialty. Nothing as spectacular as my Inn cook's flaming specialties, but even Vera Miller liked it."

"Thank you."

"The children always get so nervous when they give a party."

"I keep calm until I'm heading down the home stretch."

"Will you use paper plates?"

"Bill loathes paper plates. And I don't trust the guests with Grandmother's china, so I'll just use the everyday."

"Will there be enough plates?"

"I've accumulated cheapies for our We-Owe-Everybodies over the years. There'll be enough."

"Will you use plastic silverware?"

"No. Maybe you've noticed I don't own any stainless, Mother and Grandmother wouldn't allow it, I either had to have silver or Bill and I would have to eat with our fingers. So I'll use the silverware and hope not too much of it gets dropped in the lake. Oh, Christ again. I've forgotten to polish it."

"Let me polish it. My hands are still strong enough. I always polish the silver for the children's parties."

"Aunt Pleasie, that would be one hell of a relief. After your nap how about a sail for more rest and relaxation? We need it. The wind is gentle. I twitter, but I can handle *Nomad.*"

"I'd love a sail."

When Mary came downstairs in midafternoon, she felt she herself had won some intangible prize, some Secret Square, because she knew she had just finished the call-in talk-show painting.

Aunt Pleasantine, carrying the Oriental hat, came out of her room. They walked down to the dock. Mary took the boat cover off and stowed it away, loosened the furled sail, and helped Aunt Pleasantine in and helped her put on a life jacket.

"A snug ship," Aunt Pleasantine said.

Mary cast off. "Have you heard about the tall ships sailing to America for the Bicentennial?"

"From all parts of the world. But what *are* tall ships?"

Mary ripped at the outboard motor, which was one inanimate object which always obeyed her, probably because Bill took such prudent care of it, and the engine rumbled obediently and they motored out past the Point. "Tall ships? Remember your Masefield?"

"Oh, of course. 'And all I ask is a tall ship and a star to steer her by.' "

Mary cut the motor and began pulling the sail up the mast; watching it rise, she thought this was the tallest ship she could ever handle. She thought of riggings and heights and a dizzy crow's nest.

" 'And quiet sleep and a sweet dream when the long trick's over.' "

"Bill talks about braving the crowds in Boston to look at them, but I doubt we'll do it." The mainsail up, Mary decided not to bother with the jib and sat back down at the tiller. "Isn't it awful that if we do go we'll be too scared of bombs and snipers and pirates to enjoy the ships? I expect we'll end up watching it on TV." She tacked past Duck Island and became wary of speedboats.

Aunt Pleasantine said, "I often think of the Hubcap King's collection. I'm so glad I had a chance to see it. My cranberry glass. Mrs. Kimball's collection I inherited was enormous, but I suppose I would have kept adding to it, except for the cost."

"When you went bankrupt with the Inn, the collection went, too?"

"Yes."

They sailed and listened to the water slopping softly under the hull.

Aunt Pleasantine said, "Why do I keep having winter memories at the oddest times? I just remembered driving down from the Inn to visit your parents in—it must have been nineteen-forty. January, nineteen-forty. You were in your playpen near the kitchen wood range, and you were standing up, and when I entered the kitchen you took your first unaided steps. Three steps. You walked toward me, then grabbed the pen to keep from falling. Louisa and Arthur were there to see it, and they were delighted. Your first steps on your own accord. That afternoon Louisa and I went sledding with you. You'd been cooped up indoors because of bad weather, but that day the sun was shining on the snow, and you were very excited by it and by the sledding. I wish James and I had seen Hester's and Elizabeth's first unaided steps, but we missed both."

A speedboat towing a water-skier cut across *Nomad.* Mary turned into its wake. She lost the wind, and *Nomad* rocked and drifted. As she pushed the tiller hard over and gradually picked up the wind again, she all of a sudden realized she didn't know whether or not James was alive or dead. He could be in his late eighties or something. She had simply assumed he was dead. Had Mother ever mentioned his death?

They passed Little Triangle. Mary didn't want to risk The Broads. Preparing to come about, she studied wind and sail and asked as casually as possible, "Did James spend the rest of his life in San Francisco?"

"Do you know that song 'I Left My Heart in San Francisco'?"

"Uh-huh." Mary expected sad associations.

"I laugh and laugh whenever I hear it on the radio. 'I left my heart in San Francisco; high on a hill it calls to me.' I can't help picturing a big fat red Valentine heart on a hilltop, forlornly waving sticklike arms."

Mary, scrambling, laughed. "Coming about."

Aunt Pleasantine watched the boom. After the maneuver she said, "Is the party too much of a strain? You're looking tired this afternoon—or is it because we were awake so early?"

"I finished a painting. It's kind of cumbersome, but Bill and I'll get it downstairs to show you when it's dry."

"I could certainly manage those stairs to see your painting."

"We've lugged larger. It's got to be brought downstairs sometime anyway." Then Mary wondered if Aunt Pleasantine was hinting that she'd like to explore the workroom and the rest of upstairs. "But if you want to try the stairs—"

"Maybe tomorrow. I sympathized with Sally about selling her dolls, but I cannot imagine what courage it must take for you to sell your paintings and never see them again."

"Not all of them sell."

Aunt Pleasantine said, "The children were notified by James's wife when he died in nineteen-forty-nine. He was sixty-four, the same age Hester is now. He was six years older than I."

In nineteen-forty-nine, Mary thought, I was ten. Mother must have mentioned his death, and I didn't pay attention.

Nomad headed home. Aunt Pleasantine said, "To think I've lived twenty-six years longer than James. Somehow that doesn't seem right."

As they neared Duck Island, Aunt Pleasantine put her hand over the side and let the sun-glittering water glide around her fingers. "Even though so many television police shows are set in San Francisco you'd think nothing but crime goes on there, I've read it is a beautiful city. Restaurants. Cable cars. I know James's years must have been happy there."

"Did you ever meet his wife?"

"Good God, no. If James ever had come back East, it would have been for a fling, and I doubt if he'd have brought his wife along. I wonder if he ever returned. If so, he never visited me or the children. I wish I could have seen a picture of her. I've often wondered if she looks like me."

"Do you know her name?"

"No."

"Did they have any children?"

"I do think James would have written me if they had, to tell Hester and Elizabeth there were California half sisters or brothers." Aunt Pleasantine took her hand out of the water. "I do think James would have told me."

Duck Island was giving a performance now. A flock had arrived, and the ducks were paddling and quacking and ducking.

Aunt Pleasantine said, "I suppose James collected women the way the Hubcap King collects hubcaps. Apparently his second wife was able to put up with this."

"Maybe she collected men, and thus they were a perfect couple."

"Exactly. That's one of the many things I'm speculating about when I appear to be sitting 'old and gray and full of sleep/And nodding by the fire.' Leonard seems to have James's hobby, too."

They neared the Point, and Mary loosened the sail and started the motor. As they docked, they saw Bill's car coming up the driveway.

Aunt Pleasantine went to her room.

In the kitchen Mary asked Bill, "Leonard and William?"

"Leonard spent even more time than usual in the stockroom. Whenever there weren't customers, the old man shouted at me."

"Hell."

"Paul and I got around the question of Freddy by saying he'd unexpectedly gone to visit his father. True enough." Bill started upstairs.

Mary said, "If you want to go in the workroom, the goddamn thing is finished."

"The radio talk show?" Bill hadn't seen it; she never let him see paintings until they were done.

"Yes."

He went upstairs. She fussed with the drinks tray. Cheezits. When he came downstairs, she couldn't look at him. He said, "One of these days you're going to find yourself in the same fix as the guys who build boats in cellars too small to get the finished boats out of."

"Okay, I'll start doing the Lord's Prayer on the head of a pin."

Bill kissed her. "It's the best yet."

"Thanks."

"I do get nervous, though, when I realize I'm living with such a weirdo. Those telephone lines!"

After supper Aunt Pleasantine asked Bill to help her understand the pamphlets, and Mary used real telephone lines and phoned Connie. Uneasy about the way the last phone call had ended, she said, "Hi, it's Mary. Has the backhoe guy come?"

"Today. The stink when that backhoe went to work on the septic system was unbelievable. I shut all the windows and kept Bobby and Tommy indoors so they wouldn't fall in the trench and become part of the leach field, and they were enraged they had to watch from a window while Dave and Keith were outdoors having a glorious time watching. And the stink leaked into the house anyway. And the noise!"

"Your irises?"

"Waiting in the wheelbarrows. The guy is *supposed* to come back tomorrow and fill in the trench. It's a huge brown ditch across the lawn, Mary—"

"Grass seed—"

"The lawn will never look the same."

"Can you still come to the party?"

"The prospect of getting away from here is the only thing keeping me sane. How's Aunt Pleasantine?"

"I learned today that her daughters wanted to boot her out—"

"I wish my kids would boot me out," Connie said. Then she screamed, "Tommy, *no,* don't you *dare* go outdoors alone!" She hung up, and Mary imagined her tackling Tommy at the brink of the ditch.

Aunt Pleasantine went to bed, but Bill continued reading pamphlets. Mary returned to the Hindu Kush.

Bill said, "I think I'm getting this straight. The difference between Medicare and Medicaid is Medicare is federal and for short-term care. Medicaid is both federal and state, and it's the outfit which pays for old people, for nursing homes and stuff. I'm simplifying, it's more complicated—"

"—I'm sure it is," Mary said wearily.

"—but I hope I've convinced Aunt Pleasantine the whole business isn't a blow to her pride. We've even begun calling the Supplemental thing the SSI, shorthand, like civil servants. I get a ball park figure of about twelve bucks for her SSI a month."

"Only that much?"

"She was happy. She said, 'What a windfall!' "

"Aunt Pleasantine must be so exhausted. All these years. Hand-to-mouth existence."

Bill shuffled pamphlets. "Funny thing was, she seemed most interested in some state stuff I didn't have a chance to look at. Can't find it. Guess she took it to her room."

On the way to Kingsbridge, Mary stopped at a self-service gas station and filled up the tank. As she got back into the car, she saw that Aunt Pleasantine was smiling.

Out on the road, Aunt Pleasantine spoke for the first time during the trip. "I had forgotten."

"Forgotten what?"

"How indignant your grandmother was when our favorite Brandon grocery store expanded and put in shopping carts. We were used to phoning our orders or going into the store and telling Mr. Romano what we wanted. I always enjoyed watching him pluck down the items on top shelves with a long-handled gadget. There was the suspense of whether or not he'd drop a can of pears. But Mr. Romano moved with the times and eventually put in self-service shopping carts, and Becky never, as far as I know, never learned to feel comfortable pushing a shopping cart down aisles. And now here you are, filling your car's tank with gasoline yourself."

"Bill had to teach me."

Aunt Pleasantine was wearing a sassy peppermint-striped dress. After breakfast Mary had helped her up the stairs and shown her the bedroom and spare rooms and the workroom. Aunt Pleasantine looked at the painting for a long time. She said, "It's disturbing." Downstairs, while Aunt Pleasantine tried Lillian Crawford's number again, Mary realized this comment was a compliment. Lillian still didn't answer. Mary asked, "Want to go down there anyway? See Grandmother's house, and stop by Lillian's on the off chance she's in?" Aunt Pleasantine deliberated, then said, "If you don't mind the drive."

Mary was avoiding the turnpike and taking the old route, through towns, figuring Aunt Pleasantine would enjoy this more. But the towns seemed full of shabby shopping centers and trailer parks. Discount bread stores. Discount furniture stores. The day was humid.

After a while Aunt Pleasantine said, "Lillian did look like a lily. A tiger lily. Her father delivered meat."

"Delivered?"

"To stores. Mr. Crawford was very rugged. He could easily throw a side of beef onto his shoulder. Lillian was ashamed."

"Did her mother work?"

"Her mother had her hands full with Lillian and two brothers and a sister. Becky knew more details about the family than I do because she played at Lillian's house. I went to Lillian's only once. The house smelled like a chamber pot."

They were driving past a clump of mailboxes in front of a trailer park. One mailbox was festooned with plastic blossoms.

"And I turned up my nose," Aunt Pleasantine said.

Then she was silent again.

Mary prompted, "Did Lillian get married?"

"Lillian never married. Becky exchanged Christmas cards with her, so I heard that she took care of her widowed mother and taught forty years at Kingsbridge High School. Algebra and geometry."

"And you didn't visit her while you were living with Grace?"

"She and Grace were no longer in touch."

They approached the sprawl of cities on the tidal river. Mary couldn't tell where one city's outskirts began and another's ended; they blended into stretches of housing developments, high-rise apartment buildings, gas stations, bowling alleys, shopping malls, chain restaurants, chain stores.

Mary drove onto a bridge and said, to keep her mind off the height, "Why didn't Lillian marry?"

"I don't know. She was a beauty. She must have had offers."

In the muggy morning, Kingsbridge ahead looked thick and heavy and sweaty.

The bridge descended into the city. Mary drove past blocks of new apartment buildings and glanced at the dashboard clock, which wasn't digital, thank God. Ten of eleven. "Do you want to see Grandmother's house first?"

"If you do."

The house was on Crescent Street. It kept changing. The last time Mary had driven past, the elm in front had been cut down. Now the house had been painted a tropical pastel green. But as usual, there were bikes lying on the lawn, and toys, so another family with lots of kids must have bought this Victorian white elephant.

The car idled.

Aunt Pleasantine said, "Becky loved dolls. What a collection she had! Your mother wasn't particularly interested in the survivors, but you were."

"Especially the china-faced doll named Anne."

"One of Connie's puppies chewed her to bits."

"Yes. Do you want me to drive up the hill?"

"Please."

Mary drove up past similar houses, past other elm stumps, to where Aunt Pleasantine had lived in a sea captain's house complete with widow's walk. Now there was a Holiday Inn at a turnpike exit.

Mary said, "You can think of it as a host."

"I've tried to."

"Lillian Crawford's house is on the river?"

"Down off Main Street. On River Street."

Mary worked her way through the traffic. The heat was so bad that she expected other drivers to go crazy, to commit murder at stoplights.

"My next car," she exploded, "is going to be air-conditioned!"

Aunt Pleasantine was looking at a dress-shop window display and didn't reply, and Mary reminded herself that she was lucky to own any car at all and be able to drive it. The car in front of her had a bumper sticker which said:

SPLIT WOOD
NOT ATOMS

Mary asked, "A left here?"

"Yes."

Mary drove past mills and factories down to a sunken Cape in a wild garden. Jerry had certainly caught it with his pencil.

Aunt Pleasantine got out of the car before Mary did. Mary hurried around to her.

Beyond the jungle of lupines the river looked poisonous. On the other riverbank were more mills.

Mary said, "There isn't any car."

Aunt Pleasantine started along the path. "I expect she no longer drives. Perhaps she can still walk downtown, that's why she's been out. Her number *was* listed."

They reached the slightly open front door. Aunt Pleasantine knocked.

Mary said, "Want me to lean in and call yoo-hoo?"

"I will." Aunt Pleasantine pushed the door open a little farther. "Oh, dear God."

Mary got the smell, too. Not just chamber pots, but also cats and mildew and rot. "Shouldn't you go back to the car? I'll go in."

Aunt Pleasantine pushed harder, opening the door far enough for them to squeeze into the hallway which was filled with stacks of old newspapers and magazines. The staircase ahead was so jammed with more stacks that only tiptoe spaces were left.

Mary and Aunt Pleasantine looked into the living room. Somewhere under the junk, Mary thought, there must be furniture. Yes, she saw under heaps of little Woolworth bags an oak center table, she saw that the room was crammed with furniture beneath its layers of clutter. A cat floated onto an oak sideboard; another cat watched from the back of a threadbare sofa.

Mary stepped ahead of Aunt Pleasantine and picked a path through shopping bags which overflowed with yellowed quilting cotton, skeins of yarn, scraps of cloth. The room reeked. Something about the curl of empty afghan on the sofa told Mary that a person slept on the sofa instead of in a bed.

Aunt Pleasantine walked in and stopped near a filthy armchair which was drawn up to a huge old television set. On the small table beside the chair there was a telephone, and a volume of the *Encyclopedia Americana* from which hung edges of Kleenex. Aunt Pleasantine, obviously making an effort, picked up the volume and opened it. Between almost all the pages, someone had carefully laid a Kleenex.

Aunt Pleasantine said, "Can you imagine how bored she must be to do this?"

"Bored or berserk?"

"Or both."

Aunt Pleasantine walked back through the hallway into the kitchen. Mary followed, into the smell of rotting food. Rusty saucepans on the cold oil range held meals turned green. The sink was filled with scabby dishes. On the table, near an unopened packet of Nabs, a cracked bowl had grown a skin of soup. And everywhere on the worn and crooked floor were metal washtubs of gray sheets soaking in scummy water.

Aunt Pleasantine said, "She must try to do her laundry."

No milk remained in the cat saucers. The upper pantry shelves were piled with pots and pans and cans of ancient food. On the lower shelves were crockery, a can of Campbell's vegetable soup, a box of prunes, and two cans of cat food. Mary couldn't bring herself to look into the breadbox or refrigerator, and Aunt Pleasantine didn't either.

The bathroom door was almost closed, but the smell was fierce. Aunt Pleasantine opened the door. The toilet had overflowed. Beyond, the rest of the floor was a mess of cat shit and kitty litter.

Aunt Pleasantine walked past the washtubs and went into the ell. Mary followed. In the first room, an artificial Christmas tree was decorated with dusty tinsel. Out of moldy gift-wrapped boxes spilled years of Christmases and birthdays. None of the presents had been used. Nightgowns, scarves, handkerchiefs. Still in tissue paper in their boxes. An electric blanket, nylon slips, books, bedjackets, gift assortments of pretty little jams and jellies.

Mary went into the last downstairs room and saw a bed covered with only a dirty spread. There were stacks of ragged math textbooks, cartons of yellowed exams, and shoeboxes of canceled checks and check stubs and bills.

Mary turned and sprinted, nearly knocking over Aunt Pleasantine in the doorway, and ran back through the house, to get far ahead of Aunt Pleasantine, to find out the worst. Pressed against the railing, she dashed up the stairs past the magazines and newspapers. In one bedroom, trunks and suitcases under the eaves surrounded a single bed strewn with old clothes. She forced herself to poke among the clothes. The trunks were unlocked, and she poked too among the old clothes she found in them.

The other room was eerily tidy. It had a double bed, and on the bureau were framed family photographs and a souvenir ashtray from Niagara Falls which held hairpins. Mary opened the wardrobe and looked at more old-fashioned clothes. She opened bureau drawers. They were crammed with pink girdles, empty aspirin bottles, men's flannel pajamas.

"Her parents' room," Aunt Pleasantine said. Despite being slow-motion, she had arrived. "Lillian must be about eighteen in that photograph."

A tiger lily. Mary said, "What should we do?"

"Does one call the police at this point? Maybe she's just gone shopping."

"Let's go downstairs."

Back down in the living room, Aunt Pleasantine walked over to the mountain of junk on the center table and picked up one of the little Woolworth bags. Out of it she shook clustered safety pins. Out of another she took a box of brightly colored unsharpened pencils. Mary joined in. Spools of thread. Pads and pads of paper. Barrettes. Powder puffs. Mary remembered seeing old women in the Woolworth's in Saffron. A pad of thumbtacks. Nail polish. Buttons. Vicks cough drops. A hair net. A birthday card never sent. The cats watched.

Aunt Pleasantine said, "She walks downtown every day and buys some small thing. Something she can afford. An excuse for being in the store."

Buying a birthday card for nobody.

Mary said, "The cats would be yowling if they're hungry, wouldn't they?"

"They'd be eating the garbage in the kitchen. She's kept the cats fed, she's kept paying the phone bills, she walks downtown."

Aunt Pleasantine turned on a lamp. "She's kept paying her electricity."

Below the layers of little bags, Mary found unopened mail, newspapers, a Christmas present postmarked last year.

Aunt Pleasantine said, "She's got her wits some of the time. I hear a car."

Mary walked around the shopping bags into the hallway. The car had stopped behind the Saab, and a woman was coming down the path. She was middle-aged. Not Lillian Crawford.

"Who are you," the woman said, "and what are you doing here?"

Aunt Pleasantine had followed Mary to the hallway. "This is Mary Emerson, and I'm Pleasantine Curtis, an old schoolmate of Lillian's. The door was open, and we became worried and went in."

The woman said, "The lock's broken. It's a wonder she wasn't murdered in her bed."

The stacks of newspapers and magazines caused a crush as the woman tried to come in and Mary and Aunt Pleasantine tried to stand aside for her. The woman pushed past and went into the living room and said, "Nice sight, isn't it? It's not my fault. We never knew." She set her white pocketbook down on the *Encyclopedia Americana.* "I'm her niece from Albany, and my husband and I were driving through on our way to Maine for our vacation, and we thought we'd look in. And this is what we found."

Aunt Pleasantine said, "Where's Lillian?"

"I'm Mrs. Turmelle. We never knew. Everyone in the family always remembered her at Christmas, her birthdays."

"Where's Lillian?"

"My husband and I put her in a nursing home as fast as we could. A veterinarian's assistant is supposed to meet me here to take the cats away. You wouldn't believe what our motel is costing us throughout the ordeal. That Holiday Inn above town."

"A nursing home?" Aunt Pleasantine asked. "One of the ones in Kingsbridge?"

"Hampshire Manor. Highly recommended."

"Is she ill?"

"Why, of course she's ill. Senile, too, the doctor said. I'll tell her you stopped by, but I doubt if she'll understand."

"What will happen to this house?"

"A lighted match would probably be the smartest thing, but my husband right now is arranging about power of attorney and notifying the other relatives. And then we'll see what we shall see." The cats were moving toward the kitchen. Mrs. Turmelle looked at them, looked around the room. "Aunt Lillian," she said.

Out in the car, the house smell clung to their clothes. Aunt Pleasantine's peppermint dress had wilted.

Aunt Pleasantine said, "I remember Hampshire Manor. It's on Adams Avenue. Could we drive past?"

Mary said, "You're exhausted," but she obeyed Aunt Pleasantine's directions and drove back through the sticky downtown into streets with trees whose August leaves were limp.

"There it is," Aunt Pleasantine said.

You couldn't miss it. Mary never before had seen such a large sign in front of a nursing home. She'd supposed they tried to be as discreet as funeral homes. The sign had been the Manor's single try at jazzing the place up, however, because behind it the shabby old house was definitely not manorial.

"I should visit her." Aunt Pleasantine's tone of voice made Mary pull over to the curb without protest. Aunt Pleasantine opened her door. "I won't be long."

Now Mary did object. "Are you nuts? You're not going into that place alone."

Together they walked up the brick walk. The house's white clapboards were peeling. No one sat on the porch in the canvas-cushioned chairs and watched traffic. Aunt Pleasantine rang the doorbell, waited, rang again. Eventually a woman in a white uniform opened the door and looked at them through the screen door. Sizing Aunt Pleasantine up, Mary wondered, as a new customer?

"I'm Pleasantine Curtis, and I've been told that a friend of mine is staying here. Lillian Crawford. Would it be possible for me to see her?"

"I'm sorry. They've had their lunch, and they're resting."

"I'd be very brief," Aunt Pleasantine said. Mary glanced at her. Aunt Pleasantine was looking beautiful and frail and preparing to con the hell out of the nurse. "Lillian and I were such dear friends over seventy years ago when we were girls here in Kingsbridge. I'm making a sentimental journey to my hometown today with Mary Emerson, whose houseguest I am during a short visit North from Florida, and this would be my only chance to see Lillian ever again."

The nurse opened the screen door. "She won't recognize you. She doesn't even recognize her niece."

The room they stepped into had once been a living room, but now it was filled with narrow beds on which old men lay. The television set murmured a soap opera. The old men turned their heads and looked dully at Aunt Pleasantine and Mary, and Mary wondered if lunch had been laced with tranquilizers. One man giggled.

The nurse led them past the beds into a dining room filled with more beds. Women were white humps under coverlets.

Ahead, Aunt Pleasantine's back was very straight. Carriage, Mary thought; posture. She straightened her own back.

They walked down a hall, and the nurse said, "Miss Crawford has a double," and ushered Aunt Pleasantine and Mary into a small room. "This is Miss Crawford here. Mrs. Ellis has the window bed."

The nurse left, but Mary sensed her hovering in the hall.

Mrs. Ellis wasn't enjoying the window view, which was of trash cans and a lilac bush. She seemed comatose.

But Lillian Crawford was awake and looking at Aunt Pleasantine. Lillian lay flat, her sparse yellow-white hair hanging down the pillow. Her face was thin and taut.

Aunt Pleasantine stood at the foot of the bed. "Lillian, I don't expect you remember me, but I'm Pleasantine. We were in school together. I played at your house once."

"Rebecca."

"Becky played there too, yes, but I'm Pleasantine."

The nurse came into the room. "I told you she wouldn't recognize you."

Lillian said, "Becky."

"I'm Becky," Aunt Pleasantine said. "We played dolls. There was a china-faced doll named Anne."

Lillian closed her eyes.

The nurse said, "That's enough," and herded them out of the room. "Malnutrition is part of the problem. She's nothing but skin and bones."

They walked past the beds of old women and old men.

At the door Aunt Pleasantine said, "Thank you."

Mary helped Aunt Pleasantine into the car, got in, and thought, fuck the old route, and headed for the turnpike and leaped onto it. She sped along until the speed calmed her and she could slow down and look over at Aunt Pleasantine.

Aunt Pleasantine said, "I get hungry at the most inappropriate times. Do you?"

"Jesus, I completely forgot about our lunch. There's a Howard Johnson a few miles on."

The familiar Howard Johnson orange and turquoise annoyed Mary by comforting her so much. She even felt affection for the plastic menu, for the Twenty-eight Delicious Flavors, for Simple Simon and the Pieman.

Sitting in an orange booth, Aunt Pleasantine sipped her martini and apparently decided a cocktail-hour story was necessary even though it wasn't suppertime. "Do you remember Mrs. Smith, the woman who helped your grandmother clean house once a week? She did some baking, too."

"She made Connie and me peanut-butter cookies, the kind with fork marks across."

"Well, her predecessor wasn't very reliable. Maureen. Your grandfather didn't trust Maureen, so he started locking the liquor cabinet and taking the key with him into Boston to his office. Undoubtedly a wise tactic. However, it never occurred to him to leave the key with Becky, and it never occurred to her to ask him to. She and I liked a glass of the stuff that cheers whenever I was able to come over from Mrs. Goodhue's in the afternoon and have a visit. So the locked liquor cabinet was a challenge! I think Becky and I could have become first-class burglars if we'd put our minds to it. Becky smuggled a screwdriver up from the cellar, and we learned how to take the cabinet door off its hinges without leaving a mark. We would pour out our tipple, replace the door, and your grandfather never knew. He wasn't the sort who kept track of levels in bottles. It was very exciting, but Becky and I heaved a sigh of relief when Maureen became pregnant and was replaced by Mrs. Smith, a woman of unquestionable integrity, and the key was returned to the lock."

In the booth behind Mary a man was telling his wife about his visit to his urologist this morning. "The waiting room was so crowded I said to the receptionist, I said, 'God, you'd think you'd got a Special today.' And then what happens but when I sit down I sit next to a fellow who starts telling me his troubles and he said, he said, 'I couldn't stop pissing and I almost decided to hang an old coffee can under there.' I guess I'll have the fried clams, how about you?"

Aunt Pleasantine said, "I'm so grateful to Bill for his help. Has he told you about my SSI?"

"Some."

Reciting, Aunt Pleasantine explained, "Supplemental Security Income is a federal program that pays monthly checks to people in financial need who are sixty-five or older and to people in need at any age who are blind or disabled. People who qualify must have little or no cash income or not own much in the way of property or other things that can be turned into cash, such as stocks, bonds, jewelry. We're certain I qualify."

"So Bill said."

"In most states a person who is eligible for SSI is also eligible for Medicaid and other social services provided by the state."

"What are 'social services'?"

"I'm still trying to figure that out."

The waitress brought Mary's grilled cheese and Aunt Pleasantine's tuna fish. They ate slowly, in silence, looking at people. For dessert, Aunt Pleasantine had a dish of raspberry sherbet, and Mary suddenly craved a cigarette. Aunt Pleasantine paid her part of the check and of the tip, and Mary didn't attempt to protest.

As they were leaving, they heard one elderly woman say to another, "We might as well go to the mall. We don't have anyone at home waiting for us."

Back on the turnpike, Mary found herself driving behind a big truck stacked with wooden cages of live chickens. Instead of pulling out and passing, she stayed behind the truck. She didn't know why. She drove hypnotized by cages of chickens. Then the truck's directionals began blinking and the driver turned onto an exit ramp and one cage bounced off the truck, and there was a chicken flapping madly in a busted cage in the middle of Exit 16.

Past the exit, Mary pulled over into the breakdown lane and looked back. The truck driver hadn't stopped, probably hadn't noticed. She said, "The next person who takes that exit is going to make chicken fricassee."

"There's nothing you can do about it, Mary. The chicken was going to its just reward anyway. It'll simply go earlier and messily."

Mary drove back into the main lane.

Aunt Pleasantine didn't speak again until they reached Saffron Walden. "Blanche McGrath used to say that her motto had always been to work hard when you're young so you don't end up in the poorhouse when you're old."

They were driving past a shack whose hand-painted sign said:

HONEST ED'S TRADING POST
LICENSES
AMMO
WORMS AND CRAWLERS

Mary thought, I'd lock the liquor cabinet on Honest Ed.

Aunt Pleasantine said, "Clara Baldwin with her arthritis and other ailments. After you'd left, while we were waiting for our tea, she said, 'If I had known I would live this long, I would have taken better care of myself.' "

And when they reached the lake, Aunt Pleasantine added, "Isn't it strange how I just go on and on. I never paid much attention to taking care of myself, except for getting my figure back after the children were born and protecting my complexion always."

"You do your exercises and go for walks."

"That's now. Not then. When I was very young, I worried about consumption, because of my family history, but in those days it was a matter of fate, and you couldn't do anything about it."

At the camp Aunt Pleasantine went to her room. She was still there when Bill came home from work.

He asked, "Did you meet Lillian Crawford?"

Mary was slicing tomatoes. "Pour us a belt, and I'll tell all."

He poured, then leaned against a doorjamb, and she told.

"When we got home," she ended, "Aunt Pleasantine went off and I heard her bathtub running. I stuck around, in case she fell. She took a long bath. When I heard her go to her bedroom, I had a swim and afterwards a shower about as long as her bath."

"I'll tell her it's cocktail time."

Aunt Pleasantine came out to the porch wearing a blouse and slacks, and her story was sporty, perhaps inspired by Honest Ed's sign. "James fancied himself a fisherman. I couldn't stand wiggling worms, so I always brought a book or some sewing along instead of a fishpole. Sometimes he and your grandfather fished together, and if the blackflies were bad, Becky and I stayed in the car. We looked very innocent, sewing while the men were fishing, but we had our flask and many a laugh. Our best fishing expedition happened when James and your grandfather had gone trekking off, leaving Becky and me sewing in the car, and suddenly a man appeared out of the woods with a creel slung over his shoulder. He asked us directions and we decorously chatted, and he asked if we'd caught any fish. We said no, and for some reason —our charm?—he opened his creel and took out a lovely moss-wrapped catch of trout and gave it to us, and left. When James and your grandfather returned, Becky and I said, 'Did you catch anything?' They gloomily said they hadn't. I still remember the looks on their faces when we replied, 'We did!' and showed them the trout."

Friday morning, in the kitchen, Aunt Pleasantine began polishing the silverware. Mary did battle with the vacuum cleaner. By the time she reached Aunt Pleasantine's room she was ready to carry the damn machine down to the dock and drown it. Aunt Pleasantine's room seemed less a spare room now: the cactus on the windowsill, a book and the photograph albums on the table beside the chintz chair, a pamphlet on the bedside table, and mainly a lived-in feeling. Mary straightened up and looked at the pamphlet. It was titled:

New Hampshire Division of Welfare
Bureau of Adult Services
SHARED HOMES HANDBOOK

"Shared homes?" Mary opened the pamphlet, but the noise of the vacuum made the jargon incomprehensible—"Semi-

Independent Care—Criteria—Group Care Facilities—Sponsor Responsibilities—"

Mary realized she was sweating a sweat not caused by wrestling with the vacuum. She wanted to turn the machine off and sit down and study the pamphlet, but Aunt Pleasantine would wonder why she had stopped in her room. She read, "The sponsor will provide each resident with a clean face cloth, hand towel, and bath towel as frequently as needed but no less than once a week," and then she shut the pamphlet, put it back exactly where it had been on the bedside table, finished doing Aunt Pleasantine's room and continued the weekly routine, back out through the living room, up the stairs, lugging the canister, sweating and swearing, cleaning floors which would be made sandy by party guests. "Exercise in futility," she muttered. She lugged the canister back downstairs. She put it away, and she and Aunt Pleasantine drove into town to have their hair done, and she tried to get up the nerve to ask Aunt Pleasantine what the pamphlet was all about, but she couldn't.

Aunt Pleasantine said, "Is your—er—hairdresser on Main Street? Is it that Salon place where a grocery store used to be in my day?"

"That's the joint."

"Then it's near Irene's. I'd love to peek in, before my appointment."

"Sure. I'll walk on with you to Irene's after you have a look."

"I can walk by myself, Mary. I'll rest at shopwindows."

Mary parked near the storefront whose interior was hidden by royal blue drapes but whose gold-lettered sign announced: SALON OF GENTLEMEN'S HAIRSTYLING.

They went in. At this time of day, the customers were little boys clambering around on the plastic chairs. Their mothers either read magazines or stared into space and occasionally said, "Behave yourself."

Aunt Pleasantine surveyed the room. No pictures of hairdos on the walls; instead, a bullfight poster. No rows of dryers, no smell of permanents. The cubicles of Mr. Charles and Mr. Ronald and their assistants were curtained off with pale blue drapes. A trophy case displayed the trophies Mr. Charles and Mr. Ronald had won in hairstyling contests. "How interesting. I thought it would be more like a barbershop."

Mary said, "On Saturdays it's full of guys and the cigarette smoke can be sliced with a knife." This reminded her that she'd forgotten to dig out ashtrays for guests.

Aunt Pleasantine turned to leave. "Don't hurry doing your liquor shopping. There's plenty to read at Irene's."

And Mary was glad to see that in the six weeks since she'd last been to the Salon, a more varied assortment of magazines had accumulated on the center table. Unable to find a movie magazine, she read the "Newsmakers" section of a *Newsweek* and listened to the whining of little boys, the snipping of shears and the whoosh of blowers behind drapes, and, now and then, mothers saying tiredly:

"Behave yourself."

"Stop squirming and sit still."

"Your brother will be through in a minute."

"Do you want a spanking?"

"Behave yourself."

Mary read the obituaries. A small boy came out of Mr. Charles's cubicle, looking styled and self-conscious, and soon Mr. Charles beckoned Mary in.

Mr. Charles was probably, at the most, twenty-five years old, and the diploma on his wall said that the College of Hair Design to which he'd gone was in Manchester, New Hampshire, but he liked to act worldly-wise on all subjects, particularly business and fashion. He wore a styled goatee. And he was talkative; Mary considered talkative hairdressers almost as bad as talkative dentists. But she preferred the way he cut her hair to the way the more silent Mr. Ronald cut it, so after he'd told her all about, as he always did, his dream for the Salon, a sauna sideline, and complimented her on her newspaper photographs of the fire, she gave him something more to talk about by saying, "A friend of my grandmother's has been staying with us this summer. She's eighty-four years old and flew up here from Florida on her own."

"We don't do rinses, you know, or permanents, but I could refer her to—"

"Yes, she's at Irene's right now. She wears a French twist."

"I should think she'd find a French twist difficult. Eighty-four, you said?"

"She manages. She thinks it suits her age best."

"That's the thing for some people. Finding what suits you best. Others will always experiment, which frankly I think more exciting."

And frankly makes you money, Mary replied silently. She looked at her reflection in the mirror and guessed that she herself never would find what suited her best. She saw herself following Mr. Charles's suggestions forever, or until he turned her over to an Irene. Why had she never done a self-portrait? Mr. Charles snipped and talked, and when she left she felt very depressed.

She drove to the liquor store and pushed a cart down the aisles, consulting her booze list. The clerk who helped her carry the cartons of bottles out to the car said, "You must be going to give one hell of a blast." This made Mary feel even more depressed.

She drove back to Irene's. Aunt Pleasantine's hair was finished, and she sat waiting on the aqua sofa, reading about Richard Burton and Elizabeth Taylor and Sonny and Cher. She closed the magazine. "It's bewildering to try to keep up with what movie and TV stars are doing nowadays, but thank heavens they're no longer hiding it. So much more fun this way."

Mary, suddenly ashamed of her depression, said, "We're going to miss *Squares* no matter how we hurry. Let's not bother making lunch, let's eat out after we finish shopping. Any ideas?"

"I've never been to a McDonald's."

Mary stared at her. "McDonald's?"

They drove to the mall, and as they entered, Aunt Pleasantine said with satisfaction, "A display."

"And an electronic organ."

Woodstoves were arranged along the corridor. All sorts, New England, Scandinavian, tall, squat, lumpy, smooth, decorated with reindeer, lions, basic black, bright red, blue, dark green.

Aunt Pleasantine said, "That Franklin reminds me of the one Papa used during the War. That cooking range resembles your mother's. I hadn't realized woodstoves are in use again."

"It's thanks to the Arabs and God knows who. Our fuel bill went so high we bought a Lange—like that red one over there. We're still discussing whether or not to move my workroom and darkroom downstairs and close off the upstairs, but it'd be a hell of a project, so in the meantime in the winters we plug up the fireplace and take some of the chill off with the stove and pretend we're outwitting Gulf Oil et al."

"Winter is coming. That's why they're having this. Winter is coming."

The woman at the organ played "Hello, Dolly!" Aunt Pleasantine didn't sit down on a pink bench; she went into Purity Supreme with Mary and shopped alone for the ingredients for her specialty. Mary shopped for the rest of the party food, and her shopping cart, usually half full, became so full it looked like other people's. She had fun choosing party food at the delicatessen section, but when she saw the "hot dogs" note on her list there, she panicked. The twins. She rushed on and bought enormous jars of peanut butter and marshmallow fluff, two gallons of milk, and in the junk food section she frantically wondered what else to stuff them with. Then she remembered her students munching along the corridors of Saffron High, and she grabbed Twinkies and Charleston Chews and taffy flavored with chemists' ideas of banana and watermelon. As she paid at the checkout counter, she wondered if this awful cost for the party was what people with kids had to pay for ordinary weekly groceries. Connie had once mentioned a hundred dollars a week a few years ago; she hadn't mentioned the cost recently. Mary pushed her heavy cart out of Purity and saw Aunt Pleasantine sitting beside a paper bag on a bench. The woman at the organ was playing "I Left My Heart in San Francisco," and Aunt Pleasantine was laughing.

At The Market Basket, the early corn was in. Mrs. Nelson took time out from instructing summer people about how to pull back the husk to check each ear and came over to gush about Aunt Pleasantine's hairdo. More summer people arrived, and Aunt Pleasantine escaped into the greenhouse.

Mary chose vegetables, then joined her there. "See any plant who might like your windowsill? To keep the cactus company?"

Aunt Pleasantine blushed.

Mary thought, oh, Christ, was that a gaffe?

"The cactus," Aunt Pleasantine said, "was a present, wasn't it? For me. Not for the windowsill."

"Yes."

"I must thank you for the offer of another plant but say no, because I had better wait and see."

Plants, Mary realized, were special possessions. Living things, they needed care. And Aunt Pleasantine traveled light.

McDonald's on the bay was busy. Thunder growled faintly. Mary stood with Aunt Pleasantine in the crowd at the counter, and Aunt Pleasantine read the menu on the wall. "What on earth is an Egg McMuffin?"

"Breakfast. Bill had one once and reported it is a mystery."

"What do you recommend?"

"The Quarter-Pounder with Cheese. Look, there's a free booth, you take it and I'll give the order."

When Mary carried the tray to the booth, she found Aunt Pleasantine watching a group of little girls at a cluster of tables which had been pushed together nearby.

Aunt Pleasantine said, "It's a birthday party."

The tables were heaped with beribboned packages. The harassed woman, probably not much older than Mr. Charles, was, Mary gathered, the mother of the embarrassed little girl sitting beside her and opening the presents. All the girls wore tiny summer dresses, and their long hair was smoothly brushed, and they were chattering.

"So much wrapping," Aunt Pleasantine said. Mary thought she meant the presents' wrapping paper which had begun to pile up, then saw that Aunt Pleasantine was investigating the styrofoam box containing her Quarter-Pounder, the paper scoop of skinny French fries, the styrofoam cup of coffee.

"That's nothing," Mary said, guide to McDonald's for Aunt Pleasantine. "If you want the meal to go, it's wrapped in the National Forest."

The birthday girl was receiving mostly games. Games which Mary didn't recognize.

Aunt Pleasantine said, "A party given this way must be much simpler—you don't have to worry about cake and ice cream on the upholstery—but it seems so impersonal."

"Right now I'm ready to drag our thirty here and treat them to Quarter-Pounders. I remembered I forgot the ashtrays. What else have I forgotten?"

"I know it would be silly of me to tell you not to fret."

The birthday party meal arrived, and it immediately began getting mixed up with the presents. The birthday girl tried to sip her frappe and open a Barbie-doll wardrobe at the same time. Her mother intervened.

Mary said, "The hamburgers they're having are the cheapies. Kids don't care, I guess. Bill's theory is those hamburgers are so small they're made by taking a teaspoonful of hamburg and dropping it on the floor and stomping on it."

"Slacks are more practical, but it's nice to see little girls in dresses for a change." One girl squirted herself with catsup. "I pity their mothers, however."

"It's raining. Oh, God."

"Funny to see them still acting coy. I remember the first time you were consciously coy. It was during the January visit. You hollered for Louisa or me that you wanted to get up from your nap, and when I went into your bedroom you pretended you were asleep. But your grin didn't deceive anyone."

The rain was bouncing on the bay.

Aunt Pleasantine said, "I remember the birthday parties I gave the children. So elaborate, such as the one with the magician and Snowball. Before Al's troubles, of course. I had a cabinetmaker build a dollhouse for Hester. It was four feet high. The rooms were wallpapered. There were rugs and furniture, and in the attic there even were toy trunks. The dolls posed. The mother sat with her knitting, the father stood at the fireplace mantel, the baby lay in a miniature cradle. The weather report said just a summer shower, Mary. Tomorrow will be clear."

"I'll keep a radio check when we get home."

A cake with candles was brought, and the little girls scrambled down from their chairs and gathered around the birthday girl and squealed as she blew the candles out.

"Papa gave me my pony for my seventh birthday. That's why I named him Diamond, after my April birthstone. He didn't have a diamond on his forehead. I noticed you paid at the counter. What does my half come to?"

They drove home. While Aunt Pleasantine napped, Mary groped in the back of a cupboard and found the ashtrays. Listening to the radio, she counted glasses. Thirty. She counted plates. She didn't own thirty coffee cups, but most of the guests wouldn't give a damn about coffee. She washed glasses and plates and all the cups and mugs she had. She worried about seeing Connie. She dreaded the invasion by the twins. She wished she'd bought a dishwasher instead of an enlarger and other expensive camera equipment. The radio said, "Here's another cancellation. Tonight's Marriage Encounter Family Picnic has been postponed because of rain." She laughed insanely.

She went for a swim in the rain. Maybe she'd be struck by lightning. Another cancellation. The rain was warmer than the water. When she returned, she saw Aunt Pleasantine in the sun-porch dining room, looking at the curved glass front of the china cabinet.

"I know," Mary said. "This silver also needs doing but I don't do it until Thanksgiving. Nobody will notice."

Aunt Pleasantine opened the cabinet and took out a silver baby cup engraved MARY. "I remember Becky's writing me about buying you this. Look how battered the bottom is. I remember your banging it on your highchair, and we couldn't figure out how you dented it so badly. Connie's never got dented. Here's the Revere bowl James and I gave your grandparents. Let me polish these things. I'd enjoy it, and people are bound to wander out here and see your silver gleaming and enjoy it, too."

"If they can still see. Go right ahead, but for God's sake stop if it gets tiring. I'm going to make up beds. Who would you prefer in the other downstairs guest room? Would twins be too noisy? The younger twins usually sleep there—" Mary stopped before adding that Connie and George usually slept in Aunt Pleasantine's room, near the younger twins.

"Fine. Bobby and Tommy. I assume they'll be going to bed earlier than the others, as will I. Tomorrow night I can keep an ear out for them during the party."

Mary made the downstairs twin beds and went upstairs and made up the beds in the two other spare rooms and remembered she should get out the sleeping bags in case any guests were unable to drive home, either in car or boat, as had happened occasionally after a We-Owe-Everybody.

The rain ended.

Downstairs, Aunt Pleasantine was polishing Mother's baby cup. Mary said, "I'm going for some kindling," and took the kindling basket outdoors into the woods.

She liked dead branches. She searched and stooped and snapped them neatly. The twigs would be dry by tomorrow night. Bill called them squaw kindling; she'd never been able to get him to stop that. Gathering kindling, she brooded. *Shared Homes Handbook;* she must tell Bill. Would Leonard and Norma show up at the party? Bill, years hence, a William but still bitching about the Marina and reading about faraway places. Connie, baby sister. Winter is coming. Were three pounds of hot dogs enough for tonight's cookout? The Watercolor didn't close until Christmas; Jerry would have plenty of time to try to sell the talk-show painting, so how come she didn't want to place it there, she certainly didn't want to keep it, so how come she wished—

She heard Bill's car, then another. She ran back along the path. Up the driveway behind Bill drove a rattletrap station wagon, windows down, arms waving.

"Yes," Connie told Bobby and Tommy in the kitchen, "it's okay now, go ahead and drink Coke until your little bladders burst. Don't give them good glasses, Mary, give them cheap ones."

The kitchen seemed crowded, although Bill had gone down to the beach to start the hibachi, and the older twins, Dave and Keith, had yelled hi, yanked off their shirts and Levi's, revealing swim trunks which, like their outer clothes, didn't match, and had raced for the dock and now were swimming.

Bobby and Tommy's clothes also didn't match, because Connie believed matching clothes stunted, as she put it, twins' identity growth.

Mary poured Coke from a giant bottle into two glasses that had once contained dried beef. Aunt Pleasantine handed them out and asked, "You're Bobby?"

"I'm Tommy," Tommy said automatically but irritatedly.

Aunt Pleasantine said, "I'll learn."

Connie's husband, George, who had a tendency to overexplain things (Connie blamed this on the newspaper catechism of who-what-when-where-why), explained, "There's always a hullabaloo at every gas station. Bobby and Tommy can't seem to get it through their thick heads that the idea is to stop and piss, *not* to stop and piss and drink a Coke so a few miles later they have to stop and piss again."

"Don't spill," Connie told Bobby and Tommy, herding them out to the porch. "Sit quietly at the table and don't spill." She went over to Aunt Pleasantine and kissed her cheek. "The usual pandemonium. I didn't get a chance to say how glad I am to see you."

"And I am glad to see you, Connie. And your family."

Connie sat down and lighted a cigarette. "If any of the brats gets too noisy, just give them holy hell. I don't hear the kids' noise anymore. Mary and Bill do, I can tell by the looks on their faces."

Connie was the only person Mary knew who smoked Raleighs. Connie even saved the coupons, and whenever she mailed them off for something for the house or kids, she would say, "Well, there goes another piece of my lungs."

George called to Bill down at the beach, "Need any help?"

"Thanks, no."

"Hooray." George collapsed onto the glider.

Mary said, "I'll get the drinks." In the kitchen Mary wondered why people always knew that she and Connie were sisters. They were both blonde and the same height, but they didn't look alike and, as Mother had kept pointing out, Connie was the pretty one. Snapping ice into the ice bucket, she wondered if Aunt Pleasantine's life would have been different if she hadn't been pretty. And rich.

"Yes, all identical," George was saying when Mary returned to the porch. "It's enough to make you sick. Couldn't at least one set have been fraternal?"

Connie said, "It's my fault, of course."

George said, "That's Connie's attempt at a witty rejoinder."

The trip here, Mary gathered, must have been a lulu. Mixing drinks, she tried to make a joke. "Hey, George, don't you wish you'd had quints so you could've sold the story to *Good Housekeeping?*"

George said, "More vodka in mine."

"Mary," Connie said, "if Aunt Pleasantine wasn't present, I'd tell you to go take a flying fuck. Quintuplets!"

"Pampers," Mary said. "Think of the free Gerbers and Pampers."

"Stop," Connie said, and Mary, startled and embarrassed, realized that an end had come to the years of joking about the twins, and she babbled on, "How's the leach field? Filled in?"

"Filled in," Connie said.

George said, "To the tune of almost half a grand. Because somebody wasn't watching two somebodies."

Not daring to inquire about the irises, Mary handed out drinks and was very glad to see Bill walking up the lawn toward the porch, and she was happy that Bobby and Tommy demanded more Coke and she had to go back to the kitchen for it.

Connie invented sayings. Her favorite was: "Men always fail you when you need them." Mary found Bill doing just this when she returned with the Coke. He was asking George about the trip, as if a journey from Vermont to New Hampshire were a bold expedition. George was lying back and looking at the ceiling. Mary understood Bill was desperate when he inquired about the station wagon's gas mileage. Bobby and Tommy had changed their minds and didn't want more Coke, they wanted Dr. Pepper, which Mary didn't have, and they wanted to go to the bathroom.

Connie said, "Do you remember where the bathroom is?"

"I'll take them," Bill said, leaving a sinking ship.

George looked at the ceiling, and Connie and Aunt Pleasantine watched Dave and Keith swimming and diving.

Mary made refills.

The lake was loud, jittery with Friday-evening boats. Down the shore a summer-weekend neighbor's collie barked relentlessly.

Aunt Pleasantine said, "Your home, Connie. It's a farm?"

Connie said, "Do you ever read any of those articles about the challenges and joys of homesteading on one acre? That's the kind of farm ours is. Without livestock. George won't allow livestock because it ties you down."

"We have," George said, "quite enough livestock already."

Bill returned with Bobby and Tommy. "They want to go swimming."

This caused everyone on the porch to move down to chairs by the beach and the hibachi. Mary brought towels and the drinks tray.

Aunt Pleasantine watched Bobby and Tommy splashing. "Did you use playpens when the children were little?"

George said, "Connie thought playpens too confining for Dave and Keith. Too inhibiting. Wreck their psyches. So she let them crawl all around the house—"

Connie said, "—while you hoped someone would step on them and squash them—"

"—but when Bobby and Tommy came along, guess what? Fuck their psyches. She mailed away her coupons for a playpen."

"Notice I didn't *buy* one. Couldn't afford it."

"Another witty rejoinder."

Aunt Pleasantine said hastily, "The reason I asked is I just remembered how you reacted when you were left alone the first time in your playpen. I'd taken Mary blueberrying with me, and your mother was busy and decided to try to teach you to stay alone in your pen in the dooryard. You howled all afternoon and got so upset you couldn't sleep that night. The next morning you were peaked and on your best behavior. Your mother felt so distressed, calling it a wrong move on her part, and she wasn't comforted by your father and me saying she couldn't have known you wouldn't react as Mary had when she was first left alone in a playpen."

Connie didn't seem disconcerted that Aunt Pleasantine remembered something she'd been too young to remember. "How did Mary react?"

"The older child, she was used to playing alone anywhere."

"Big sister." Connie lighted a cigarette.

"Mary was so tickled when you were born. It was the off-season at the Inn, and I was glad I could come and help while Louisa was in the hospital. Mary kept asking about your mother and you and whether or not Louisa would be able to bend down when she got home. And when you came home, she asked to hold you after your bath the second day. She was much interested in seeing Louisa nurse you, and one time Mary came over and stuck her toy duck in my bosom and said, 'Duck get milk from Aunt Pleasantine's tummy.' "

George said, "Connie was very public about her nursing. Whipping tits out all over the place."

Connie said, "Saved us money for a while, didn't it?"

Dave and Keith, waterlogged, came running along the dock looking hungry, and Mary and Bill threw hot dogs onto the hibachi. The project of supper distracted Connie and George and they put aside their fight to referee twins' squabbles over piccalilli and mustard, and after supper the twins wanted a sail and George decided to go along, so Bill squeezed them all into *Nomad,* and Mary and Connie and Aunt Pleasantine did dishes in the kitchen.

Connie dried a plate. "A divorce is another thing I can't afford."

Mary washed some silverware and Aunt Pleasantine dried a glass.

Connie said, "How could I support myself, let alone me and

the kids. Getting child support from George would be wringing blood from a stone."

Mary asked, "Can you still take shorthand?"

"Rustily. One stupid year of one stupid business school. I should've gone to—I should have done—oh, I don't know." Connie flung away the dish towel and went outdoors, down the path toward the end of the Point.

Aunt Pleasantine said, "Some couples thrive on fights. Your grandparents, for instance. They were known, in an affectionate way, as the Battling Fosters."

"Mmm," Mary said absently.

Aunt Pleasantine dried a plate. "People are so odd. And when they combine in marriage, they get even odder."

That night Mary placed on her bedside table the Transactional Analysis books, got into bed, opened one book, closed it, turned off the lamp, and rolled over toward Bill, who was snoring.

The next morning Bill set up the sawhorses-and-planks buffet table along the inside wall of the porch and managed to talk Dave and Keith into mowing the lawn at an outrageous price. He went to work, they mowed, George slept until noon, and Aunt Pleasantine kept an eye on Bobby and Tommy and their Lincoln Logs on the porch, while in the kitchen Mary made potato salad and Connie made coleslaw, the recipes for which, Mary reflected, had been Mother's and Grandmother's and maybe even Aunt Pleasantine's Grandma's—

Connie said, "You know how Mother categorized things. Did she ever categorize Aunt Pleasantine?"

Mary chopped a potato and pondered. "They got along. I remember noticing that Mother laughed more when Aunt Pleasantine was around."

"A category, though. Invent one if we can't remember. 'Aunt Pleasie is plucky but injudicious.' "

" 'Aunt Pleasantine is a prey for rascals.' "

"How the hell did she get up the guts to divorce her husband back in those dark ages?"

"Her pride. And she didn't expect to go broke." Mixing the salad, Mary told Connie the details about James and Al.

Connie said, "She had two kids. I've got a population explosion."

Mary racked her brain for a polite reply. "Unintentional."

"If only I'd stopped after Dave and Keith, if only I hadn't tried for a girl."

"Bobby and Tommy are awfully cute," Mary said, and unfortunately they rushed in at that moment yelling for Dr. Pepper. They got Coke. Aunt Pleasantine followed them in and began making her specialty.

Bobby said, "I'm sick of Lincoln Logs."

"We'll go swimming this afternoon," Connie said. "Go play Bionic Man."

Tommy said, "When Mary and Bill get married, will they have toys?"

"Huh?" Mary said.

Connie mixed coleslaw. "They think you're not married because you don't have kids. Shoo, brats, but stay indoors."

During the afternoon Dave and Keith swam, George napped on the chaise in the sun, and Connie played at the beach with Bobby and Tommy. Mary dusted the house, made dips, studied her gardens and cut the flowers for the party.

Aunt Pleasantine came out to the kitchen after her nap and saw Mary getting frantic with vases and flowers and said, "An artist I am not, but I can arrange flowers. Let me help."

So they worked with the flowers as they had worked with the herbs. This time, however, Aunt Pleasantine didn't figuratively let her hair down. She was silent, while Mary wanted to shout, *"What are Shared Homes?"*

Then Connie came in with four sons who had to be fed early, and Bill came home and drove the horseshoe posts into the lawn, and George realized he'd got sunburned and began complaining, and Mary and Aunt Pleasantine spread tablecloths on the buffet table, showers were taken, clothes changed, and, twins constantly in the way, Mary and Connie and Aunt Pleasantine set out the buffet.

In the kitchen Connie peeled rims from circles of salami. "You kids touch the buffet before the guests get here and I'll amputate your hands. Did you make that dress, Mary?"

Unmolding the pâté, Mary said, "Yes, does it look it?"

"You know yours don't. Mine do."

Aunt Pleasantine was checking her refrigerated bisque. Suddenly Mary wondered if Aunt Pleasantine had anybody to describe this party to in a letter, as she had described her daughters' parties to Mary. Would she write her daughters, her grandchildren?

Connie carried the cold cuts and Italian rolls out to the porch. Mary followed, carrying hors d'oeuvres. Connie said, "Maybe when we're recovering together from our face-lifts, you could teach me the secret of sewing."

Aunt Pleasantine fussed with a vase of flowers.

Mary said, "Mother taught you too, Connie. The secret of sewing is an ironing board."

"Face-lifts?" Aunt Pleasantine said, and Connie grabbed Bobby away from the olives, and cars and boats began arriving.

An hour later—or two or three—Mary went searching for Aunt Pleasantine. Mary and Bill had introduced everyone to her, and, sitting white and delicate in the fan-backed chair, wearing her pale pink pantsuit, she looked decidedly out of place in the midst of suntans and bikinis and shrieks and Bermudas and guffaws and backless dresses. Mary had seen her listening to some teachers and Aunt Pleasantine had winked at her, and when Mary brought her a fresh drink, Aunt Pleasantine said, "Most teachers' voices get to be like actors', don't they. Pitched at the last row in the balcony." Then Mary had lost track of her. The Hubcap King and his cloud of red curls now sat in her chair; he was discussing ocean sailing versus lake sailing with Bill's brother Paul. Mary doubted that Aunt Pleasantine was down with the people on the dock or playing horseshoes with Dave and Keith and a group of men, a group which included Leonard who had shown up with his wife, Janice. Norma had shown up too, alone, and she and Leonard ignored each other. Mary pushed slowly through the porch crowd, being hostess, aiming toward the living room and Aunt Pleasantine's hallway, and all around her people were drinking and eating and saying:

"Is that a fact?"

"I told the manager four dollars and fifteen cents for a pound of shrimp was highway robbery—"

"It's hotter than Tophet in here, let's go swimming."

Teresa, the Hubcap King's wife, said to Bill, "If you try satin sheets, you'll never want to sleep on anything else," and Philip Altman, the newspaper photographer, was saying, "Can't wait for next year's primary—" and someone replied, "Yes, New Hampshire's big moment comes only once every four years," and Philip said, "Next year, instead of photographing the campaigns, I'd like to concentrate on photographing the clothes the politicians and network reporters wear; they're always bundled up like they think they've come to the Arctic."

"Sheepskin coats," someone agreed.

"Russian hats," Mary joined in, "mufflers, fur-lined gloves," and she moved on, avoiding the home-ec teacher who, perhaps as fate's revenge for Mary's smugness about sewing, had trapped Mary earlier and instructed her in detail about the proper way to peel a hard-boiled egg. Mary also avoided the group of hockey fans known as rink rats and squeezed past people into the living room, where the record player was playing Judy Garland, and she spotted Aunt Pleasantine sitting in a chair near the unnecessary fire in the fireplace. Aunt Pleasantine was listening to Janice say, "How I dread shopping for back-to-school clothes. I don't know where the summer has gone, and it's only August ninth."

Janice sat on the arm of a sofa. She had a narrow face which seemed pinched toward her overbite, but she was attractive and, Mary had discovered, surprisingly photogenic throughout those ghastly Christmas-card-picture sessions.

Aunt Pleasantine said, "Shopping is like doing a crossword puzzle. Sometimes nothing works out right, sometimes you're stymied awhile, and sometimes everything clicks together. Do you live on the lake, too?"

"No," Janice said. "Leonard says he sees enough of the lake at work, though we do have a boat. We moved from Greenwood Court to Parkvista Heights two years ago, and last year we put in a swimming pool."

Mary said, "Anyone need a refill? Did you get a sandwich, Aunt Pleasantine?"

"Jerry helped me assemble it, and he packed it with everything. I thought of your first birthday, and what a lovely day you had. I came down from the Inn for the occasion. Your parents gave you a cloth doll and your grandmother sent a coat and bonnet and two dresses and a dark-blue flannel wrapper, and your grandfather sent money. I gave you a picture book. You attempted to eat the book, as well as Louisa's rouge pot, a cigarette package, and a pencil, and you did consume a jelly sandwich."

"What was in the picture book?"

"Alphabet letters. If you run across Connie, could you tell her I've just checked Bobby and Tommy and they're still sound asleep, despite the guests using the bathroom."

Mary heard a hesitation, as though Aunt Pleasantine had almost said "my bathroom" but caught herself.

Janice was saying, "And now that Robyn is starting school I

can't imagine what I'm going to do with an empty house and all that spare time."

Sally of The Watercolor stopped and said briskly, "You'll find plenty to do, believe me."

"But you've got your dolls all winter. I've been thinking I should have a hobby."

Mary didn't look at Aunt Pleasantine and knew Aunt Pleasantine was deliberately not looking at her.

Sally tossed her cigarette into the fireplace. "How about adopting? Jerry and I would adopt again if we could afford another kid, Mike has fitted in so beautifully."

"I thought of it when Vietnam fell and everyone was adopting war orphans, but Leonard said absolutely not. He'd rather have another of his own, though he doesn't want any more at all. But every time I see those foster-parent ads in magazines, those babies in rags, or when I see one of Norma Wentworth's paintings of such pathetic children, I do wish we'd adopted a war orphan."

Teresa, careening past toward the bathroom, said, "I wish to Christ I'd adopted both our kids and spared myself my gorgeous stretchmarks."

Mary was glad the neighbors had been invited to the party and had come, so they wouldn't call the cops about the noise. Dainty Teresa looked ready to kick a policeman in the balls.

Janice said, "I've heard cocoa butter helps, but I don't know."

Mary moved on to the kitchen, where she found a group of teachers trying to describe conditions at Saffron Walden High School to some of Bill's summer-people customers who seemed to think all schools north of Boston were pastoral.

"And," a teacher said, "the cafeteria doesn't give out knives anymore because the kids kept stealing them."

One of the customers wore a Madras sport jacket which had bled successfully. "Then how do they cut their food?"

"With forks."

"How do they butter things?"

"With their forks," a teacher said patiently. "Weird sight."

"And," said another teacher, "last year so many *forks* got stolen we're wondering if this year only spoons will be issued."

Another teacher said, "Let the fuckers eat out of dog bowls on the floor."

Another said, "Did you see that food fight the next to last day of school?"

"Yes," another said. "You mean the one that ended with the guy smashing his tray over his girlfriend's head?"

"Ouch," Mary said.

"Well, it was Melmac."

Mary went out the back door and walked around the side of the house. She saw Donna, Paul's wife, standing in the sunporch alone. Donna still wore her neck brace, and she was holding a highball glass and looking intently at the china cabinet full of shiny silver pieces polished by Aunt Pleasantine. Mary realized she'd never before seen Donna alone, without children or adults around, and she had never before seen Donna concentrating on anything. Donna stared at the silver.

On the lawn, horseshoes thudded. Dave and Keith, still hungry after their early supper, were cramming huge bites of Italian sandwiches into their mouths between turns, and Mary guessed they must be winning because the men players were gulping drinks between turns. She avoided Leonard and asked the twins, "Is Connie here?"

Keith swallowed. "At the beach."

Beyond the porch lights and the dock lights the beach was shadowy. Connie, wearing her rubber sandals, jumped up and down in the shallow water and said to Norma, sprawled in a beach chair, "If Dave and Keith decided to run away, I'd pack their suitcases for them. Hi, Mary. Who am I?"

"Gene Kelly."

"Remember when we had such hots for him? I need yesterday's rain, but I'm improvising. 'I'm singing in the rain,' " Connie sang and jumped and splashed. "I'll bet I could pack their suitcases in two seconds flat."

Mary said lightly, "I thought kids were supposed to run away from home with their clothes wadded into a red bandanna tied onto a stick."

"There are stages," Norma said. "I'm over the crying, I'm over the guilts. Am I over being angry? Am I getting resigned?"

A drunken horseshoe landed dangerously close. Mary yelled, "Watch it, you guys!"

Leonard yelled back, "Watch it yourself!"

Norma said, "Donna told me the comment Freddy came in on."

" 'What a glorious feeling,' " Connie splashed, " 'I'm happy again!' "

Norma groped around the sand, located her glass, and took a sip. "In the supermarket this morning I thought: one less mouth to feed. Another one less mouth. And in a few weeks Ginger will be gone, and there'll be just my mouth. Okay, I said to myself in the supermarket, that makes all the more for me! And I bought some extra-sharp cheddar. Freddy hated extra-sharp."

"Have you heard from Stan again—or Freddy?"

"When Stan and I split up, I bought a beige sweater. Stan hated me in beige, but I think beige is subtle. Don't you agree beige is subtle?"

Another horseshoe bounced onto the beach.

Norma said, "Ginger hates broccoli, but so do I. What will I buy next month?"

Connie said, "Buy broccoli anyway." Splash, splash, splash.

Mary said, "Aunt Pleasantine reports Bobby and Tommy are still sound asleep," and, hostess-circulating, she went out onto the dock, and Ray Brunelle, the boys' gym coach, said, "Why do Frenchmen put shit on the altar?" and Mary said, "Why?" and he said, "To keep the flies off the bride," which reminded Mary of screen-sneaky flies who might have found the buffet and she went up to the porch and as she was checking the food she encountered Watercolor Jerry devouring a mound of potato salad.

Jerry said, "I'm getting ready for my Alka-Seltzers. Are you an Alka-Seltzer addict? I'm looking forward to an Alka-Seltzer nightcap when I get home."

"I can't burp."

"You can't burp?"

"Bill's tried to teach me, but I can't. I once took an Alka-Seltzer and sat around like a time bomb worrying about which way it was going to go off. It never did."

"I thought everyone could burp."

Bill, only a voice and a hand gripping a glass until he'd shouldered himself the rest of the way through the crowd, said, "She can't wiggle her ears either. I can."

Mary raised an eyebrow. "I can raise one eyebrow, and you can't."

"I can talk like Donald Duck and you can't." Bill dunked a Frito into a dip and said, "!@#$%¢&*!"

Mary said, "But they don't understand him at Duck Island."

Jerry asked her, "Can you fart?" and Mary got lost in another crowd, where the high school librarian was saying, "I go over to the study carrels to tell them to keep the noise level down, and what do I hear but this kid telling another kid, 'For a Big Mac you can get yourself a blow job,' and I said, 'From whom?' —"

In the living room, music had changed to comedy, George Carlin's *Class Clown,* and Aunt Pleasantine said as Mary came over to her, "Such a funny man, but I think one has to be brought up Catholic to understand all the jokes."

A summer-people woman asked another, "Are you sure it was Elizabeth Janeway who said that appearance equals value in women?"

"Baloney!" said a summer-people man.

Mary said, "I told Connie."

"Thank you," Aunt Pleasantine said. "I've checked them again, and they're still asleep. I know I ought to be, too, but it's such a good party. One of your neighbors explained to me all about ice hockey, and the driver-education teacher discussed his job. He drives with students in his summer vacation, too. Terrifying work, I should think, but he seemed instead rather—"

"Numb," Mary finished. "Need a refill?"

"No, thank you. And the girls' gym coach told me how she used to take a busman's holiday during her lunch period and free period and run ten miles."

"Making the rest of us feel like sloths." Mary wondered if Aunt Pleasantine was writing her a letter aloud. "*Used* to?"

"The school board has ruled that the poor girl can't run during school hours. They were afraid the townspeople thought she was wasting their tax money. She was on the brink of tears."

"She wants to be the first woman to win the Boston Marathon."

Nearby, George explained to Philip Altman, "If it weren't for my responsibilities, I'd be free-lancing—"

"Food stamps," a neighbor said. "Disgraceful."

An English teacher said, "The priceless line is the one the principal sent out in his bulletin about class pictures. I'll never forget it. 'PLEASE NOTE: Upon seeing your pictures if you have decided NOT to purchase, then it will be impossible to get them at that time, however.' "

Mary saw the back door open and Kitty and William come into the kitchen.

"Bill." Frantic, Mary looked around. "He was on the porch. Where's Bill?"

Aunt Pleasantine said, "I didn't realize they were invited."

"They never are. Wrong age group—I mean—"

"When Bill was last here in the living room, he was restraining Teresa from strangling a guidance counselor who said collecting hubcaps is childish."

"Mary!" Kitty swooped into the living room. "We were passing by on our way home from the Muirheads' and we couldn't resist your bright lights."

William said, "Just one for the road," and went out to the porch.

Kitty snubbed Aunt Pleasantine and followed him, tugging Mary along. "All my boys are here?"

Janice appeared. "Yes. Your Firstborn and your Baby and Whatshisname in between." Janice was very drunk, the first time Mary had ever seen her that way, and Donna appeared, still brooding, and said to Mary over the neck brace, "I don't know how you can live with so many things from dead people."

The high school librarian said, "And every time the library is empty some kid runs in and jumps on the Xerox machine and pulls down his pants and makes a copy of his ass—"

"Fulfillment," Kitty said, taking the drink William handed her. "I want to talk to Mary about fulfillment."

Mary said, "Kitty, I haven't the faintest idea what words like that are supposed to mean," and saw Aunt Pleasantine coming out to the porch and Connie coming in from the beach, but she couldn't spot Bill anywhere. Connie was dragging Dave and Keith, a silly sight because they towered over her, yet when Connie said, "No more food. Bed, and goddamnit, I mean *bed!*" they obediently headed toward the stairway. Mary wondered if they'd get past the Carlin record collection. Kitty said, "Connie, did you know that your sister allowed Bill to have a vasectomy?"

"My husband had one, too," Connie said.

Mary said, "But he and Bill didn't have them together."

"No, not like our face-lifts."

Kitty said, "Your situation, Connie, is entirely different. Face-lifts?"

"Dead people," Donna said. "Creepy. When I—"

Janice said, "Oh, for God's sake, we're all sick and tired of your brush with death."

Aunt Pleasantine said, "My children have often discussed face-lifts—"

Mary saw herself living with Connie in a bungalow in Florida.

Janice said, "And we're all positive you're just wearing that brace as a reminder. You don't need it anymore. Take it off."

Leonard arrived at the drinks table. "Take what off?"

Connie said, "You mean she should take it off like in those movies when the crippled female villain—"

Mary said, "—in a wheelchair—"

"—is tricked into proving—"

"—she can really walk!"

Janice said, "And if you think it's smart to keep reminding Paul you might've died, let me tell you what he told Leonard—"

"Shut up," Leonard said.

"Protect the Baby," Janice said. "As usual."

Ray Brunelle said, "Heard the one about the Frenchman who had diarrhea and thought he was melting?"

"Motherless children," Donna said. "If I had died, he'd appreciate me. He'd have to hire a full-time baby-sitter. He'd have to hire a housekeeper and a cook and a maid and a chauffeur. Maybe he could get Mary to come over for free and polish my silver."

"You don't own any silver," Janice pointed out. "You couldn't make up your mind, so I talked you into stainless. Less work."

"And cheaper," Donna said. "Low wife on the totem pole." Kitty said, "Now, Donna, don't be ridiculous," and Donna said, "Dead things from dead people," and Mary stepped back and took Aunt Pleasantine's arm and said, "Did you get a chance to sample your specialty?" and led her away to the dessert end of the buffet table, where the bisque had already been gobbled up by guests.

Aunt Pleasantine picked up a peach. "When I die, I want no services. I told the children during the flu, but they didn't listen. I want cremation and no grave, no trouble to anyone, and definitely no memorial service. Any words said over my remains would have no significance when my spirit has gone."

"Gone where?"

"I've never been able to decide. I'm glad Unitarians are vague."

Mary got brave. "Aunt Pleasie, while I was vacuuming your room I saw that Shared Homes pamphlet. What does it mean?"

"Your grandmother used to tease me and say I should want to be buried, because I would enjoy the pinks which bloom in cemeteries. Oh, there's Bill."

Bill wasn't talking like Donald Duck now. He was yelling at William, "And it's just too fucking bad if I don't dream of the day we can walk across the lake without getting our feet wet, Jesus Christs of Emersons' Marina!"

"Progress—" William was yelling.

"Stepping from boat to boat, wall-to-wall stinkpots across the lake—"

"Barbecue," Kitty was saying to Janice and Donna, "William's famous shish kebabs, and you bring your—"

Aunt Pleasantine said, "Do you remember, Mary, when I took you to the circus?"

"No."

"Connie was a baby. Your mother thought you were old enough and ought to see the circus which had come to town, and she asked me to take you because she was so busy with the canning. The day was very hot. The fairground was dusty and smelled of animals and people and candy. I had described high-wire acts to you, and you were eager to see a high-wire girl balancing with a parasol. We went into the tent and walked across the sawdust and I found us seats up in the bleachers. In the ring, clowns somersaulted and horses circled and midgets tumbled and elephants reared and trumpeted. After the elephants left, some small dark men climbed on each other's shoulders, and after that a girl in jodhpurs snapped a whip at three thin tigers.

I recited silently the Hodgson poem. But you weren't interested in the ring. You watched the top of the tent, waiting for a girl with a parasol. There were only, however, trapeze artists."

"I was never scared of heights until my thirties."

"You watched the top. But then you noticed six chimpanzees dancing down in the ring. They were wearing crinoline petticoats, and they were waving parasols. They curtsied, they twirled, they grinned out from under their hair ribbons, and you began to scream."

"Oh, dear. I gather that whenever I screamed, I really screamed."

"You screamed blue bloody murder. Everyone around us started frowning and shushing, so I picked you up and pushed my way down the bleachers and ran with you out the nearest flap. Unfortunately, it wasn't an opening to the outdoors but to another part of the tent. Where the elephants had been taken. It's amazing how huge elephants are. Great hulks. Legs like pillars. The chimps had just frightened and disappointed you; the elephants terrified you. You went rigid and intensified your screams. I didn't know what to do. Later, when I told your parents about it, they said the elephants must have been chained, but I swear they were not. They moved, and one blocked the flap I'd come through, and they seemed intrigued by your screaming, and they came toward us. I remember I could hear the band playing for the performers beyond that flap. I couldn't see a keeper or trainer. You and I were alone in this part of the tent, and the elephants were naturally curious about us. I think I must have gone crazy. Fearing we were about to be trampled to death, I ordered the elephants, 'Leave us a path.' I don't remember the rest clearly, but I know the hulks shifted, and I walked very firmly, very sternly, carrying you, among the elephants and out the flap on the far side of the tent, out to the fairground."

"—tax deductions!" William yelled.

"You're goddamn right," Bill yelled, "except you've got it

backwards. People should get deductions for *not* having kids!"

Aunt Pleasantine said, "Shared Homes is a Welfare Program. If I am accepted for Supplemental Security Income, I automatically become a Welfare recipient and thus eligible to be a resident in a Shared Home."

"Run that past me again."

Aunt Pleasantine did. "There are two types of Shared Homes. A Group Care facility is a home capable of taking care of four or more residents, and a Family Care facility handles less than four. I would prefer being a lone resident, of course, in a Family Care."

"You've lost me. It's not a nursing home?"

"No. One of the criteria for Sponsor Certification is that the sponsor has to be making enough money to support himself without any residents. So it's not a business."

"It's a regular house? Like this house?"

"But a sponsor can't be related to the resident or get paid by the resident's relatives. The money comes from Welfare."

"How much?"

"Two hundred and forty dollars a month for a Group Care and two hundred dollars a month for the Family Care. The payments cover the fee the sponsor and resident agree on—"

"Fee? Like rent?"

"Room and board. Linen, an available telephone, laundry service. My two hundred dollars would pay for these as well as for my clothes and odds and ends."

"Postage stamps et cetera."

"That's the way I understand it. The thoughtful thing is, the monthly checks would be paid to *me.* So I myself, not the government, would pay my fee to my sponsor. The government really is paying, but—you know what I mean. It seems a small thing, but it is most important."

"Gotcha."

"Do Bill and William argue this fiercely often?"

"What?" Mary was thinking: we aren't relatives. We qualify as sponsors, and Aunt Pleasantine is saying she could become our boarder, not guest, and maintain her pride. "Oh, yes, they always fight. William may be the sort who thrives on battles, but Bill isn't."

A neighbor said, "The biggest surprise of *my* fraternity haze came the next morning when all us pledges pissed green."

Janice and Donna had left the porch, and Kitty was discussing Christmas dolls with Sally, and Leonard was eying Connie and Teresa.

William yelled, "First you break your mother's heart by growing that beard, and now—"

"The beard," Mary said to Aunt Pleasantine, "was grown eleven years ago. How long will they harp on the vasectomy?"

Bill heard her. As he looked at her, his face went strange. "Twang twang," he said, "forever," and he slammed out the screen door and ran down the steps to the lawn.

Connie and Teresa stood at the wrecked buffet. Connie said, "Try what I did, that'll cure Hub of leaving the toilet seat up. George used to, and finally one morning I got so mad about it I threw his hairbrush in the toilet. Then we had breakfast, and then George went to the bathroom and shit on his hairbrush. Oh, Aunt Pleasantine, there you are, I've figured everything out, and I want to see if you agree."

"Excuse me?" Aunt Pleasantine said.

"I've figured everything out."

Mary said, "What out?"

"Life," Connie said, "and don't say that's sophomoric, Mary. Indulge me, I never had a sophomore year. You were the smart one, remember?"

Aunt Pleasantine said quickly, "Louisa was apt to oversimplify."

Connie said, "Yes, but this time Mother was right. Mary was

smart enough to figure the whole thing out early. The important thing in life is to have something to do. So Mary started drawing."

Mary said, "I didn't figure anything," while trying to figure how drunk Connie was. "And in my sophomore year I used to compare the something-to-do with the fox inside the Spartan boy's shirt. Not too swell, having something to do."

"Better than nothing," Connie said. "Agree, Aunt Pleasie? I wanted to ask you, for obvious reasons."

Teresa yelled at Leonard, "Cruising for a bruising!"

"Your drink? Sorry, thought it was mine. Mary ever painted you?"

Aunt Pleasantine said, "I'm not the person to ask. Age hasn't brought me wisdom. I've had fun and I've survived, that's all. Surviving has taken some ingenuity, and now I am proud as a peacock to discover I'm probably eligible for Welfare." She turned to Mary. "I couldn't have learned this without Bill, and I planned to tell you and him about Shared Homes the day after tomorrow, when you had recovered from the party."

Mary said, "Bill. Where the fuck's he gone?" She ran down the steps and looked past the lawn groups of silhouettes and saw that *Nomad* was still at the dock.

People said:

"And the office lottery prize was a cord of wood!"

"Is that a fact?"

"Good old Governor Meldrim Thomson's done something stupid again—"

"Meldrim? I call him Mildew."

"And they took the corridor doors off the boys' lavs because the boys were busting the lavs up, tearing off toilet seats and the stall doors, throwing cherry bombs into toilets—"

Mary said, "Hairbrushes are more imaginative," and moved on through the groups, her nerves twitching faster and faster, and people said:

"Raccoons got the corn—"

"Ford's pardon—"

"No way!"

"Winterize the camp—"

"Put a four-lane turnpike through the Notch and tourists can see the scenic grandeur at eighty miles an hour—"

"If the scenic grandeur hasn't been blasted to bits."

Janice said to Donna, "Sometimes Paul wishes the roof of your car *had* caved in—" and Donna said, "All right, I've held my tongue long enough, do you know what the whole town is talking about—" and Mary thought oh God and hurried on, and people said:

"Can I bum a cigarette, I'm tapering off."

"That son of a gun!"

"A forty-six footer—"

Mary heard through the voices her voice in her head reciting dum *dum*-dum-dum dum *dum* dum; heaven help me, she thought, it's:

> John Anderson, my jo, John,
>   When we were first acquent,
> Your locks were like the raven,
>   Your bonnie brow was brent;
> But now your brow is bald, John,
>   Your locks are like the snow;
> But blessings on your frosty pow,
>   John Anderson, my jo!

I'm coming unglued, she thought, and she left the porch lights, the dock lights, the silhouettes, the red dots of cigarettes. She took the shore path into the woods to the Point. She knew the path so well that she didn't need the moonlight or the lakelight, but she was watching her footing when she bumped into Bill.

He said, "Did the gatecrashers leave?"

"Kitty is negotiating with Sally about dolls to give the grandchildren. William is having more than one for the road. And among the invited guests, Donna is blabbing to Janice."

"Inevitable."

"Would you believe what I've just remembered?" Mary recited:

> John Anderson, my jo, John,
>   We clamb the hill thegither;
> And mony a canty day, John,
>   We've had wi' ane anither:
> Now we maun totter down, John,
>   But hand in hand we'll go,
> And sleep thegither at the foot,
>   John Anderson, my jo.

"Jesus Christ," Bill said. "First you read *Widow* and have me die before you do, and now we're tottering down a fucking hill to a cozy grave. Enough's enough."

"Sorry."

"Besides, your Burns burr is awful."

"I know."

"I'm going to quit."

She said, "Like you'll never judge another race? Sure you are."

"I mean it."

"That's booze talking. Midnight talk."

"I am."

The shock hit. She started shivering.

He said, "We'll sell the house and buy a bigger boat and sail South for the winter."

In the hot August night, her teeth chattered. "Something out of a kid's book. Armchair dream. We'll starve, you bastard."

"After that vacation I'll look for another boatyard. Back up North. My own."

"Another lake?"

"As far away as possible." He took her by the shoulders. "Stop shaking. Your work is portable, right? So is mine, and I'm through here. Stop shaking. You quit once, remember? You quit teaching. I should have quit here long ago."

"Mine was safe quitting, not dangerous, and teaching wasn't my real work."

"The old man refuses to specialize in sailboats. I will. Stop shaking. No kids. Free."

"But Aunt Pleasantine!"

"She'll have to return to her daughters."

"They'll slap her into a nursing home."

"I'll call her grandchildren and tell them the situation. Ask them to keep watch."

"We could be sponsors!"

"What?"

"There's an arrangement, she'd pay us rent. Remember I told you about the Shared Homes pamphlet in her room? She was waiting until after this goddamn party to tell us."

Bill sagged. "Oh, hell."

Mary remembered life before Aunt Pleasantine. The house to herself all day. She hadn't realized how much she'd savored that. The suppers and evenings alone with Bill. Free. Only a few weeks ago she had hoped Aunt Pleasantine's being here wouldn't change anything.

She said, "The money'd help Connie and George, but they can't be sponsors, there's no room in their house, and anyway I don't know if Vermont has Shared Homes."

"Aunt Pleasantine isn't our responsibility."

"How about if we rented her an apartment until we're settled somewhere and then had her move in with us?"

"We're going to need every cent we've got."

Money.

Bill said, "No. She *is* our responsibility. What's the pamphlet's arrangement?"

"You don't think you, the Firstborn, have any other responsibilities?"

"I didn't ask to be born, first or any time. They owe me nothing, I owe them nothing, the world owes nobody anything. Like in that Stephen Crane poem about the man saying to the universe, 'I exist!' and the universe replies that the man's existence hasn't created in the universe a sense of obligation."

"You're running away. Freddy."

"Freddy ran to a parent."

Mary said, "Aunt Pleasantine could live fifteen more years."

"We'd be as tied down as Connie and George are."

"But it's safe here."

"And soon we'll be fat and forty. *DAMN!*" Bill yelled. Then he turned her around, and as they walked back toward the camp, he said, his voice shaky now, too, "Tell me what the arrangement is. We'll have to stay here."

The party had ebbed. Car headlights moved down the driveway, and a boat at the dock revved loudly and left.

Mary saw the big safe camp above the lawn where she'd created flower beds. She'd lived here fourteen years. Fifteen more?

Jerry stumbled across the beach, eating an Edam cheese. "Your aunt says you've done this great painting, where is it?"

Mary said, "I'll bring it in Monday."

Sally grabbed him. "Home, teddy bear. Time for home and Alka-Seltzer. Good party, Mary, thanks so much. Your sister's over there crying."

Crouched beside the empty herb garden, Connie sobbed to Hub, "I dug up the entire iris bed, and the fucker left his backhoe in the front yard—"

Hub said, "If you look at it from a contractor's point of view—"

On the porch steps Aunt Pleasantine was standing in as hostess to the few guests who remembered to thank a hostess, and she was saying to Philip Altman, "I'll tell Mary you enjoyed the evening. Your primary idea is brilliant," and to a neighbor she said, "The Red Sox? So exciting, not since nineteen-sixty-seven—"

Mary, knowing she should relieve Aunt Pleasantine, guiltily followed Bill through the shadows to the driveway. He halted.

The Emersons were leaving. As they got into their cars, Kitty was crying, William was staggering, Janice was screaming at Leonard, "How long did you think I wouldn't hear!" and Donna, neck brace gone, shouted at Paul, "—we deserve a swimming pool, too!"

Engines roared and they drove off.

Bill said, "Okay. The coast is clear."

He and Mary went indoors. Dave and Keith were alone in the living room. Keith had fallen asleep on the floor, and Dave was listening to the "Teenage Masturbation" section of Carlin's *An Evening with Wally Londo.*

And on the porch George was asleep on the glider, and Aunt Pleasantine said good-bye to Ray Brunelle and his wife and Ray didn't tell another French joke.

The house, almost drained of guests now, still seemed to quiver.

Mary said to Aunt Pleasantine, "Thank you for taking over. I'm sorry—"

"I was glad to help." Aunt Pleasantine came into the porch and sat down. "You'll be interested to learn that Norma left with the driver-education teacher. He told me earlier he was divorced. Er—the Emersons—"

"Yes, we saw them leave."

Then they heard Teresa out on the lawn, yelling and running at Connie and Hub.

"Husband-stealing bitch, I'll kill you!"

Instantly, Mary reacted. A grammar school reaction. She leaped off the porch steps and tore across the lawn.

Teresa screeched, "I'll *murder* you!"

The reaction was, of course, unnecessary. Hub reached out in a practiced manner and held flailing Teresa away from Connie, and Mary didn't have to go swinging into a fight to protect her.

Connie wiped her eyes. "Teresa, we were just discussing my leach field, for Christ's sake."

Hub said, "Thanks for the party," and carried Teresa off.

Connie said, "He told me he'd give us free hubcaps. Our rear two are missing."

Mary said, "Thank God Teresa didn't hear that, she'd've really killed you."

"Where's George?"

"Asleep."

They walked up the lawn. Connie said, "Remember in high school when we went through a phase of wearing our watch faces on the inside of our wrists and our cardigans draped empty-sleeved over our shoulders?"

"What on earth made you remember that?"

"Thinking about my shorthand, I guess."

Bill was pacing on the porch, and Aunt Pleasantine was watching the lake traffic. Connie walked past George into the living room and said to Dave, "Throw an afghan over Keith and go upstairs to bed."

Mary said, "I've got a couple of sleeping bags."

"That'd just wake Keith and George up. Let them be lame tomorrow." Connie went down the hall and checked Bobby and Tommy. She came back to the porch. "Thanks, Aunt Pleasantine."

"They slept right through."

Mary, exhausted, looked around at the mess. Remembering her obliterated cartoon on Norma's kitchen cupboard, she walked over to the buffet and straightened a vase which had spilled flowers and water across the coleslaw. "I wonder if we can hold off even longer giving our next We-Owe-Everybody. Or we could be shameless and never give another." She unplugged the electric coffeepot.

Aunt Pleasantine said, "Long ago I discovered a trick that came in handy whenever I was able to use it. After the guests have left, you yourself leave. Go for a drive and let the house cool off."

"Cool off?" Bill said.

"From their presence. And then wait until tomorrow to relive the party. Mary, are you worrying about if there was something you might have had or done to make it better? I think all hostesses do that after entertaining. I know I used to. But there's more perspective the next day."

"Okay," Bill said, "let's go for a drive. Connie? Aunt Pleasantine?"

Aunt Pleasantine said, "You go with them, Connie. I'll stay up and wake George if—you know what I mean. An emergency."

Connie lighted a cigarette. "No. I'll stay here. I don't get a lake vacation often."

Aunt Pleasantine rose. "Then I'm off to bed."

Bill said, "Aunt Pleasantine, if you're not too tired, I'd like you to come with us."

Aunt Pleasantine looked from him to Mary.

Mary said, "As stand-in hostess you ought to let the house cool off, too."

Aunt Pleasantine looked again at Bill. Flustered, she said vaguely, "I always like a drive," and went with them out to Bill's car where Mary got into the back seat and Bill helped her into the front passenger seat.

They drove up the east side of the lake. Among the sleeping dark camps, other camps shone with the aftermath of the party. Late-late TV, nightcaps, talk, arguments.

Bill said, "Mary has told me about the Shared Homes. When Connie and her gang are gone tomorrow, let's all go over the pamphlet, and Monday we can discuss the arrangement with the Welfare Office, but let's get this part settled now. We're happy to be your sponsors. We're happy you've found a way to stay that suits your independence."

Aunt Pleasantine said, "Oh, but—"

"But what?"

Silence. The road veered closer to the shore, along the public beach, then swung out again around camps.

"Damn," Aunt Pleasantine said. "I didn't make myself clear. I can't ask you to be sponsors. But may I ask for your help with the red tape of finding one?"

"Why can't you?" Bill said. "If you're worrying about our qualifications, no sweat. From what Mary told me about the sponsor requirements, we sound like paragons. There'll be no problem."

"How do I thank you? Such a generous offer. But I never meant to live with you because one should never live with one's children. I've said that before, I'm repeating myself. My age."

Mary said, "Aunt Pleasantine, you *have* gone gaga if you think we're your children."

"That's why I've been telling you my memories of you. The circus and everything."

"What circus?" Bill said.

Aunt Pleasantine said, "I had nursemaids who took care of my children, Mary, when the children were as young as you and Connie were during my stay at the farm. I didn't know Hester and Elizabeth at those ages the way I came to know you two because I was busy with my social life. And I later watched you and Connie grow up during your visits to me and through Louisa's letters. How can I say this tactfully? You aren't my children, but you're too close."

Mary, dazed, sensed Bill's controlling his wild relief.

"Kingsbridge," Aunt Pleasantine said. "Shared Homes is a statewide program, and I hope with your help I can find a sponsor in Kingsbridge. God knows that town has changed since my childhood. But."

October. As they drove south to Kingsbridge, Aunt Pleasantine watched the foliage colors reverse from faded to bright and remarked, "It's like seeing two autumns at once."

In the mother-in-law seat, Mary asked, "How come autumn isn't on your list of things that make you feel peaceful? It makes some people feel snug, getting ready for winter."

"Oh, no, autumn is a restless time."

Beside Mary on the seat were Aunt Pleasantine's suitcase, the cactus, and a seascape Aunt Pleasantine had chosen when Mary begged her to take a painting with her.

Bill drove across the turnpike bridge and down past the Holiday Inn, past Grandmother's house, and along Main Street out to the housing developments.

Mary and Bill and Aunt Pleasantine had come here before with the Welfare woman to meet Mrs. Fortin, so Bill didn't get lost in the straight and angled streets. He found the small house on a corner. Mary looked at all the other same houses down the other streets and imagined houses stretching for miles and miles in all directions.

But this house would be Aunt Pleasantine's address now. 49 Birchbrook Drive, c/o Mrs. Ethel Fortin.

Bill parked behind the Chevrolet Impala in the driveway. "She certainly keeps her hedges neatly clipped."

"Because of her husband," Aunt Pleasantine said. "When he was alive, he spent the years of his retirement cultivating the hedges. Ethel told me he was a hedge sculptor, doing globes and things. Her son, the one who's supposed to be the 'responsible adult' I'm to call if I'm alone in an emergency, does the clipping when he comes over and helps her out with chores, but he sticks to straight edges."

Bill walked around and opened Aunt Pleasantine's door. Mary opened her own door, got out, hesitated, forced herself to reach in for the suitcase, which she passed to Bill. Mary lifted out the cactus and the painting.

The front door of the house opened, and Ethel Fortin, smiling, came bustling down the walk.

When they'd met, Ethel and Aunt Pleasantine had, as Aunt Pleasantine put it, "clicked immediately." In her mid-sixties, Ethel was small and plump and busy; she seethed with energy. She'd started working for a real estate agency after her children grew up, and continued working there after her husband's retirement and death. Aunt Pleasantine had said as they drove home from that meeting, "She's a doer. Keeping busy is very important. But she's lonesome, too." In Saffron she'd added, sounding quietly pleased, "Ethel says I'll usually have the house to myself most of the day."

Aunt Pleasantine took Bill's offered arm and walked toward Ethel, who escorted her into the house, into the living room. Venetian blinds and overstuffed furniture. Ethel helped Aunt

Pleasantine off with the winter coat Mary and Bill had insisted on giving her as a good-bye gift.

Bill said, "I'll take your suitcase to your room."

Mary followed him up the stairs to one of the three bedrooms. Ethel's was the largest; the smallest was used for clutter. Aunt Pleasantine's room had girlish wallpaper chosen years ago by Ethel's daughter. The dormer window looked down onto the street, and the other window looked onto a neighbor's sideyard. Mary put the cactus on a windowsill and said, "I can't stand this."

"You've got to. She is."

Mary propped the painting against a wall. "I suppose the son can hang it when he comes to do chores."

Downstairs, they found Aunt Pleasantine and Ethel in the kitchen. Ethel was at the sink, filling a teakettle. Aunt Pleasantine sat at the dinette table.

Ethel said, "Pleasantine says you'll want to be on your way. You can't stay for a cup of tea?"

Aunt Pleasantine said, "They have people coming to look at their house today," a downright lie but a perfect excuse to a real-estate person, and Aunt Pleasantine silently dared Mary and Bill to say the next house appointment was tomorrow.

Mary remembered arriving on campus with her parents the first day of college and how urgently she had wanted them to stop fussing, to leave, to let her break away from the familiar and safe and start settling into a new world. "Yes," she said, "we've got to get back." She leaned down and kissed Aunt Pleasantine's cheek. "I'll be writing."

"So will I."

Bill kissed Aunt Pleasantine, and they left.

January 2, 1976

Dear Mary and Bill,

Whatever am I going to do with you! You are far too generous. The shades of pink are my especial favorites, and I am a very warm glamor girl now in my new winter pantsuit and turtleneck. No need to worry about exchanging—your accurate eyes judged my size absolutely correctly. I thank you very much. I wore the outfit to a New Year's Eve party, and before we toasted the Bicentennial Year, I mentally toasted you both.

I'm glad you agree with me that Christmas is crazy in Florida, and I'm sure your photos and paintings of it, Mary, are wonderful. I'm glad too that you miss New England—I look forward to your return North. I know that you will be very successful, Bill, *in your own business.*

Please don't be anxious about me. I must be part cat, because I always land on my feet.

Why, just the other day I "won" a Secret Square which included $300 worth of Bonanza Steak House steaks and *another* Honda motorcycle.

I am being spoiled rotten here with Ethel, as I was with you, and loving every minute of it. Ethel usually takes me shopping with her, and sometimes I go along for the drive when she is checking out a new house for her agency, so I am keeping tabs on the town.

I cannot say I am sorry about Lillian's death. It was a blessing for her. But her house and land were bought by the shoe factory next door to it, and the house and the lupines are gone now, replaced by a cinder-block addition to the factory and a parking lot.

I'm sure you know how I felt one day this November when I glanced out a window and realized the gray weather had begun to spit snow.

The New Year's Eve party was in the old part of town—*my* part of town—and Ethel asked me to accompany her. It was given by some satisfied customers of hers. They have made a showplace of a rather neglected house, and the party was a humdinger. Its color scheme, naturally, was red, white, and blue, even the canapés, and . . . .